FRIC

Joe Stretch was born in 1982 and brought up in Lancashire. He moved to Manchester at the age of 18 to study politics at Manchester University. His band, (we are) Performance, in which he is the lead singer and lyricist, released their debut album in 2007. *Friction* is his first novel.

JOE STRETCH

Friction

VINTAGE BOOKS
London

Published by Vintage 2008

2 4 6 8 10 9 7 5 3 1

Copyright © Joe Stretch 2007

Joe Stretch has asserted his right under the Copyright, Designs
and Patents Act 1988 to be identified as the author of this work

First published in Great Britain in 2008 by
Vintage
Random House, 20 Vauxhall Bridge Road,
London SW1V 2SA

www.vintage-books.co.uk

Addresses for companies within
The Random House Group Limited can be found at:
www.randomhouse.co.uk/offices.htm

The Random House Group Limited Reg. No. 954009

A CIP catalogue record for this book
is available from the British Library

ISBN 9780099515968

The Random House Group Limited makes every effort to ensure
that the papers used in its books are made from trees that have been
legally sourced from well-managed and credibly certified forests. Our paper
procurement policy can be found at:
www.rbooks.co.uk/environment

Typeset in Sabon by Palimpsest Book Production Limited,
Grangemouth, Stirlingshire

Printed and bound in Germany by
GGP Media GmbH, Poessneck

FOR PELHAM

CONTENTS

Prologue

I

II

Prologue

NUMBERS HAVE ENTERED my brain with a blink and a bleep. Details have become cool and chewed in my stomach. Every fact has landed with a crack. I cannot tell you my name.

The people that surround me would go mad if I told you. People tend to do this. Go mad, I mean. Particularly in here. They're energised, you see, and there are few things more foul and embarrassing than a fully energised person. They run from room to room, checking up on us, encouraging us, sighing if they catch us with our pants down or hunched over a line of dog dirt. And yes, they go mad. If we try to talk about information, like, say, if we talk about civilisation, or about order, or about the insides of our underpants, then they hit the roof.

But I am no longer afraid. Not at all. I'm about to horse-crap myself forwards into a wide sea of trouble. And you, my friend, are coming too. Because my research tells me that we humans die as we are born: simple. We complicate ourselves between two terribly grand simplicities. We enjoy it; we enjoy ourselves. We used to dance in buildings, to beats and flashing lights. We used to chat and chat and chat. But I have never done that. No, I have never spoken crap. Never leant against a wall and sang of understanding or of love. Not until recently, at least.

You see, I have been staring at information. I should not have been allowed to do this. When I sneaked into the system, about six months ago, someone should have stopped me, you know, dragged me backwards, someone should have injected me, punched my lights out. But they didn't. Consequently, I have swallowed facts like others used to swallow bollocks. I have eaten information with a spoon. They will regret their error. I'm a fucker. Nowadays, I am a fucker. I will make them lament each of their blind eyes. I'm going to, yes, horse-crap myself forwards into a wide sea of trouble.

They often make us begin our stories by describing our environment. Well, this room is like a cheap kitchen. The floor is linoleum, but is patterned in such a way as to imitate wooden floorboards. There are even small black circles where I'm meant to believe different pieces of wood have been nailed into place. The flooring is very old-fashioned, actually. It virtually disappeared at some point. Probably because society suddenly realised how absurd it looked, and collectively blushed. Apart from that, the furniture here is made from pine. There is a table, a chair and a bed. Combined with the lino, the effect is vile: a yellow haze. It is in this room that I will tell my story. It is in this room that I will kill time.

I have read many accounts of people talking out of their arses. I do not think that this is what I do. But nor do I talk from my heart, which is certainly what is required of me.

2

They want a story that will allow them to love me and think me safe. I've seen it all before. Such a story will not get written. Not by me. They will howl in response to my tale. It will be quite funny. Even if they kill me, it will be quite funny. They won't kill me. No, they won't, because this is all their fault. I'm sure they allowed me to sneak up on the truth. Big mistake. They should never have held me by the ankle and dangled me into such cold, informative water.

The point is this: I get myself. For the first time in my life, I get myself. Hee hee. I do. The only thing I don't get is this world, and that world. It's just incredible. You are actually in it. Hee hee. Are we vulnerable? What's it about? Is it about bras that take the piss out of tits and tits that take the piss out of bras? Girls become round with power. Brilliant. Boys with invisible dicks and impeccable skeletons sway. Jump on my back. You know how to ride like a piggy. Put your arms around my neck. I will hold each of your thighs. I will run and you will bounce around on my shoulders, laughing and shouting, stop, stop, slow down. And I will say, no, it's a story, a true story, we're getting into trouble. Slow down. No. And you'll be like. And I'll be like. And you'll be like. And I'll be like.

I can see my eyes reflected in the screen. Data on my face.

How did this begin?

I

1

The Starter

IN THE BEGINNING it was casual. Before all the fizzing and the thrusting, everything was laid back, posed and fashionable. In the beginning people drifted. They were decorated, toned and full of elastic love. They twanged along the streets of Manchester like life was the greatest game: fulfilling, but a piece of piss also. Naturally, there was a flowing undercurrent of bullshit. But there is always a flowing undercurrent of bullshit, so no one cared. No one cared because everything was reclined and perfect. Each night small trucks cleaned the streets, swallowing rubbish with their circling wire brushes. People were happy. Each year brought seasons of fashion and vast quantities of cool. Yes, in the beginning it was certainly casual. No one seemed to notice that the sewers were rising. That the bullshit was, in fact, bubbling.

Justin, a sort of boy, is walking terribly hard. He walks along Cross Street and down on to South King Street. Actually, he's more of a young man. His hair a lightly shaved brown, his body hidden by average design: a loose white shirt and boot-cut blue jeans. He grips the chrome handle of the restaurant door, his image ghosting in the polished glass. Already he can see his mother. She sits with her legs tightly crossed at a table in the centre of the restaurant, a menu smiling in her lap.

Justin pulls at the door and in he goes. The restaurant is all light and crap plants. Various exotic shrubs planted to convince people that this isn't Manchester at all, but a foreign place where happiness is typical. Well-washed waiters slide along the floor and pirouette around tables, placing plates of Italian food in front of the hungerless. Justin's mother is called Diane. Twenty-four years have mumbled by since Diane gave birth to Justin. Now a waiter is taking his coat and he is approaching her.

'He's dead, then?' says Justin, taking a seat, wincing at the burdened fabric that holds his mother's tits in place. The winch-like bra, the nylon of her struggling blouse. His throat tightens. His mother's body is preparing to spill. Certainly. Years are ganging up on her, making her looser and creased. Soon her breasts will finally fall, her chin will burst and turn to scrambled egg. She sucks the gums of her cheeks into her teeth and sighs at the menu. 'Yes, Justin, he is dead.'

Should it be made clear that Justin loathes his mother? I suppose it should. He's been estranged from both his parents since he left home because they remind him that he was conceived. Probably in the dark. This doesn't make sense. Justin doesn't feel conceived. He hasn't met his mother like this in years. He considers his mother to have a foul addiction to sexiness. Many women do. She refuses to surrender her body to ugliness and let the prospect of a

8

final fuck fade. She'd banged strangers throughout his childhood, paraded around the kitchen in blood-red underwear, performed blow jobs on boys barely his senior and divorced the dad who is finally dead.

'He wanted you to know that he loved you very much,' says Diane. 'He wished you all the best for the future.'

Justin's bottom squirms so extremely that he's convinced the crap plastic of his chair is going to crack and leave him lonely on the floor with a dead dad and a sickly, horny mum. The chair holds. Justin's throat tightens still. Is this how it begins? He grips the menu, scans over the Italian beers, the bruschettas, the pizzas. Fuck this, he decides, fuck this. He's seen a thousand menus like this before; he's swallowed pizzas with his mum and pizzas with his dad. I should have gone to see him, he thinks. No, no, I shouldn't have, the cancerous pansy.

'Can I get you guys some drinks?'

A waiter appears with an electronic notepad in his hand and a smile skirting sheepishly across his lips.

'I'll take a mineral water, and I'll also take some bruschetta.'

'A White Russian,' says Justin. 'I'm not eating.'

Late in the twentieth century, certain people stopped 'having' things in restaurants and began 'taking' them instead. It wasn't a crime. They still paid. It's an American influence. The waiter leaves and Justin watches as his mum perfects her lips with a small brush and a pot of colourless gloss. Any minute, he thinks, it will happen at any minute. Her lips will turn the texture of bark and the seams of her trousers will rip, revealing legs that can no longer be injected into tight jeans and a disobedient arse that will not be packed into a trendy, sexy shape.

Justin is losing. He's lost his dad to cancer and his mum to a world of endless fucking and body banging. One week ago he lost his girlfriend, who discovered he was cheating on her with an almost identical-looking girl. He's not sure why he cheated. Both girls tucked similar jeans into similarly suede boots, improved similar tits with similarly enhancing bras. They laughed at the same jokes, kissed and fucked the same. It's over for me, thinks Justin. Sex. Gone. Love is over for me.

'Say something, Justin, you look awful.'

Justin says nothing. He looks awful. Do I? he wonders. What does looking awful mean? He thinks about it for a moment and decides he likes the idea of looking awful, of looking like shit. Because it's over for him. Love. He knows it. He has noticed the brown muck curving round the grids of Manchester's drains. Noticed the foul smell around the shops and the squares.

'How much?' he says at last. 'How much am I getting?'

The drinks arrive and Justin gulps immediately from his White Russian, his eyes fixed on his mother, who beams at her bruschetta and blushes as the waiter pours her water. Justin's blood begins to simmer: the bruschetta won't stop flirting with his mum. The little chunks of tomato won't stop winking at her, the bread's nodding suggestively. Typical, thinks Justin, she's going to fuck her starter.

'How much am I getting?' he asks again, as his mother's glossed lips meet the machine-washed metal of her fork. But Diane's eyes close, her jaw munches in a circle, her lips scrunched, humming approval.

Why did I shag two girls who were so alike? thinks Justin, turning to where the summer light is brightened by the restaurant's large windows. They were on the same course at university, both fascinated by Virginia Woolf. He recalls the moment he realised they'd found out. He watched as they exited the Union Building on Oxford Road and approached him. He remembers their similar strides, their folders held tightly to their chests, the same purple betrayal in their eyes.

'I thought they were the same girl!' he says, suddenly, out loud.

'Pardon?' coughs Diane, a chunk of tomato dropping to the floor, causing her cheeks to redden. She swallows hard then says, 'Sixty thousand pounds, you'll get sixty thousand pounds.' A leaf of basil stumbles knackered on to Diane's bottom lip and Justin concludes that his life has changed course. He downs his cocktail in one. It's gone, he thinks. It has ended or it has begun. I need to find new ways of having sex.

2

Modern Arse

YOU'RE YOU AND I'm me. Neither of us is Steve. Steve is twisting in his bed, eyes squinting, preparing to once again behold the immaculate glory of his Green Quarter apartment. Beside Steve is Carly, the girlfriend, twisting too. Both were battered last night, hammered at the bar. Both returned home with zig-zag legs and zig-zag tongues and began doting on each other. Too much drinking. Sex with no clothes on. Life with no legs on.

Steve's eyes open: two used condoms gossip about him beside the bed, one filled and tied, the other untied and containing only a squirt. British boys have British brains, the texture of a mushroom. They can be prised apart like fruit. His throat is the asphalt of a car park.

Steve lifts himself up on to his elbows, exhaling loudly as he does so. His hair is bleached blonde, though memories of its original black streak through it. This is fashion. Steve's haircut cost sixty quid and is a constant source of pride. As is the room that surrounds him: the excellent stereo, the cool wardrobe containing brilliant clothes, the skirting boards painted Duck Egg Blue, the fit girlfriend.

'I feel like shit,' he observes, sitting up completely, breathing into his cupped hands and then recoiling in disgust. 'My breath stinks of shit,' he adds.

Steve glances again at the condoms beside the bed; they're still whispering to each other. Discussing, no doubt, their experiences of a few hours earlier. Steve had torn their foil wrappers with his teeth and slid them on to his marauding cock. I was great, thinks Steve, turning to Carly who lies beside him, both times I was brilliant.

'I'm not going to work,' says Carly, stirring. 'I'm still fucked.' Her right hand creeps across the covers towards a packet of cigarettes on the bedside table; it fumbles open the lid and removes a fag, shaking the packet on to the floor as it does so. Her hand then returns to her face and places the fag between her lips. She can't be bothered to light it. It remains unlit. Carly works in a shoe shop. She and Steve have been together for two years.

'I can't believe my arse is still trendy,' says Carly, the fag bouncing in her dry lips, her voice muffled. 'It's such good news.'

Steve nods. 'Yeh, it is good news.'

For weeks Carly has been fretting about her arse. She's been craning her neck to get a proper look at it, chasing her buttocks round and round like a dog chases its tail. Ever since she saw a late-night documentary suggesting that arse fashion was changing, she's been shitting it. Her bottom is small and compact, whereas the programme suggested that bigger and more rounded bums were marching into fashion. She was devastated, ordered Steve to take a photo with his phone and spent a day staring at her denim behind,

14

imploring it to stay in fashion. It did. Although not before Carly had investigated the surgical options on the Internet and decided she'd get her arse enlarged if it meant remaining fit. Eager to prevent this, Steve did his own research, concluding that the programme was really just reflecting African American tastes and that the British bottom was likely to remain untouched. Last night they celebrated this news. Carly wore a boob tube and a very short skirt.

One thing's for sure nowadays, you can't beat a sexy girl. One that is as fit as fuck. Steve doesn't know any man who can resist a girl who is as fit as fuck. And Carly, who twists awkwardly beside him in bed, is exactly that. She is precisely as fit as fuck. Her face is open, its features perfectly spaced and in total agreement. Her breasts bob and flirt with physics. Her hair is a rich brown and journeys down over her shoulders before curling perfectly above each nipple.

'You spanked me last night, didn't you, baby?' asks Carly, sitting up finally and reaching for her lighter.

'Yes.'

There's a spark and the fag is lit. Carly spits out the first uninhaled cloud of white and smiles. 'Thank you.'

It was exactly Carly's beauty that ended Steve's ambitions. Two years ago he was about to start work on an MA thesis, investigating the merits of globalisation. But then a door opened in a bar on Deansgate and Carly walked through it. Steve froze. Ambition puffed fart-like from his arse. He put down his drink and approached her. The conversation was twenty seconds old when Steve discovered that Carly had just one interest: money. He sighed, wafted the odour of his ambition from his nostrils and simply changed his mind, cancelled his MA and started independently investing on the stock market. So came style, the sixty-pound haircuts, the fajitas and the goats' cheese, the lifting of weights and the financing of Carly's sprees.

To be a shagger of others, particularly a shagger of girls like Carly, demands sacrifice. So it is that Steve smiles carefully when she returns from town with numerous shopping bags, or when she points her finger at certain garments in various catalogues. He doesn't complain. Carly is a choice: the glorious twenty-first-century choice between fantasy and mind. Carly makes Steve feel exactly like a man. Extremely like a man. A cock god, a swordsman, a sexpert, etc.

'How many times was it last night, Stevie?'

Steve listens as the condoms titter below. 'Twice,' he says, turning away from Carly's smoke and shutting his eyes tight.

'I could go all night. Really. I could fuck all day,' says Carly, stubbing out her fag and reaching round Steve's arse cheeks to where his cock and balls discuss the meaning of life. She gently jigs his webbed testicles, taps at his cock until it moves like a flag flown in mourning, to half-mast.

'I'm not going on top.'

'I'm too fucked.'

'Just wank me off.'

This is life. This is glorious life. There is a burst of activity as Carly drags Steve on to his back and makes for his middle. She gets herself into a comfortable position and, with a soft grip, begins to wank him off, as agreed. One thing has been proved: boys love friction, and being wanked off by a girl is the easiest source of it. It's stress free, guilt free, and needn't be repaid. Unlike a blow job, which is world-splittingly political and requires a measured, softly spoken diplomacy. Carly's strokes begin to get more vigorous and Steve feels he owes her nothing.

16

An area of the blue duvet is going up and down like a fast heart beating under thin skin. Steve's eyes shut, capturing situations of sex inside his head. A mixture of fantasy and icicled reality: the begging eyes of a conquered female, the round African American arses he clocked on the web, the merits of globalisation, a pop star round his cock, a film star at his balls.

It's as if all Steve has are his looks, which are so good they virtually guarantee him intercourse with any girl in the Western world. Lots and lots of lifting weights occupy a great deal of Steve's time on earth. Up and down, making his body bigger and bigger. He's changing and, deep down, he blames Carly, he reckons she makes him less refined. Carly doesn't give a shit.

She thinks of products as her wrist moves up and down. She pictures clothes. She sees lifestyle in her hand: ripped jeans, stiletto heels, her tortilla palm wrapped round alert cock.

There is a desperate silence in this room, broken only by Steve's silly groans. He knows it. She knows it. The condoms beside the bed know it. The sewers are rising.

3

Only Joking

SOUTH FROM CENTRAL Manchester down Oxford Road gets you to Fallowfield. Two gloriously young students, Johnny and Rebecca, enter Platt Fields Park with their arms loosely linked. They're not lovers. Linking arms is very popular in the early twenty-first century, even amongst friends. Today the sun is scarlet and the sky seems almost green. A young man glides by on rollerblades, headphones in his ears, swaying from side to side. Rollerblading is getting less popular these days. Never trust a rollerblader. They're a bunch of fucking nihilists. They don't believe in anything.

Johnny and Rebecca are wearing shoes. Rebecca watches their pacing feet through aviator shades, the ice-cold sweat from Johnny's T-shirt is troubling her naked arm. 'The lads in my flat have stuck porn all over the kitchen wall,' she says, disentangling her arm from Johnny's and brushing it gently with her palm.

Johnny is crap at replying. So he doesn't. He simply allows his awkward, stooping posture to become more extreme. The mere mention of pornography causes the teeth of his brain to chatter. He can't imagine porn. Has never seen it. Loosely linking arms with Rebecca is as close as Johnny has come to sex. And now our arms are no longer linked, he notices. Because of my sweat, he concludes, she disliked the cold, wet sensation of my sweat.

'It's a real montage. Hardcore on almost every wall. It strikes me as rather odd. What were they thinking?'

The path ahead of them ends and opens out into a large expanse of grass. Fellow students roll around with each other, some read in the shade of trees. Boys kick footballs to each other over long distances. Johnny takes his chance and sprints ahead of Rebecca.

'Where are you going?'

Johnny's crap at replying so he just runs off. Rebecca watches as he escapes towards a tree. He climbs it quickly and hangs from a branch. Rebecca is Johnny's only friend. She knows this. That's why she sets aside time to walk with him or cook him dinner. For Johnny has an ugly little face, friendly, but so unfortunate. His features positioned like darts thrown drunkenly at a board. His eyes like underwater organisms, forced to breathe the air. Hanging from a tree, the large discs of sweat under each of his arms are conspicuous. His frame is long and gangly; he's what people call a lanky bastard. Certainly, he's a lanky bastard. Limbs like lengths of inflexible rope.

'I am the Milky Bar Kid!' shouts Johnny, swinging in the breeze, his voice retaining its adolescent croak. 'The Milky Bar Kid is strong and tough. He is a figment of the male imagination!' Johnny only ever speaks in joke.

Rebecca passes the tree, smiling, embarrassed. She is short in stature, her body contains curves, her haircut is a sedate chestnut bob and her face is a face, a pretty one, soft, as if shielded by a light mist. She watches as Johnny drops from the branch and accidentally crumples into a small heap. He has the knees of a child; muddy and many-sided. He ambles after Rebecca with the unfortunate lurching movements of doomed youth.

Johnny, of course, is in love with Rebecca. On the first day of term he tripped and fell at her feet. Her ankles, Jesus, thighs, the darkness up her skirt, in love, instantly. His little mind is full of her and his little heart is full of arrows. Her cleavage; it reminds him of not breathing. But he's a lanky bastard. He has unfashionable genes. Fucked about by fate. A colourful acne flows from ear to ear.

'I don't understand it. What am I meant to believe is in your mind, Johnny? I mean men, in general?'

Johnny's mind contains broken swings and a knackered roundabout around which tracksuited villains sip cider, throw stones and make him think and do stupid things. Especially around Rebecca.

'Men are rank, really, men are really rank,' says Rebecca, finding a place on the grass and falling backwards into it. She's thoughtful. Wonderful. A full middle-class figure that speaks of swimming lessons, trips to France, passing your driving test and being rewarded with a car. Beside her, Johnny is attempting to sit down. But he's not even cool enough to sit, can't find where to put his legs. He can be quite funny, I suppose, but beyond that his talents are eating, shitting, getting ill and breathing.

One of the things that Johnny loves about Rebecca is her mild political commitment. This consists of her making one or both of the following points on a monthly basis, usually on occasions of personal failure or moderate fatigue.

Point one: 'How, Johnny, can we inhabit a planet where

half the population is starving, and the other half is deliberately starving themselves?'

Point two: '[Politician A] is only interested in creating a context in which [multinational corporation X] can successfully and safely establish factories in [poor country Y], the guy doesn't give a fuck about human rights, just free fucking trade.'

Point one is actually more of a question, albeit rhetorical, so as compensation here's the usual extension of point two: 'I'll tell you something, Johnny, free trade has got nothing to do with freedom.'

This more than constitutes profundity in many of man's days and ages. Rebecca is to be applauded for her efforts.

Clap. Clap. Clap. Clap.

In Johnny's eyes Rebecca is the vanguard of the proletariat, with an intimidating set of tits to match. She stretches out in the sun and his eyes roll like marbles down the mysterious contours of her body. He barely knows what a tit is. Can't really imagine one, its consistency, its texture.

'When I graduate, I think I'd like to teach in a prison,' says Rebecca, uprooting clumps of grass and placing them on the inch of flesh that is revealed between her shirt and her skirt. When I graduate I'd like to be that little clump of grass, thinks Johnny, like little green pubes. I'd like to be natural. I'd like to hide where your buttocks meet your thighs and not be found.

'Definitely,' continues Rebecca, absently brushing away the grass, 'I'd really like to work with sex offenders, get inside their heads.'

Just as Johnny's trying to work out what sexual offence he could commit so as to land Rebecca as his teacher, the sun disappears behind a cloud and a football bounces between the two of them and comes to rest. It becomes noticeably colder. A wind blows. I'm not capable of rape, thinks Johnny. Can you go to prison for simply staring at girls?

Johnny drifts off, wondering whether wolf-whistling is a sex crime. Rebecca looks to where the football came from and watches as a young man begins to jog in their direction. She smiles. It wouldn't cross Johnny's mind to kick the ball back. He couldn't kick air.

The jogging boy wears no top; his pectoral muscles jump fiercely up and down with every foot that hits the ground. Rebecca scans down his body to the neatly tensed six-pack, the seams of his perfectly baggy shorts, sharp shins flanked by calf, trainered feet, dancing laces. Rebecca gets a lurching feeling. A sense of being alive and a sense of being fooled.

'I feel sick,' she says suddenly, 'what's that smell?' Rebecca knows. She has smelt the danger, seen it in the lines that define the muscles of young men's chests.

'I'll never be a sex offender,' says Johnny, noticing the football for the first time and wincing at its muddy, worn leather, at it horrendous kinetic potential. He sees the boy, too, and turns away.

Rebecca doesn't. Her eyes are on the football. It moved. Slightly. The seams that bind the pentagons of black and white leather begin to prise apart. Rebecca sits up. The football is mouthing something to her, trying to communicate, an expression of terrible fear on its kicked and muddied face. Thudding footsteps get louder. The boy arrives, the skin that binds his skeleton tensing and relaxing with his gasping mouth.

'Sorry,' he says, addressing Rebecca. Johnny looks at the young man's face and instinctively raises a hand to his own, running it across the bloody terrain of his cheeks. He returns his eyes to the ground, which he gouges with a stick.

'No problem,' says Rebecca, rolling the ball towards the young man's feet but not wishing to look at it, in case it starts talking again. She doesn't wish to be warned or persuaded by a football. It wouldn't be right. The boy runs the sole of his shoe over the ball and begins dribbling in the direction of his friends, hoofing it towards them after a few metres and running on.

His eyes, thinks Johnny, recalling how the young man had observed Rebecca, did his eyes get erections?

'You OK, Johnny?' asks Rebecca, taking a tissue from her bag.

Is this how it has to be, thinks Johnny, sex sewn into my brain, like air inside a ball? It's Rebecca, he thinks, she's making my brain go red. Johnny turns to Rebecca with a smile pulled across his face like a zip. Gentle Johnny, a sex offender? No. His brain blushes. He's only joking: 'Tonight, Rebecca, I'm going to drill a drizzly minge!'

'Pardon?'

'I'm going to hammer away at a twat!'

Rebecca gets up from the grass. She's offended. A twat? She's not laughing. She's frowning, a tissue held against her face. What would Johnny want with a twat? thinks Rebecca. What's the smell? Is it the stench of young men thinking?

The bullshit is carried on the breeze. Rebecca and Johnny both sense danger. Sense that a previously perfect system of interlocking shapes has somehow fallen out of synch and that this spells trouble. Rebecca brushes grass and dried earth from her long khaki skirt and turns to observe the group of footballing boys. They're crowding around a hedge, poking at it with long sticks, retreating cautiously after each jab. The football has rolled into a wasps' nest.

4

Cash and Waste

WE CAN'T STAND still. We don't wear rollerblades. We have more characters to meet. Last night the air was stuffy, as ever, stuffy with sirens, shouts and short skirts. Rented limousines crawled through the city centre, from Corporation Street, down Cross Street, Deansgate, through Castlefield. Drinks flow in England. Weekends arrive with gifts for the thirsty, leaving behind only trickles of piss.

Boy 1 and Boy 2 meet at 'The Bar' for lunch at three o'clock. The Bar, pronounced 'Thee Bar', is not quite *the* bar to frequent, but as franchises go, it's good. Boy 1 takes a steak sandwich and Boy 2 takes a BLT. The steak sandwich, as it must from 1998 onwards, contains caramelised red onion. Caramelised red onion is seen as really, really delicious. Boy 1 wants to be rich, he wants to be fucking rock and he wants the high life: red onions, houmous, focaccia, fit-as-fuck bird. Food having been consumed, both boys are left feeling powerful. The weekend looms above them dressed in hilarious drag, it offers them its creased and open palm.

At five o'clock the lager living begins. The lager loving begins. Boy 1 goes to the bar, returning with two pints of Stella and a handful of change. At first it's moderate, the drinking. But subtle sips give way to greedy gulps and their hearts begin to darken. After four pints they begin to piss and a banal chaos starts up; neither can go half a pint without jogging to the bogs and spraying into the urinal, a clenched fist held against the white tiled walls for support. At seven o'clock a fleeting lethargy hits them both and the subject of Colin is raised.

'We should call him,' says Boy 2, belatedly tugging up his flies.

'Should we?' Boy 1 replies, his eyes fixed on the girls that by now are pouring into The Bar.

'Yeh, man, we should.'

Colin is heading down Sackville Street when his phone vibrates in his pocket and he comes to a stop. The display glows against the night, the words 'Boy 2' flashing across the middle. Answer?

'You sound fucked,' says Colin, as the lager-lipped tone of Boy 2's voice creeps from the earpiece. Colin agrees to join the two boys at The Bar. He does this reluctantly, because he has to. He does this because, nowadays, opting out of social occasions is a form of self-mutilation. The social is everything. Colin suspects that when removed from the glass gazes of others, he is nothing. And it hurts.

Colin ends the call, turns around and starts walking in the direction of The Bar. He temps at the University of Manchester, admin for the English Department. Having worked late, he is still in his work clothes. Don't worry. Luckily for Colin, the sartorial code at the university is

26

pretty casual. He's wearing a pair of smart jeans and a well-ironed blue shirt. (Apart from the odd, short-lived experiment with the idea of an intentionally creased shirt, by about 2004, the well-ironed shirt has achieved supremacy.) Colin skips onto Whitworth Street, past the croaking, toad-like building of Oxford Road train station and on towards south Deansgate and The Bar.

He crosses one of the many wooden bridges that lead on to Deansgate Locks. The Bar looms, its cheap sign lit up, its doorway cordoned off with red rope and brass stands. It's getting busier.

There are plenty of couples. Colin's head begins to spin. The couple is still going strong. There are long tanned legs, bunches of birds that you could screw up, smash, straightening their limbs with red hot tongs. Spinning fast. Lovely arses for Colin to look at coldly. Couples seem vile to Colin. These men and women are the wettest, most vile, idiotic, sick, compromised cowards he's ever seen. He looks at beefed-up men like they're hideous idiots, preoccupied with some misunderstood idea. Cocks. Colin doesn't want a bird, fit as fuck or not. But he'd burn the clothes of these turd-tanned slappers, burn their push-up bras off their bodies just to show them. Colin's girlfriend left him a year ago and, at this stage, he isn't sure whether he'll ever be able to have sex again. He pays at the door, entering the club that The Bar has become.

The majestic boozers of this damp century wade around the dance floor. It's dark but the room is full of psychedelic drinks: girls and boy sucking on neon liquids, pouring golden fluid, animated by flashing lights and colours, down their throats and into their stomachs.

This is what we people live for, a lot of us think. Great

27

times. Great times. The music is running as fast as it can and the dance floor is heaving with fabrics and different skins. The place is burnt hollow with cleavage, with skirts short enough to reveal the beginnings of hard, curved bums. There are tight T-shirts, see-through tops, muscles, perfectly ironed shirts of white, of red, of blue. Oh, they drink a shitload, they do. These are those who will live and die but this is a generation that mustn't get old; so great is its responsibility to the nihilism of its youth. Colin waits fifteen minutes for a pint of Stella and joins Boy 1 and Boy 2 at the edge of the dance floor.

'All right, mate!'

'Yeh!'

'How was work?'

'Fine. You're fucking wasted!'

'We've been here all day!'

These three are idle young men. This is a room full of idle young men in pursuit of idle young women in pursuit of idle young men. Cyclical and unchanging. Paceless. Anger warms and finally burns. It creeps up on you on the dance floor or outside the club. It ruins your night, then is thrown off and forgotten in the course of some restless, semi-comatose sleep. Sex is some hard-throated bout of power play. Girls and boys passing time. Staring, looking, touching, fucking, leaving, missing, abandoning, living, trying and fucking up and trying again, anal, stopping, taxi-rank fights, bus blow jobs, orgasms, excitement, experimentation, fetish and a frantic smell of spermicide.

Boy 1 and Boy 2 sway on the dance floor, stumbling in the direction of tits, their gelled hair the texture of barbed wire. Colin watches with a choking throat and dried-up eyes as the rest of the club work themselves up into a frenzy,

28

pair off, fight and leave. Colin is a granite statue with flickering marble eyes. He surveys the girls. He weighs them, unwraps them, cuts and prices them. It's slaughter, quick, it's slaughter.

'Look at her.'

'That twat's pointing at me.'

'Come on.'

'Knockers. Quick, fuck. Look at the knockers.'

'I've got no chance.'

Somewhere among the lights, fun is located, invisible to the untrained eye. This is the age of excess, of silence, of stillness, of getting fucked up, of inebriated and uninhibited sex or hard morning wanks. This is the age of cash and waste.

At around midnight Colin seeks refuge in a toilet cubicle, leaving Boys 1 and 2 on the dance floor. He takes a piss and then lowers the toilet seat and the lid, wiping away the residue of cocaine and urine before sitting down and resting his elbows on his knees. The music is muffled but still seems deafening. 'Y2K' reads a note on the door, graffiti, 'Y2K: Kev fucked Sal.' What became of that moment? thinks Colin, noticing a pair of black brogues entering the adjacent cubicle. What became of Kev? He fucked Sal, of course, but then what? What did Sal and Kev do afterwards? Dance, maybe, yes, thinks Colin, Kev danced with a dirty dick, and Sal with an altered minge.

Colin falls forwards on to the wet floor, turning and lifting the lid, vomiting an odorous yellow into the toilet water.

'You all right in there, mate?'

Am I all right in here? Colin wipes a hand across his mouth. It's decay, he thinks, pinching his Adam's apple between his fingers and thumb. It's some fucked-up decay. He looks down; the toilet lets out a deep, gurgling belly laugh.

'All right, son, out you come.'

Colin looks up to see a very white face staring down at him over the divide. A very large fat face, the telling shine of black bomber jacket beyond its neck. A bouncer. Bollocks. A bouncer balancing on next door's toilet. Colin sighs. The bouncer jumps off the toilet and comes round to meet Colin as he leaves the cubicle.

'Let's go, sunshine.'

With a fat white hand on each shoulder, Colin is pushed slowly through The Bar. The crowd parts in front of him. Wankers turn to watch. Bitches whisper and Colin finds himself outside with Boys 1 and 2.

'You've been chucked out, too?' he says, straightening his collar. 'What for?'

'Fighting,' says Boy 2, quietly into his sleeve.

'Wanking,' screams Boy 1, over his shoulder, running quickly towards a bus.

The following morning. Colin suggests that they all eat breakfast at the hospital. The others follow for one import-ant reason: for the hell of it. They walk from Boy 2's flat in Victoria Park to the Infirmary off Oxford Road by the University of Manchester. On the second floor they find the Wishing Well, a grim cafeteria where the light is the yellow of vomit and the air is always grey. The pregnant and the dying shuffle here, trays in their hands, hair terri-fied by nocturnal static.

All three boys order English breakfasts. Since being guided from The Bar last night, Colin is sure that something has changed. That the intricate pipes of his brain have been tampered with, or one little tube has slumped accidentally from its socket and has begun to leak into his open skull, closing off a hemisphere of feeling and thought.

'I can't be arsed going out any more. All those wankers, chasing cunts – I can't be fucked with that.' Colin watches Boys 1 and 2 closely. His veins seem to course with fizzy blood. Or something bitter, perhaps. Boy 2 forks an entire sausage with one jab and allows it to hover in front of his face.

'You don't have to go out, Colin. You can shag prostitutes.'

'They make you wear condoms and you can't kiss 'em.'

'So?'

'I don't know,' Colin snaps and Boy 2 crunches at the sausage. 'What do you think of these women?' asks Colin cautiously, causing Boy 2 to look around with difficulty, his eyesight impaired by his munching cheeks. The room is full of pregnant women. The room is full of heaving bellies. Unseen faces and torsos nestle and develop in happy wombs, waiting for birth. Boy 1 and Boy 2 scan the cafeteria, unable to avoid the smells and the presence of the unborn.

'You don't want to shag a pregnant bird, do you? Colin?'

Colin lays his cutlery across the half-eaten breakfast. His eyes widen, he inhales, his fingers grow crooked with tension. Why did Sal bother fucking Kev? Where did I come from? His lips purse and he exhales. Boys 1 and 2 regret that they are under his control, subject to these strange moods.

'No, Boy 2,' says Colin, drops of moisture round his eyes, 'I won't shag a pregnant one.'

5

New Sex

BACK DOWN SOUTH King Street to the restaurant where Justin is watching his mother foreplaying with her tuna Niçoise. The salad's loving it, its leaves writhe in their dressing and, of course, all olives adore a little middle-aged sex. Justin is wondering whether inheriting sixty thousand pounds is enough. Surely, he thinks, with sixty grand I'll never have to see her again, she can fuck off to Greece and shag a schoolboy. I'm free, he guesses, free to find new ways of loving.

He's watching the space where his mother's left arm meets with her left shoulder. He's watching the way the excess fat on both body parts meets; he imagines this area of skin is sticky to the touch.

'Your father wasn't a rich man, Justin, and I'm barely taking any for myself.'

Justin nods. He's wondering what his mother's body was like before she met him, before she gave birth to him. He feels that her large bosoms have always been dependent on a degree of obesity. He imagines their size fluctuating in

33

accordance with her varying weight. He imagines this process sped up. Bigger then smaller. Bigger then smaller. Could you plot a graph that showed how moments of good fortune and happiness coincided with periods when she was a good weight, when her breasts were firm and more taut, still large but not droopy? He imagines the graph and tries to imagine his mother's current misery.

'Have you any idea how you'll spend the money?'

'Well,' Justin begins, quickly deciding that sixty grand is enough and that'll he'll never have to see his mother again. 'I was thinking of conducting an experiment.'

Diane's eyebrows arch into something like an interested expression.

'Yeh, Mum, you see, I've been shagging very similar girls recently. So similar, in fact, that I can no longer tell one from the other. And, in truth, I doubt they can distinguish me from other boys either.'

A paper napkin begins to dance in Diane's hand, nervously waltzing with her fingers. She sighs at her tuna salad; the sex is over, her son having interrupted.

'So what I thought,' continues Justin, 'was that I could do an experiment.' He gulps the remainder of another White Russian, leaving a milky residue across his top lip. His mother's eyes begin to quiver. Justin rises and leans forwards till his face is only thin air from her own: 'Mum,' he says, slowly and quietly, 'I'm going to save us all. I'm going to find brand new ways of having sex.'

Justin leaves Diane silent on her chair, a half-shagged tuna salad lying in front of her. He grabs his coat and smears grease over the shite glass door as he pushes it open. Air congratulates him as he leaves, summer runs to him and slaps him on the back. Brilliant, he thinks. New ways of having sex.

He walks to the Chop House pub on Cross Street and sits at the counter at the window. 'White Russian, mate.'

He takes out his mobile phone and finds the number of Old Trafford football stadium. His call connects and he quickly quits his job as a steward because it's fucking bollocks and because sixty thousand pounds are bleep-bleeping their way to his bank account. His drink arrives and he sinks half of it immediately. His legs jig on the high stool. He is looking for adventure.

Outside, the shoppers of Cross Street shop. Babies get pushed in buggies while buses get waited for. I'll put a stop to this, Justin confirms, I'm going to save us all. He orders another White Russian and begins to feel noticeably drunk. He shouldn't be drinking cocktails in the Chop House at all, it's a traditional English pub. But something is changing, is getting lost, is dying, etc. We have entered the age of lager and fruit, the age of cocktails and pop. Although I sense that if you were in this pub, you'd get a pint of real ale, as would I. 'I really fancy a pint of real ale,' I'd say to you, and you would agree, I hope. If you didn't want one, I'd try to persuade you. 'Go on, mate,' I'd say, 'lager's shit, cocktails too, have a real ale.' We are mates, right?

Yes, yes, I'm me and you're you. Neither of us is Justin. Justin sits on his high stool, leaning forward on to the thin counter that works its way round the walls and windows of the pub. He's looking out at the people of Cross Street, but he's not much of a people-watcher. He's not the kind of person who would think *fuck*, who are all these slaves? Who are these drones with their shopping bags and their nauseating, broken, dishevelled bodies? No, Justin wouldn't think that at all. He's more likely to think *fuck*, my dad's dead and I seem to be consciously indifferent to the fact, what should I do? Or even more likely, he thinks *fuck*, certain events have occurred that have rocked my hitherto firm belief in the merits of love, what should I do?

But Justin knows what to do. The plan is simple. The plan is to find a happy sexual experience, or at least a sexual experience that makes him happy. New ways of having sex. He sips his drink and scores lines in a beer mat with his fingernail. You can only fall in love once, he thinks, twice at the most. The human heart is a butcher's nightmare, quick to shrivel, to lose flavour. Justin's out of time, out of chances. He's pissed too much affection up the wall. Told too many girls of his ridiculous love for them. It's dumb and regular, love. He should have avoided the idea of it until later in life. He should have covered the basics like first kiss, first blow job, loss of virginity, first girlfriend, without ever flirting with the notion of actually loving another human being.

He gulps the last of his drink and uses a straw to manoeuvre the residue of frothed milk around the glass. It is afternoon and the sun is out. This is an experiment, he thinks, indeed everything that has preceded this moment was an experiment. But the experiment must now be changed in light of certain failures, in light of the unforeseen collapse of love and its long, life-affirming story. The project is, he supposes, happiness. Or more broadly, the project is life. Or more narrowly, the project is sex and a calmed mind. Love has been eliminated; it failed. New things must now be tried: new sexes, contexts and techniques. The project is, he maintains, happiness.

The trouble, Justin believes, is that once experienced, everything becomes dull. The tracksuited goon of experience harms itself. It scrapes away at its own features with its gold-ringed fingers. Just when you suspect you're experiencing something enjoyable, you're abandoned. Just when you feel ready to gorge yourself, when you've sharpened your knife and tucked a napkin into your collar – just at that moment when you're ready to feast, you lose your appetite. I can never do that again, you say of some activity. No, I can never do that again. It has become dull. I hadn't noticed, but I am already full and must find new appetites.

Justin asks at the bar for paper and a pen. The barman prints out a ream of blank till paper and hands it to him with a biro.

'Cheers, mate,' says Justin, catching sight of a staff photo Blu-tacked to the till. In it, various employees embrace, wet and drunk. A boob has fallen out of a turquoise top and the nipple is purple, like an exotic beak. Faces smile, fingers are held up to the camera.

A shiver tip-toes up Justin's neck.

'New sex,' he whispers.

'Pardon, mate?'

'Nothing,' says Justin, blinking, smiling at the barman and removing the pen lid. 'Nothing, mate.'

Returning to the counter by the window, Justin jots down three points, each preceded by a large black dot:

- Experience all sex.
- Spend freely, bankrupt sex.
- Find new sex.

He exits the bar and heads towards Deansgate, leaving the list behind.

6

The Curious Wanker

CARLY WATCHES WITHOUT interest as Steve's cock begins to dance. She turns away as it begins to spurt, choosing instead to watch Steve's face as he performs his trademark little twists and grunts and begins to cough with joy. The wank is over. Steve is dragged irresistibly back to sleep.

Carly climbs over him and steps down from the bed, carefully avoiding the condoms which yellow by its side. She opens the top drawer of Steve's bureau and removes two hundred and fifty quid. Her mind has been on products since her wrist began to move. She could think of nothing but cash as she wanked Steve off, to the extent that the branding on his boxer shorts triggered fantasies of purchase, newness and the brands the day might bring.

Carly is an exceptional shopper. Really, really good at it. She showers, dresses, then heads for town down Corporation Street. She hits Market Street and her lungs begin to open, her pupils dilate and the shopper in her screams with joy. She is surrounded by shops. In her element.

39

Her peripheral vision works overtime, making out shapes, colours, textures and cut, judging them instantly, ensuring a well-paced and heavenly glide through each shop. This is the way to buy: smoothly, elegantly, exactly. Girls like Carly don't pause and stagger, don't finger garments for minutes on end or agonise over decisions. Carly is a killer. Few people bother holding garments up against themselves any more. Everyone can shop. Everyone knows their bodies, their capacity to fit into fabric, their ability to hide their shame. If it doesn't fit then fuck it. Take it back. Give it away. Forget you ever bought it. Garments begin to amass on Carly's arm: slashed skirts, capri pants, military styles, tracksuit bottoms for chilling out in.

Her presence in the shops is akin to that of a celebrity. She has an aura; so slender, decisive, erotic and fast. People are rooted to the spot. The eyes of boys and girls roll after her, admiring her bottom, her breasts, her long, dark brown hair, her delicately tanned arms. It isn't unheard of for young men to approach Carly during the day.

'I realise you must get this all the time, but I think you're the most beautiful girl I've ever seen.'

'You're beautiful. You're incredibly beautiful.'

'I'm serious, I don't mean to put you on the spot . . . a drink maybe?'

'Are you familiar with the films of Pedro Almodovar? I'd love to take you to his latest.'

'Dinner?'

'You are so fucking fit.'

'Latte?'

My name is Carly and I advise such diamond wankers to fuck themselves. Carly is tough. Three weeks ago, at twenty-five minutes to four on a Saturday morning, she was arrested. She gave a black eye to a boy called Brad and beat the shit out of his girlfriend. By the time the police arrived the pavement was covered in blood. The girl was unconscious. Steve legged it after the first punch; he turned red with shame as his bird began battering the couple. It took six people to pull Carly away. She doesn't know. Just likes a drink. Loses it. Fuck this. Hates things. Feels like shit. In a month's time she will go to court and be charged with actual bodily harm. So?

At noon Carly meets a friend, Girl 1, in the Breathing Room on Deansgate. The Breathing Room is a bogusly plush affair: velvet pillows stuffed with crap, pockets stuffed with cash, lips stuffed with arse fat. The two of them take a table outside, in front of a group of boys who seem to suffocate as Carly sits. Carly's legs cross like lovers. Girl 1's bulbous midriff is revealed and sags to obscure a lurid gold belt. Her hair is a lank yellow and her skin is the colour of an orange felt tip. Carly recounts the theft of Steve's cash and Girl 1 is breathless with admiration.

'He won't kill me,' says Carly, reaching for her pint. 'He'll probably just get his cock out at the breakfast bar, you know?'

'Make you suck it?'

'Of course, yeh, which is fine. I mean, look at this.'

Carly lifts a denim jacket from one of her many bags, it has the words 'The Pistols' scribbled in pink across its back.

'It's like clockwork: I rob his cash, spend it, then suck him off in the kitchen.'

'I'd love to,' says Girl 1, dreaming into the bags.

'Love to what?'

'Suck him off.'

'You're too fat,' says Carly, snatching back the jacket and lighting a fag.

41

'I know.'

Yes, it's the twenty-first century and Girl 1 is too fat. A gold crucifix dangles on a silver chain from her belly button. But her belly button can't be seen, the jewellery squirms from within fat like a tasteless umbilical cord. She stares knowingly at the midriff between her belt and her pink T-shirt. The midriff, she thinks. My midriff, she thinks again, then drinks.

'We're going to Versus next,' says Carly, suddenly bored with watching Girl 1 wallow in self-loathing. 'I'm going to try the Relentless Bliss.' She inhales hard on her fag: 'In fact, there's part of me that just fucking loves machines, but they don't have any money, do they? No, they don't, because they're just sex machines.'

'Steve is so fit,' says Girl 1, 'and dead posh.'

'I know, and he's got a cock like a dildo, but . . .'

'Really?'

'Yeh, but it's as if he . . . I don't know . . . it's so easy.'

'Does he make you laugh?'

Carly stubs out her fag and begins gathering her bags together, boys behind her dying, smiling at her arse and dying.

'I don't wanna laugh. Let's go to Versus.'

Carly and Girl 1 head towards Exchange Square. Shoppers sulk around them, drowning in bags, killed by accoutrement, murdered by the special offer. Funny fucking freedom. Carly strides by, head held high, thighs pumping. Girl 1 waddles to keep up.

Designer clothes, mobile phones, sunlight. Sometimes it seems as if this isn't a world at all, but something entirely different. A land of the new, ageless and forever fulfilling. Just a context, a secret space, a hell. A virtual reality in which our petty miseries and our joys can coexist with our need to move, to shop, to die. There is a deceit here, these days. It's in the crucifixes jiggling with the pigskin midriffs. Something's coming. Something dirt-cheap.

Sex shops for women became popular in the 1990s. Shirley Rivers was the first to prosper but is now on the slide. Its twelve-inch glass dildos fail to impress. As do the four-inch butt plugs, the nipple clamps and the rather dated selection of one hundred per cent leather lingerie. It was an all-too-belated attempt to win back a clientele who had already gone elsewhere for kicks. Nowadays, the discerning consumer of sex accessories is going to Versus.

They're wet with lust, the Versus stores. They're as close as most people get to actually having sex with a shop. A popular fantasy. The atmosphere is dark and dingy. Neon is used to laudable effect. Pornographic videos beam and blast across the store, accompanied by loud groans and the sound of extremely athletic intercourse. The products vary greatly. A thousand different models of vibrator are on offer. Booths are provided where one can test the products; issues of hygiene are largely ignored. No one gives a shit about their innards.

'Flesh seems total shit to me,' says Carly, as they pass by the large glass entrance of the latest annexe of the Arndale Centre. So see-through it might not even be there.

'I haven't touched anyone in ages,' says Girl 1.

'It's because you're too fat.'

'I know.'

Versus is situated towards the south end of the Northern Quarter. To build it, a row of old sex shops that pretended to be bookshops had to be demolished. Boys used to buy

American magazines here, with erections, penetration, etc. Nowadays girls buy dildos. While men continue to peer awkwardly at the top shelves of newsagents, or shit themselves in illicit massage parlours with thin carpets and peeling wallpaper, women are legitimate players in the lucrative economy of sex.

'Right,' says Carly, smirking at a group of boys who loiter nervously at the entrance to Versus. 'The Autopen Relentless Bliss.'

'I can't believe you're gonna try it.'

Autopen is the name of the corporation; it's American. It has existed in some capacity since the eighties, but is yet to manufacture a product capable of disrupting the dildo/vibrator-orientated market. But word is that's all about to change.

The Autopen Relentless Bliss comes in a box the size of a small suitcase. It opens out to form two A-frames which support a phallus eight inches in length. When the Autopen Relentless Bliss is switched on, the cock pumps back and forth over a distance of about sixteen inches. It vibrates internally. Riding the phallus is a missile-like device, the clit fizzer, which vibrates too, though more fiercely. To use the contraption, the girl simply erects it and lies between the two A-frames. She then positions herself in relation to the driving rubber cock, the speed of which is controlled by a handheld device.

Carly and Girl 1 enter Versus. It's busy. Few girls bother to view the lingerie situated by the entrance. Most are towards the back, comparing the lengths and motions of battery-operated phalluses.

Carly discovers the Autopen Relentless Bliss in the centre of Versus. It is floodlit, elevated on a platform and surrounded by women. It's like some Jesus, balancing on a crate.

'Fumbling Lovers Are a Thing of the Past. Make Multiple Orgasms a Part of Your Future' reads a banner. Another says simply: 'Better Than Him'. Overhead, six large TV screens depict six different women using and enjoying the Relentless Bliss. 'Who Needs a Kiss, When You Could Have Relentless Bliss?'

Who indeed? Carly looks up at the screens. On the first, a woman is using the Relentless Bliss in a very conventional manner. She reclines on a well-made bed in a room decorated in fashionable colours: browns, blacks, creams and navy blues. The Relentless Bliss shudders at her loins, working its alleged magic. Her eyes are closed and her lips curl downwards at either side of her mouth, which is open wide and making a loud noise.

On the second TV, a girl is in a spacious bathroom, lying on a floor of shining white tiles – imitation marble. It looks as though she's only recently got out of the shower. She's holding the hand-held controller in both hands, raising it high above her head. With careful flicks of her index finger she makes the Relentless Bliss fuck her at a variety of paces. Slow, faster, faster, faster, then slow once more, then fast again and again. On each of the screens, the girls get more and more experimental. The kitchen table, a blonde with cream smeared like sewage over her chest. The garden during the summer, surrounded by flower petals. On the fifth screen, two girls use the Relentless Bliss together, same room I mean – they're using separate machines. All the footage is looped, as if these girls will be fucked for eternity. At least until someone pulls the plug.

Curiously, on the final screen, we're back in the bedroom

from screen one. The difference is that a man has walked over to the side of the bed, and has undone his flies. He's currently massaging what surely must be his fully erect cock; he's wanking. He looks like a right dick. This is glorious life. It's an odd sight, the man's muttering to himself. What does a man wanking over a woman being screwed by a machine mutter to himself? 'That's it, come on, oh yeh.'

Something along those lines. But, in truth, the language hasn't been invented for these sorts of occasions. He's powerless, has to rely on what they taught him in the pornos or at drama school.

'Keep going, oh fuck, shit, shit, come on, bitch.'

How does he feel about the machine? Maybe he's intimidated. Maybe he's relieved that he no longer has to fuck his bird; a machine does it, like it does the laundry and the dirty pots and pans. Or maybe he just gets paid to have a fake wank. She seems to be loving it though. She's saying things like, 'euughh, aaahhgg, eeuugh, aaahgh, nooooooo, eughhh, aaahgh, yes yes yes yes yes.'

Carly joins the queue. Moments later she's ushered into a cubicle by a girl in a T-shirt. It reads: 'The Autopen Relentless Bliss – God's gift to Woman'. Inside the cubicle, the Relentless Bliss is already erected. In her left hand, she has an eight-inch rubber cock, which she's been told is easy to attach to the machine. It's true, everything slots into place. Versus is a brilliant shop. Everything is done perfectly. The light is dim; just enough to see what you're doing, what goes where. The cubicle walls are thin, but succeed in blocking out most of the noise coming from the main floor of the shop. What little noise remains is covered up by ambient music. Flutes with beats and synthetic bass. The calming music is necessary; this is a nervous and potentially embarrassing occasion.

Carly removes her jeans and places them on a chair, actually, it's more like a chaise-longue. Oh, it's a tasteful shop. This commercial space is like a peacock, or a coral reef; so perfect that it makes one inclined to believe in God. Determined, Carly removes her knickers quickly. Within seconds, she's lying on a velvet cushion between the A-frames, touching her clitoris and reaching for the hand-held operating device. Nobody had foreseen quite how erotic such scenarios could be. Nobody had predicted they'd make quite so much sense.

It winks before it's introduced, the dildo, it winks and then smiles. The machine whirrs and enters calmly, like an expert. Carly naturally benefits from its ability to vibrate softly in accordance with the average woman's needs and preference. Her eyes shut and her brain holds its breath and sinks into the milky swamp at the bottom of her skull. The clit fizzer fizzes and Carly inhales fast. She's surprised by the sensitivity of the controls. She quickly teaches it the depth, power and pace she prefers. The machine is ecstatic, happy to oblige. After a few minutes, though, predictably, it is Carly who is being taught. What she had hitherto considered to be the limits of her enjoyment, toleration and stamina are exceeded. Easily. Her index finger enjoys a pragmatic dialogue with her brain. The machine is soon approaching full speed and Carly is careless, content to enjoy the effect of its inhuman motions. The machine does not waver, it only laughs as the girl begins to tense and stretch beneath it. By the time she unknowingly brings the Autopen Relentless Bliss to a stop, Carly has torn a hole in her jumper and her bra is twisted and damaged around her waist. Her cheeks are reddened and raised by a rare smile and her throat is bared and lined with scratch marks.

She returns the cock in a transparent plastic bag and walks quickly through the store, past the whips and the various plugs, past the screened girls who scream, past the lingerie and into open air.

'Jesus,' she says, putting her forearm against her sweltering forehead, her mouth half open, cheeks reddened, 'flesh seems like total shit to me.'

'How was it?' says Girl 1, sidestepping out of Versus to avoid a young girl with a pushchair. 'Did you get off?'

Carly puts a cigarette between her lips and lights it. She pictures Steve. His muscular body turning in his sleep, all its stinks and its leakages, its sweaty crevices. She swallows hard and uncomfortably, turning to Girl 1.

'Yes,' she says, 'it was fucking incredible.'

7

OUCH. MY BACK is aching. Too much time spent curved and crooked, I expect. I need a moment's rest. After thinking about the wide grin of that sex machine pressing against human innards, I need to feel seriously chilled. I'm like.

There is no sound here. Just the tap of fingertip on key and my occasional sigh. No objects either. Just the small desk and the bed. How long have I been here? Years. Years.

I need an ally and it's going to be you. Whoever you are, I like you.

Yes, I'm a good sort. Eager to please. Not one of the bastards who speed-writes after snorting lines of dog dirt from the toilet seat. I know what fun is. I know how to kill time, laugh my arse off and survive. You're going to be safe with me. You're going to enjoy yourself.

Already I'm getting confused. We've barely begun. But already I'm being silly. All this dreadful recreation is making me low. It's making me weird. All this talk of sex machines and parks, young people, open air and the market. Who am

I trying to kid? What do I know of women and men? Only the facts. Maybe these will count for something.

I am pleased to announce that my research continues. The Authority is a weakling. I am working extremely hard and apparently no one can stop me. It must seem strange to you. A mischief like me partaking in such scholarly activity. Perhaps it seems boring, a little unadventurous? But survival is my task – not yours. When I was younger, I tried killing time in more basic ways. I snorted my fair share of dirt with the other prisoners; the drugs, whether snorted or injected, got me into a great deal of trouble. In fact, I'd go as far as to say I was a ringleader. Indeed, this shiny little hell of mine has had a few parties thrown around it. Protest binges. Assaults. The odd moment of mayhem. But the hedonist's path is difficult to tread in here.

The others; I ought to mention them. We're separated into two categories: those who, like myself, were effectively born into this institution and those who misbehaved in the outside world and were brought here. To avoid confusion, the Authority chose not to let the two sets mix, and it's a decision I'm rather grateful for. You see, I'm what is known as a 'real lifer'. As such, I'd rather not spend my days slopping around with the rapists and the deviants of the 'actual offenders' wing. It's a question of one's guilt: I don't feel guilty. My crime is, in effect, yet to be committed.

Today, as once again I found my way on to the Evernet system, I discovered an urban CCTV archive. I like to imagine myself on an old grey road in one of the cities. I am waving both my arms as if inviting someone to strike me. I am shouting: fucking come on then, fucking come on then, fucking come on.

Life is a struggle.

But all is as it should be. No worries. The machines have begun to whir and jab. The footballs are speaking and the condoms natter. Grab my hand. Forgive my fantasies of you and me. It's just survival. I bullshit you with mystery when I ought just to proceed. Another story. More beginnings. Where were we?

The park. Of course. The park . . .

8

Tinned Hearts

WE'RE GOING SOUTH again, down Oxford Road to Fallowfield and the park. Rebecca watches from afar as the football is freed from the wasps' nest. A vested boy jabs hard with a broken tree branch, the football rolls out pursued by buzzing black dots, causing the boys to retreat in unison. Moment later they're playing again. Rebecca turns to Johnny.

'I don't like you using the word "twat", Johnny. What do you mean, you're going to hammer away at a twat?'

'I was joking.'

'I hate that word.'

'Fanny?'

Rebecca turns to leave, causing Johnny to scramble to his feet and begin his shamed and lolloping pursuit. Really, Rebecca doesn't give a shit what words come from Johnny's mouth. But lately she's grown tired of the endless mindlessness. She's tired of silly boys. Stale males. With gentle Johnny, Rebecca feels she ought to make a stand, to improve his sexual vocab.

'Forgive me, Rebecca, I was joking.'

'I can't bear boys saying that, using the word "twat", it's offensive.'

'Pussy?'

'Fuck off, Johnny.'

Johnny grabs Rebecca by the shoulder, trying desperately to slow her down. His horrible hand against her delicate skin, it seems so out of place, the result of some alternative and far fouler evolution. The evolution of man; rank in comparison to the laboratorial development of woman.

I only said 'twat', thinks Johnny, that's funny, right? Daring? No. Clearly not. Rebecca is pulling one of those classic twenty-first-century faces: seemingly serious and actually serious. But, deep down, as bullshittingly false as all the other smiles, frowns and lovey-dovey dogshit expressions that we pull so sincerely. No, she won't forgive, in spite of Johnny's efforts.

'It's not funny, Johnny.'

'Maybe you just don't get it.'

'I get it, Johnny, it's offensive.'

'You just don't get me.'

These days, the idea of 'getting' things and people is important. It relates almost directly to the idea of understanding. Johnny feels that Rebecca doesn't 'get' him, that she doesn't understand him. Do you get me?

'Oh for God's sake, Johnny, don't cry.'

'I'm not fucking crying, Rebecca.'

He is, actually. As the confrontation began, tears started to congregate in the corners of his eyes. Now they're collapsing under their own weight; the first tear has just rolled down his cheek.

'Johnny, I don't want you using those words. I won't tolerate that kind of vulgarity from you.'

Oh, dearest Johnny. He listens to Rebecca, wearing a face of weary surprise. He really has nothing. Nothing except Rebecca, whose friendship gives him hope, happiness and access to a cooler, more interesting stratum of student society.

'Vulgar, you think I'm vulgar?' demands Johnny, his red cheeks wet and beaming.

Rebecca shrugs, her face the colour of treated pine. Natural but impenetrable. 'I can't love you, Johnny. You know that, don't you?'

Five seconds pass. Johnny imagines that he doesn't contain bones, but simply a sparkling selection of inter-locking blades. He stares at Rebecca as she walks away. She doesn't love him. He knows. He stops and stares at the ground, watching the stretch of grass that grows between them as Rebecca walks away.

'Yes,' he says, 'I know.'

Rebecca's footsteps do not fail, she strides away. Johnny continues to admire the ground. His eyes twitch and more tears tumble over their ridges on to his uneven, unfair face. The park becomes a blur, as if his eyes decide to function less, like they can't be arsed to work properly, weary as they are of beholding rubbish, melancholy occasions.

If you remember correctly, though, Johnny referred to the female genitals as a 'twat'. This is almost certainly vulgar, particularly in the presence of a girl of Rebecca's intellect. The word 'twat', you see, is more commonly known as a generic swear word, a moderately severe insult. So it's certainly a little risky to use the word in the old sense – as a signifier of the vagina. 'Cunt' is a slightly different story. It holds on more successfully to its sexual connotations, despite also being simply an insult.

Many of the swear words and insults of the 1990s and early twenty-first century originate as vernacular signifiers of the female sex organ. Cunt, twat, pussy, to name exactly three. It is, predictably, also true of words used to describe the male sex organs. Cock, prick, knob and dick are all legitimate insults, if a little less severe than those relating to the twat – or rather vagina. Fuck it. Words are fallen leaves.

Rebecca reaches Oxford Road and hails a bus. As she takes her seat her phone rings. It's the university, calling to discuss a problem with one of next year's modules.

'I was going to do the Dostoevsky module,' she says. Through the grey of the bus window she notices Johnny exiting the park, his spine curved into a tragic arch, hands inside his endless pockets.

'No, no. I'm in town. I'll come in and sort it out now.'

Johnny's eyes have certainly gone to shit. He can barely see a thing as he leaves the park. His mind tumbledries in a cycle of alternating bullshits. She can't love me, he thinks. I told her that I knew. I don't know anything. No one should ever 'know' anything, Johnny confirms. 'Knowing' things is exactly what makes life so tedious and boring. If we're going to start knowing things then we might as well be dead.

But yes, tumbledrying bullshit. Cycles cycle. Laugh or cry. Laugh or cry. So hard to choose. Johnny's always assumed the former to be of more use and fun, but now he just can't be sure. By the time the dog of history cocks its leg and sprays out the twenty-first century, everybody is laughing their arses off. Comedy's all over the TV, almost everything is pissless. Despite wars and the odd moment of schedule-halting aggression, everybody is very much amused by life. It's hard to say whether that's good or bad. Laughter is, of course, normally part of being happy. But there is something sinister about twenty-first-century tee-heeing. Everybody's wetting themselves. What's so funny?

Johnny strides towards central Fallowfield. As the shops begin to scroll, the promoters begin to leaflet. Boys with triangular torsos and girls with the best boobs thrust pieces of card at the pedestrians. Only, not for Johnny. He watches as each outstretched hand is hastily retracted as he walks by, watches as the flyers are returned neatly to the pile until a more suitable person walks by. Johnny can only glimpse the flyers, briefly hold the airbrushed eyes that advertise nights of sexy music, sexy dancing, sexy puking and fucking.

'Here you are, mate, you'll enjoy this.'

At the corner of Braemar Road Johnny does receive a flyer, from a boy in a pink vest with eyes like upturned beetles. He looks down at it, 'Shag Tag at Robinskis: Everyone Will Pull'. Johnny rests the flyer on top of an over-flowing bin. Everyone will pull. I wouldn't, thinks Johnny, I couldn't pull string. But pulling, yes, it's vital for a good youth. Did you pull? your fellow young will ask. Who did you pull and were they absolutely as fit as fuck? Were they a lump of congealed sexiness with naked legs falling fit-as-fuckly from their arse? Did they have the muscles of a mutant and the smile of a magazine? Did they have shag-ging medals around their neck and was it happy screwing and was their bedroom brilliant in the morning? Did you pull? Did they fuck you stupid?

Johnny passes Bar Revolution where the wealthy students learn to look down on those destined for little. Boys swing car keys around their fingers, flip-flops on their feet and ace haircuts all over their scalps. Girls talk shit and so do boys. The fit get whistled at and giggle, giggle because they hear the tones of fate in the whistling, hear the great youth that their perfect bodies will bring. Johnny shuffles by.

'Not for me,' he says to himself, not knowing quite what he's referring to. 'Not for me.'

He turns into a supermarket, reminding himself of his talents, listing them out loud.

'Shitting, getting ill, breathing, eating.'

He gets funny looks. But something is changing. Getting broken down.

The entrance to the supermarket is dominated not by food but by magazines. Johnny feels like shit. He's covered in sweat and everything's a blur since his eyes ceased to see the point in seeing. Where is it? thinks Johnny. Where is my happy life?

Through the blur, a pair of tits leap from the magazine rack and staple both his eyes to the back of his skull. Jesus, thinks Johnny, his bowels loosening as if he might have to instantly shit. Such incredible breasts. They must belong to Lucy Something or other, she's got her hands all over them. Her fingers are surreptitiously placed over each nipple in accordance with certain laws passed in parliament. Chances are, if you were to buy the magazine, she'd put her arms down by her sides or in her mouth or on her hips. Either way you'd be able to see her nipples.

'I could buy you,' says Johnny to the magazine. 'Couldn't I? I could buy you and then that would be me, happy.'

Lads' magazines have been popular from the 1990s onwards. Johnny has never bought one but is familiar with the content: articles on reasonably inexpensive cars, special reports about African tribes who plant trees in their arses, stuff on watches with global positioning technology, photographs and interviews with beautiful girls.

Right now Johnny can think of nothing else but returning home, throwing a large towel into a steaming hot shower, erecting his penis and slowly making love to the hot, wet fabric. He can't though. He's only got one towel and he hasn't got the guts.

He imagines what it would be like to get hold of the tits. Imagine if he found them in the street, without Lucy. Imagine if he just found them lying on their own, no blood, of course. He could take them home, be with them, touch them and have a really good time with each boob.

'I could buy you,' he says again to the magazine, 'that's exactly how it works!'

Johnny becomes aware of a figure behind him.

'Are you gonna buy that, mate? It's the last copy.'

Johnny turns to see nothing but perfectly hairy muscles. A topless young man with his T-shirt folded and hanging out of his baggy white football shorts. It's not for me, thinks Johnny, none of this was intended for me.

'No,' he says, putting the magazine into the young man's hand, 'you take it.'

'Cheers.'

Johnny watches as Lucy enters the young guy's grip, his thumb creasing her slightly, offering a strange perspective on her breasts. As if they're disconnected from her, and simply stand in front like a couple of painfully inflated skins.

Quite alone, Johnny walks the aisles of the supermarket. They shine, the products, each one shines with contentment.

People choose them. Student boys with calf-length shorts and three-day stubble. Girls with oversized canvas handbags and sunglasses branded in gold. Socks match trainers and lips match nails. Oh, they shine, the humans, each one shines with contentment. But not Johnny. He spots his reflection in the glass of a refrigerator and for a second hopes that he too is up for sale, priced like the ice creams and the Chicago pizzas, a look of lonely misery frozen on to his face.

No, thinks Johnny, turning from the fridge, I am not a product. Products are perfect. They have beautifully designed labels that wrap around perfect tin. Their innards are sealed in and preserved. Wonderful people design products, people with disposable income, takeaway coffee in their hands. They sit round tables and have lengthy discussions about target markets, cross-cutting commercial cleavages, lifestyle, image, the hard sell. I was designed by a dick, thinks Johnny, a lazy dick with no knowledge of the market. There was no table, no takeaway coffees, no talk of commercial possibility or love. I'm rotting inside. Unpreserved. I was aimed at no one, designed with no one in mind, shaped to fit the hands of nothing.

Johnny stands among the cereals, shoulders hunched with envy. Which aisle contains the tinned hearts? Under which heading has love been preserved?

9

The Rat

THE SMELL OF rotting rubbish has made its way down the lane, through a closed window and into Colin's nostrils. They flare in disgust. His bedroom is filthy; the sheets that surround him haven't been washed in over a year. He knows he has one more minute in bed before he has to get up, before an alarm will sound and he will have to shower and go to work.

If you were in the room, you'd find it difficult to determine the origin of the smell of rotting food and dog shit. Outside, you'd say, surely outside. But then your eyes would be drawn to the infested chest of drawers, choking on its wet, brown contents. On the floor, there are many piles of dirty plates, clothes and magazines. This is a room that a girl will never be brought back to. This is a room that only Colin will see. He is secretly, and ever so gently, breaking apart.

The infestation starts somewhere in the recesses of his brain; if you were to try, that's where you'd diagnose the first signs of rot and fury. How do you begin to pick apart a brain? I guess you'd try to find some idea or principle, some memory or piece of faith that suddenly went bad, turned, changed, was hollowed out by some unknown and careful bacteria. Too late now. His whole brain's gone rotten, both milky hemispheres. Disdain and unhealth mess up his insides, stake him out, fuck about with his eyes. A light goes out. His body is weary, struggling. Colin is a boy burnt out by strange failures in his brain.

The infestation spreads. It smokes out of his pores and into his room. Everything in here looks as if it could never be moved, as if the contents have grown naturally into these discarded and obscene shapes, have grown brittle and will never regain flexibility, or be used again. The walls rejected Colin's posters long ago; they wilted and have since been destroyed, ripped underfoot, forgotten. He is running out of plates and cutlery; empty pizza boxes have been screwed up tight and thrown into one corner. His sheets are damp with dirt. The entire area by the window is wet to the touch.

Summer heats the room, causes it to boil. The stench of waste cannot be avoided and the infestation will only get worse. Colin is still able to wash, sanitise himself, spare the outside world for the time being, at least. But something has to give. Colin is aware that the pile of pizza boxes and at least two piles of clothes have developed communities. He's seen the spiders, he's seen the millipedes and the rat. He has allowed them to live. The insects are fickle – quick to feed on the fallen. They are reactionaries. Early converts to the culture of loathing. Colin hears the calling. He is the propagandist, the king of the parasites, equipped with an instinct for hurt, an unavoidable reflex to destroy.

Colin rolls over in bed, his face restless, cheeks flinching because of the sweat. Since being chucked out of The Bar his mind has been on women. He'd spewed to think of them. He's been thinking about his last girlfriend, Marion, who left only last year.

He forced her away, wore her down, isolated her with quiet. On reflection, Colin has always been infested, has always had an uneasy grasp of silence and slow anger. Marion certainly saw it, was even attracted to it in the early days. Colin is the boy with the look of unease, the element of doubt. Lonely and inarticulate, he moves effortlessly with the crowd. Marion ran because she saw too much. Saw he was getting worse. First was the drinking. Then the inaudible, stationary rage.

He hasn't had sex since Marion. Her body gradually and almost cunningly became repulsive to him. It happened so slowly he couldn't work out what was going on. Small nuances in her configuration subtly evolved into things that made him breathless with revulsion. His mind was constantly playing tricks on him. He remembers her attempts to turn him on: the lingerie, the words, the caresses and the look in her eye, unknowing and humili- ated. He also recalls her fear and her collapsed body on the kitchen floor.

Colin's friends remember the day he recovered. They'd been aware that he'd been going through a tough time. Marion had told them about his strange and overwhelming moods, his inability to speak or touch. About a month after Marion left, Colin seemed fine again. Less prone to those long silences that would envelop entire rooms until you could hear a pin drop. He started phoning people again, Boy 1 and Boy 2. He went out for drinks with them, picked up kebabs on the way home, watched the football in the pub on Saturday. He had no interest in girls, but that was his right. Sure it was, not everyone has to be into girls. Gay men, for example. Yes, he was happy to just have a drink.

Now, Colin looks like just another idle lad. Does fuck all but who gives a fuck? He works, as we know, in a departmental office at the university. Colin is disguised; Colin is private. He irons his shirts, washes thoroughly each morning, keeps up with the fashions of the high street. Colin appears normal, is normal, hurting, rotten to the core.

Beep beep beep. Beep beep beep. Beep beep beep. Beep beep beep. Beep beep beep.

His minute's up. Fastest minute of my life, he thinks, as he leaves his bed and picks his way across the room to the door.

Colin's glad to get out of his bedroom, glad to get to the shower where there's fresh water and a more optimistic light. He lives in Withington, south Manchester. He always pays his bills on time. He has a highly strung, rakish frame. Resting between his nipples is a thatch of black hair, the texture of dried earth.

He gets out of the shower and dries himself with a thin yellow towel. Having sprayed each grizzly pit, he puts on those of his clothes which are already clean and ironed. Underwear, socks and a pale blue Hugo Boss shirt. He walks downstairs, erects the ironing board and turns on the TV.

It's morning. Morning TV is on. Currently, a man is being interviewed by two greying, playfully obese presenters. The man has written a book on body language and has a face that seems entirely comprised of pink soap. Body language is a very fashionable subject in the twenty-first century. The idea being that the way we move our bodies says a lot about who we are, why we succeed and why we fail. This guy is all hands, limbs and smile, a voice that sounds like a trumpet slurring the notes of some major arpeggio. He's sitting forward on the soft couch, eagerly and expressively making his points, trying, no doubt, to tell us he's a tit.

'You'd be amazed by what I've learnt about you in the past five minutes, Jemima.'

'Would I?'

'Yes, you would.'

'Oh goodness, I dread to think.'

'You'd be amazed how naked our behaviour makes us. Your movements will always betray your mind.'

'Oh, I feel so embarrassed. Am I really so transparent?'

'Yes, I'm afraid you are.'

The guy reckons he can discover what a person's like in bed just by shaking their hands. Dominant, submissive, playful, shit. Shake my hand, thinks Colin, shake my fucking hand, you twat. Of course, the guy can't, because he's on TV. Too bad, thinks Colin, looking down at his hand. It's gripping the iron, smoothly guiding it over his jeans. What does this mean?

'Tits,' says Colin to himself. The iron hisses steam and Colin coughs into his fist. 'Nothing,' he says, continuing to iron.

Along with football, bird-shagging is a major national pastime; it's odd that Colin no longer gets involved. He tries to ignore his feelings. He remembers Marion's cellulite. How it began to shimmer and quiver on her thighs towards the end of their time together. How it reminded him of enormous blisters; the scars that the victims of fire are left with. She had tried so hard to win him back. She bought gels from Versus, toys, videos. She had pleaded, bent herself over the kitchen table and pulled up her skirt. 'Fuck me, Colin. Teach me a lesson.'

With every effort Marion made, Colin got colder and colder. As if he was just some debris drifting in space; an old flag or a piece from a shuttle, floating away from the world of touch and love. He's barely been touched since Marion, even the bouncer had held him by the collar while escorting him from The Bar. Occasionally someone will brush past him in a busy place, or he'll be forced to shake the hand of a new colleague at work. But apart from the odd social nicety, Colin remains completely untouched.

Jeans still warm from the iron, Colin is walking down Wilmslow Road towards the bus stop. It'll be hot today. Chesty vests, mini skirts, what is he missing? Even the most slender and beautiful of girls leave him with an inexplicable rage. Is it simply a question of hatred? Does he simply hate women because they're stupid, weak and shallow? He's not sure, and in truth, you can care about these mysteries too much. Fuck it. Live with it.

Oxford Road is bathed in early morning sun. Students on voguishly battered bikes weave between the buses. Colin drifts. The Wishing Well has been on his mind since he ate there yesterday morning, with Boy 1 and Boy 2. If he looks east, out towards Upper Brook Street, he can just make out the glass structure of the hospital. But the hospital has to wait. He takes a short cut through a car park behind the Union building, avoiding the crowds of chilled idiots that slouch around the front door. He manages to get to his building without encountering youth. But the Wishing Well, yes, he's desperate to dine there again.

Because pregnancy is on Colin's mind. He's never really considered the reality of childbirth before, and in some small way, believes he couldn't possibly have been pushed into the world from his mother's womb. He climbs the stairs of the Arts Faculty, oblivious to the girls, thinking only of the women at the Wishing Well. Their bellies like Allied helmets of the Second World War. Their horse-head tits. The children living inside them; shouldn't we all be a little bit more amazed by this? he thinks. Those women walk differently, they lean back in order to bear the weight of their baby. Colin likes their slippers and their moth-eaten dressing gowns. He feels, perhaps, that they possess a rare kind of honour.

'Hello,' he says, as he enters the office, making for the relative sanctuary of his desk, as if under gunfire. It is certainly summer. There's not too much work to be done at the university, a bit of prep but nothing too strenuous. Not until the term starts again in September.

'Hello.'

'Hello, Colin.'

His colleagues: a selection of dreary objects with whom he shares nothing, not even the petty ennui that the job offers them. A job is a job, believes Colin.

'Lovely weather today.'

True enough. Colin boots up his computer and flicks through a pile of questionnaires returned to him by the boys and girls starting university in September. Fresh meat, as they're known in the office. Today will be spent feeding this information into a spreadsheet. Names, hobbies, dates of birth, preferred course and living arrangements. Colin will fulfil his duties to the best of his ability. He never complains. His mind will not wander and his breaks will not exceed their permitted duration. He will not say a word.

At six o'clock, just as he's preparing to leave, a girl called Rebecca will come in to sort out a problem with the Dostoevsky module. He will watch the episode with eyes of glass. Snobby bitch, he will think. Slag.

10

Business and Pleasure

STEVE IS STILL in bed, wanked off where we left him. It's my fault. I'm letting time get the better of me. The characters are streaming off into different zones. We should have worn rollerblades, you and I, given ourselves a better chance of keeping up with these various unfortunates. Of course, as we return to Steve, Carly is being seduced by a sex machine in one of the cubicles of Versus. We know this. Steve does not. Such is life.

It's almost midday by the time Steve wakes up. A block of sunlight lies on the floor beside the bed; the used condoms bathe in it like a couple of nattering holiday makers. Steve looks towards his bureau, its top drawer ajar. She's robbed me again, he quickly concludes, Carly has robbed me again.

Steve has given the matter some thought, he's calculated that ejaculation perpetrated by Carly results in a five-minute period during which he is drawn to her, loves her and is inclined to cherish the girl. But then it fades. It faded as he drifted inevitably back to sleep, emptied and content. Steve can imagine a time when this feeling of affection fades almost instantly. He will ejaculate, experience a fleeting moment of affection, then nothing. The flash of something close to love dissolves. A bark of romance, then suddenly nothing at all.

Steve jumps from his bed and shuts the drawer of his bureau. Carly robs him regularly. She robs him because she loves to shop, because Steve is her fit, rich boyfriend and can afford to be robbed. Steve, mostly, allows the robberies to go unnoticed. For Carly is his fit-as-fuck girlfriend and therefore must, he supposes, be granted certain privileges. Normally, after such occasions of theft, Steve will produce his cock at the breakfast bar or in the lounge and suggest, quite forcefully, that Carly suck it. Which she does, has to, really, because she robbed him.

This transaction lies at the heart of Carly and Steve's relationship and they both treat it with respect. Under normal circumstances, of course, a penis unleashed at a breakfast bar would possess only a slim chance of getting sucked. It would stride purposefully from its fly like a monarch on to a balcony, only to find that no subjects have turned up to applaud its arrival. After theft though, it's quite different. Carly knows this as much as Steve. People cheer and wave flags. Carly reverentially drops to her knees.

In the shower, Steve lets the water run over him. His hands follow the trendy contours of his body. His six-pack scrums with itself, his abdomen drops triangularly to what he feels must certainly be his deadly dick. But the break-fast bar, must justice really be found at the breakfast bar? A brightly lit blow job? Appliances humming gently in the background? What a well-lit and lonely fate. Steve shuts his eyes from the soap and sees the cardiganed girls of his university past. Yes, his colleagues on his economics BA, the ponytailed frigids that had marvelled at his beauty and at the confident strides with which he entered the lecture theatre. Perhaps, thinks Steve, drying himself, I should have married one of them, seduced a little Mary or a little Jane, bought her fancy lingerie and had kids and discussed the misery and injustices of the open market, the merits of globalisation.

'No,' he says to himself, rising like a dancer to meet his gaze in the mirror, the red towel falling off his blond hair.

'No way,' he says again, shocked anew by the symmetry of his features. His haircut perched on his scalp like an endangered bird. No way, indeed. Because you die, he thinks, yeah, because you die and should never miss the chance to feel some real beauty. He leaves the bathroom and returns to the bedroom, picks up the condoms and flings them towards the bin. They go straight in. Good. Because you die.

An hour later, as Steve pulls his Audi TT out of the underground car park of his apartment block, the decision has been made. No more bullshit blow jobs at the breakfast bar. Anal, that's the ticket. All the rucksacked girls of his middle youth are gone, only Carly remains. Carly, whose knickers match her brain and whose bra matches her heart. Carly, it's impossible to imagine her heart as anything but tailored, designed with tomorrow's sex in mind. She has thighs that remind the normal boys of absolute joy. Perfectly curved. But anal, thinks Steve, rejecting distraction, anal's the ticket.

Steve pulls the car on to Upper Brook Street, heading south, past the instantly outdated flats built around the turn of the twentieth century. He feels perfectly entitled to play the economy of sex. Sex is his way of solving things. Before now he might have spoken, turned a phrase or placed a kiss. But few turn phrases nowadays. Most bang away at another, eyes shut, just breathy hissing coming from their tightened lips. Carly robbed me, he thinks, anal will make me a man once more. Traffic lights go red, he checks his phone: no word from Carly. The lights go green.

He turns right off Upper Brook Street, down Moseley Road, through Fallowfield, then Withington, past the cancer hospital and its air of glassy, transparent dread, then further south to Didsbury. There is sunlight and the streets have been cleaned. Didsbury 'Village', as it's curiously known, is dominated by franchise restaurants. Steve parks up then buys a copy of the *Financial Times* in a newsagent's. He exits the shop, the pink paper folded under his arm. A man walks by with cardboard coffee cups for hands. No, not that. Normality. A brunette jogs past in tight shorts and sports bra, her tongue visible like the tip of a violet lipstick. No, no, normality. Steve crosses the road.

He has travelled to Didsbury to meet Frank. Frank is a fat twat. He's sitting sipping a latte on the terrace of a franchise Italian. He has a papier-mâché head and a gut like an incoming tide. Frank is Steve's guru, an expert in investment and risk, the reason for Steve's burgeoning wealth. Frank spends his days relocating his money and watching his bank account swell. His nights are spent bantering with the prostitutes of Cheshire. Invariably, as the sun rises, Frank finds himself drunk, protruding like a human-shaped tumour out of the back of some high-quality call girl.

'I've done it again, my boy,' says Frank, through a terribly deep, Adam's-appley laugh. 'I've done it again. Waiter. Another latte!'

Steve takes a seat opposite Frank, the glass table a circle of bright reflection, as if a miniature sun shines between them, supporting drinks. He waits for the guttural reverb of Frank's laugh to fade, then watches as the rough, fatty tides of Frank's cheeks turn to a ripple and then settle around his wet, maroon mouth.

'Have you told Carly?'

'No, I don't think I will. How much do we stand to make, exactly?'

'Frankly, my boy, millions. All Autopen stock has risen six hundred per cent.'

Steve's lips sprawl awkwardly into a half-smile, all uneven, unsure whether happiness is quite the right feeling. But it is. Yes, it is, so he lets out a cautious chuckle. Frank and Steve invested heavily in the Autopen Corporation. Frank got the tip, the Relentless Bliss is going to go huge.

The waiter returns with the coffees. There is tense silence as they're placed down, then the two men lean forward and sip at the light brown lattes, their eyes meet, shining like silver coins in the sun.

'We're rich, my boy,' says Frank. 'It seems as though girls are extremely keen on machines.'

Steve sighs, a hand in his hair, his fingers tensed and spread equally like the bristles of a brush. He'd been reluctant to invest in the Autopen sex machines, had to be persuaded by Frank. Don't you understand, boy, Frank had blared, Autopen is the future. All of us men, we will be replaced. Sexually, we are absolutely replaceable. This wasn't an idea Steve was keen to agree with. The beauty of man, believes Steve, the beauty of himself, is the future. His hair of various shades of blond and its original black, his wonderful clothes, clean and distressed, his ringed toe, brass bracelets, necklaces, moisturiser, tattoos, perfume, gel. Beautiful man is the future. Beautiful me.

'I don't buy it,' says Steve. 'It's a fad. I say we sell soon.'

'You don't think, Steve, that your darling, fuck-puppet, Carly, could be pleasured by a machine? Can you not conceive of that?'

'No,' Steve replies, the tone of his 'no' failing slightly and becoming more of a 'nahh'. He reaches for his coffee, gazing uncertainly beyond Frank's huge left shoulder, which curves like the gradual, endless throat of a docile whale. It's possible, I think, that on some level we humans know everything. That we choose simply to ignore the knowledge brought to us by the more cosmic, bowel-based, mystical senses. So it is that Steve shifts in his seat at the suggestion that his own lover could defect to the machines. Deep down, whatever that means, he knows she could. On some level, he's suppressing the clouded, only vague image of Carly, spreadeagled in the cubicle of Versus, the machine moving in and out, vibrating fiercely and perfectly.

'No, Carly won't go for machines,' he says eventually. 'I fuck like one.'

'I see.' Frank leans back on to the layers of fat that congregate above his belt. 'We will sell,' he says, suppressing a burp. 'In many ways, you're right. Autopen is a fad. The Americans are far too keen on the idea of replicating penetration. It's nonsense.'

'Nonsense?'

'Of course. Penetration is a trap we keep falling into, a needless homage to a Stone Age ritual. The future lies on the outside, in the superficial stimulation of the exterior, with electricity.'

Steve bows his head, placing both his hands on the table.

74

He looks at his diamond-encrusted watch. What is time doing? If I am anything, thinks Steve, I am a penetrator. Markets, fashions, cunts, arseholes, elites, parties, mouths. I'm a penetrator. Running out of time.

'I'm going to take a trip,' continues Frank, his fingers fiddling with each other like lovers at an orgy for the fat. 'I'm going to go to Japan, find the company with the best sex machine. Then we'll invest. The electronic orgasm, that's where we're headed. Don't look so glum, my boy.'

'I'm not glum, Frank.'

'Has Carly been robbing you again?'

Steve moves his empty glass to one side. Milk dried like crystals to the rim. His watch. Diamonds. What is time doing?

'Carly's fine,' says Steve. 'I'm fine. Look at me.'

'You're a beautiful young man, Steve, a beautiful young man.'

'I know I am.'

'Of course you do. Of course you do.'

Frank begins to bang on about something, prostitutes, perhaps, they're constantly frustrating him, but Steve decides to not listen. His relationship with Frank is far from comfortable. Where are the tweeded economists of my youth? he thinks. Where is my respected brain? The lever-arch files, tutorials, ambition, the cups of tea and talk of Keynes. Steve feels his mobile phone vibrate in his jacket pocket, buzzing next to his heart. A text. It's Carly, no doubt, but he doesn't look. He feigns interest as Frank talks him through the economic future of mechanical sex. He is, he realises, surrounded by choice. Coated in the stuff, his palms sticky with it. Choice. The fat twat Frank who cares for cash and painfully thin prostitutes with siliconed tits like overkicked footballs. The fit-as-fuck Carly who cares for cash, boob tubes, alcohol, whatever. So much choice. It's hilarious. Is it possible I've made so many choices?

After declining Frank's invitation to go to one of Didsbury's five-star massage parlours, Steve returns to his car and checks his phone.

> *Sorry babe. should*
> *have asked. soz, really soz.*
> *in town with Girl 1 x x*

Anal then, logically. Because I am still a penetrator, thinks Steve, twisting the key in the ignition. And because you die. Because I'm beautiful and I'm young.

11

The Satsuma

AFTER ABANDONING JOHNNY in the park and talking Dostoevsky at the university, Rebecca is late for work. The sun has dropped below the Town Hall, casting a shadow on to Deansgate. The last of the shoppers beat hasty retreats. They make for car parks, dragging bags and children, aware that night is falling and that they risk being out when the party starts. They feel the beat of the boozers drumming beneath their feet. And they run.

But, yes, Rebecca. She works in a strip club on Deansgate. She's an unlikely stripper, really, what with her occasional moral outbursts. But on arriving in Manchester she was keen to become one. Because as much as she resents the cobwebbed corners of the male mind, she cannot help but investigate them. Tonight she's late for her shift. It's almost seven by the time she passes through the scarlet curtains and walks down the steps into the Nude Factory.

In truth, Rebecca had been lucky to get a job as a stripper. Her breasts don't droop, but nor could they have your eye out. When she came for the interview she knew she was borderline. She had shivered topless in the centre of a back room as men tapped their lower lips, sending clouds of grey smoke towards her. 'She's girl next door,' the manager, Marcus, had said at last. 'And we need a real pair.' She got the job. She had smiled and got dressed. As she left the interview she heard a bouncer whispering to himself. 'Wicked nipples,' he had said.

In the Nude Factory the light is purple and cheap. The air is smoky and greased. Rebecca smiles at the manager, at Marcus, the fat black man who sits at the bar in a cloud of smoke, bomber jackets and men. Marcus is medically incapable of smiling.

'You're late,' he shouts, his voice like a desperate engine.

'I know,' she calls, 'traffic was a nightmare.'

Rebecca makes straight for the changing room. She enjoys being the girl next door. She enjoys the job in general. The money is amazing and the other girls are good company. Invariably, she arrives to find a streaked-orange stripper hunched tearfully over her huge tits, weeping about a man whose name sounds like it ought to belong to a pair of trainers. Yes, she enjoys them, the other girls. Those that aren't students are simply fascinating tragedies, their lives grated to shreds by drugs, men and age.

Rebecca removes the green khaki skirt which has made her legs invisible all day. Her midriff, she knows, contains just enough definition. She is the girl next door. She is changing into matching underwear, a black contraption. She removes her faded day bra. It's like the unblindfolding of a particularly sexy terrorist. Her breasts look like halogen lights under water.

Rebecca runs a comb through her neat brown bob, thickens her eyelashes with mascara and steps into a pair of stilettos she purchased specifically for work. As she clops into the bar, the music razors her ears. She thinks it's fucking shit; so do I, so would you. Crap chart dance with thick beats and inane lyrics sung with ridiculous conviction, usually by a black woman. She makes for the bar where she's handed a gin and tonic. Inebriation is the stripper's secret; they are all getting completely fucked. Pills are forbidden, because it makes them dance badly. They lose eroticism and then money. Some do them anyway. There's coke in the back room if you can stomach the attention of the resident dealer. Most can, it's the only way to endure the boredom and the incessant nudity.

'If you're late again, you're fired.' Marcus takes the gin and tonic from Rebecca's hand and places it on the bar. 'And you're dancing for Pete.'

'Oh, for fuck's sake,' says Rebecca, because Pete is a regular and a nutter, a lonely idiot, and now she has to go and show him her breasts – bring them up close to his misty eyes and his chapped lips. This is punishment. She was late and now she must dance for the dirty nutter. Fine. She swigs from her drink and sets off in Pete's direction. The bar is half full. Shockingly shite and nicotine-yellow chandeliers hang like meat from the low, red ceiling. Disgusting curdling laughs rise above the music as men buy dances for one another. The Nude Factory caters for the old-fashioned wanker, little business is done here, customers count coppers for one final dance. Rebecca exchanges smiles with some of the other girls as she takes a seat next to Pete on a poorly upholstered banquette.

'Pete.'

'Oh hello, girly, thank you, I should say, thank you. Been slow for me, so slow so thank you.'

'What?'

'No no, it's OK, girly. Drinky? Can I buy you a drinky?'

He isn't mad, Pete, just a bit lost. Another corduroyed, disorientated anybody that the city seems to secrete. On his cheeks, dirt and wiry grey hair gather around healed white scars. A look in his eye suggests abuse. Many forms of abuse.

Marcus's eyes are fixed on Rebecca; there's no way of getting out of this. Marcus is a sack-happy twat. Never thinks twice. Resents the fact he's forced to employ students. Feels they fail to maintain ideas of glamour and celebrity that ought to characterise a decent strip club. Rebecca removes the 'Nude Token' from Pete's hand, places his arms down by his sides and pushes his back straight against the back of the seat.

'Oh, yes, Rebecca. Becky lovely jugs,' mumbles Pete, a yellow cheese-like substance thickly coating his front teeth.

Rebecca opens her ears briefly to register the tempo and tone of the song she must dance to. Having done so, she returns to the concentrated silence she's perfected in the six months she's worked here. She begins to sway and gyrate gently in front of the regular, the nutter, the lonely idiot. After exactly thirty seconds of moderate thrusting, swaying and stroking, she bends down and brings her face up close to his. This is misdirection. While Pete attempts to cope with the proximity of a youthful, seemingly aroused face, her hands are undoing her bra. Imagine his surprise as she rises to reveal breasts. Her breasts will be enjoyed by Pete for exactly a minute. She will support them, squeeze them, tease them and tweak them in precisely that order. Of course, he is forbidden to touch.

'Your hooters, Becky. Honk honking hooters!'

Rebecca runs the index finger of her left hand down Pete's scrambled egg face. He looks up at her through Perspex eyes. The club sounds like shouting underwater. It's time to take a shit.

'Taking a shit' is how the girls refer to the task of lap dancing for particularly grotesque men. It was coined by Rebecca's good friend Sidney. 'Right, I'm just gonna go and wipe my arse, back in a sec,' Sidney would say, after grinding on the crotch of some cheese-dicked punter. The kind of guy whose crotch feels like a countryside footpath, eroded by rain. Before the invasion of American clubs, such men wouldn't have even been let in. The Nude Factory survived easily without recourse to the flimsy capital of the under-class. Nowadays, virtually everyone is welcome. Marcus can't afford a dress code or strict behavioural guidelines, and he hates to see nudity go to waste. It must be watched and paid for.

Rebecca turns her back on Pete and stands with her feet one pace apart. She slowly bends over so her hair falls down over her head and her face is only inches from the ground. Blood runs to her eyeballs. If you were Pete, you'd see the skin on Rebecca's legs pulled tight enough to reveal the muscles and bones of her thighs and her arse. You'd see the strain on her reddening face and the fingers of her right hand half-heartedly simulating masturbation.

'Girly, girly, beautiful.'

Then down in one firm movement on to his crotch, the feeling of muddy corduroy all over her clean bottom. This is the worst part, actually metaphorically taking the shit. It's impossible to remain distant during this phase of the dance, for fear the erection you inevitably find yourself sitting on takes you by surprise. In Pete's case,

Rebecca is aware of something hard in his pants, but feels it can't possibly be considered cylindrical. It feels like a satsuma. Rebecca hopes the physicality of dirty, elderly penises will remain a mystery to her always. Nevertheless, she endures a minute of squirming about on Pete's crotch and she performs her customary lean-back manoeuvre. This involves throwing her head back over the customer's right shoulder then lifting and toying with her tits. This provides a great view for the customer, a sexy view, she supposes. This moment is the secret to her good tips. As she tweaks each of her nipples, the satsuma in Pete's trousers begins to pulsate violently. Time to stop. Sick bastard. Old shit. What an incredible lap dancer I am.

'OK?' she says to Marcus as she returns to the bar clutching the crumpled tenner given to her by Pete. Now, Pete is trying to camouflage his hard satsuma as he side-steps across the bar en route to the toilet to piss and wank, or rather, wank then piss. Rebecca takes her drink from the bar and goes to greet Sidney, her friend, who leans, smoking, against the back wall.

'What time do you call this?' says Sidney, a fellow English student with a self-financed boob job and hair the colour of soft sand.

'I know, but the Dostoevsky module's full, I had to go in and beg.'

Sidney holds her cigarette to Rebecca's lips. She inhales deeply.

'I was out with Johnny, too, until he started going on about twats and minges.'

'I see. Have your flatmates taken the porn down yet?'

'No, they've coated my cupboard in cum-shots.'

'Ha.'

Sidney laughs and Rebecca almost stumbles amid an-all-too brief rush of nicotine.

Rebecca finds it difficult to reconcile the male as sexual agent with the male as intellectual agent in her overall view of men. Dostoevsky is a case in point. The question is, how did Dostoevsky feel about women? Did he do a bit of writing, then go to a club and stare at girls? Stiffen his satsuma over vodka? How famous was Dostoevsky when he was alive? She isn't sure but she needs to know. She knows that Baudelaire visited prostitutes; was this a clue? Perhaps. Do all men harbour pulsating satsumas and thoughts and instincts darker than the human eye can see?

'I'm fucking tired of men,' Rebecca says to Sidney.

'I know. It's weird how they're all wankers.'

What, wonders Rebecca, did Dostoevsky wank about? Something cool, perhaps. Like hairy armpits. But no, she thinks, tits. Certainly tits.

Rebecca's sexual history is limited to exactly three relationships, all carried out between the ages of sixteen and eighteen while she was growing up in the Lake District. All three of these relationships were with boys of around twenty-four; farm hands, small-time rural drug dealers. These relationships were founded less on love and more on the allure of the motor car, cigarettes and the novelty of cock. She has never really been able to understand men since she became older and the attraction of cider and sex in barns waned. Rebecca firmly believes that boys are comprised of two entirely separate halves that simply betray, battle and deny each other. Perhaps Johnny is one half sensitive, funny man, and one half sex-starved goblin. Maybe this is why he tries telling jokes about twats and minges. Because his mind is being driven to overdrive by a thinly veiled desire for heavy metal sex.

Rebecca turns to Sidney to find that she has disappeared. She scans down to one side and locates her, she's taking a shit on a skinny businessman with a floral tie.

'Sidney,' asks Rebecca, 'how do you feel about sex?' Sidney pauses mid-gyration and thinks; the businessman grimaces.

'Well, I think it's meant to be good fun,' replies Sidney. 'But weirdly, it rarely is.' The face of the businessman dissolves into peach mush. He appears to die beneath Sidney's near perfect buttocks.

No use. Rebecca can't work this out alone; she needs to speak to Dostoevsky. I need to date Dostoevsky, she thinks. I think. He faced a firing squad in Moscow at a very young age. They didn't fire but he stood there for a while, blindfolded, shitting it presumably, waiting for the roar of the guns. After surviving that, everything must be valued and pretty euphoric. Sex must be kind of evangelical. Happy, clappy, thankful and kind, eyes open, drinking in the occasion. What a guy.

'If you want to talk about sex,' says Sidney, rising to reveal an elevated area of pulsating pinstripe around the businessman's fly, then turning to take a tenner from his weak grip, 'then you should go and talk to that guy over there.'

Rebecca follows Sidney's finger to where a young man is making notes on various scraps of paper, sipping regularly from a cocktail.

'Take him a White Russian. He's been downing them since he got here. It's good money, too. Funny fucking weirdo.'

The young man has a shaved head and wet eyes, pale

blue with defined eyebrows. He looks like a rather primitive line drawing, but handsome, definitely handsome. Rebecca turns and heads towards the bar.

Of course, the young man is Justin. This should have become clear when you learned about his chosen drink – yet another reference to the White Russian. It wasn't just a coincidence or a comment on twenty-first-century cocktail consumption, as you might have thought. I guess what happened was that he left the pub on Cross Street, retraced his steps back through St Ann's Square, on to Deansgate and down into the Nude Factory. His being here makes sense. Think about it. Beyond buying a porn mag, a visit to the Nude Factory is the first logical step on his journey to happy sex and steady living.

Justin looks up from his notes to see a stripper's finger pointed directly at him. Sidney? Was that her name? She'd gyrated on his lap an hour or so ago. He hadn't enjoyed it. Her purplish pimply nipples had seemed absurd, perched, as they were, on top of her somehow translucent skin. He could almost see the silicone beneath. He watches as another stripper visits the bar, returning moments later to his table, placing a White Russian directly in front of him.

Having placed the drink down, Rebecca takes a seat opposite Justin. She's intrigued. She stares at him, sending ice cubes clinking around her gin and tonic with a straw. They sit in warm darkness. Unknown to one another. The music blares and naked girls dance. The two of them exchange a look. Thank God they met. And yes, of course, thank fuck. They begin to blabber through the near darkness of the club.

'Hello,' says Justin.

'Hello.'

'I've had this idea, quite a big idea.'

'Right.'

'Shall I pay you now?'

'Yes, do you want a dance?'

'No, thank you.'

'OK.'

'I've had six already.'

Rebecca removes two twenty-pound notes from Justin's hand and screws them up tight in her fist. Justin is clearly drunk, overly so. He's had a skinful, if you think back to the pub and the restaurant and to his mother. Justin sips from his drink and tweaks his nose lightly. Rebecca wonders whether Justin could survive a firing squad. It's unlikely, he could barely stand.

'I'm a man,' Justin begins. 'And you, well, you're . . .'

'I'm a woman,' Rebecca intervenes.

'Of course you are, and I, well, I've had this great idea.'

Rebecca looks down beneath the table to where her legs are tightly crossed around the thin fabric of her underwear. It's a silly business, life, she thinks, full of fine lines. She wishes to know what men are, or, more precisely, where sexuality and personality meet in them. Justin burps, bringing his hand to his mouth in an attempt to pass it off as a cough. Never. His jaw drops. Words, more words.

'The narrative of love has been written, it is completed. It has been read and understood, now the manuscript must be burned and . . .'

Justin fumbles over the first line of his oration. With Sidney he'd been more on the ball, more lucid, less hammered. Now the booze is making his head ache and Rebecca is causing his mind to trip. Is she the girl next door? And doesn't Rebecca have fucking amazing tits? His eyes buzz.

'What's your name?'

'Rebecca, what's yours?'

'Justin.'

Technically, Rebecca should have told him her name is Claudette. Every girl in the bar has a stripper name, Claudette is her 'nom de nudité', as she calls it. Around them, the Nude Factory is getting busy. The entrance chokes on male, tracksuited youngsters, their yellow eyes magnified by desire. The music ploughs on, soul-shaftingly bad. Rebecca looks at Justin, imploring genius and the ability to survive a firing squad. Bang! No, no, he's dead, he's dead. Justin feels a squelch in his brain, as it momentarily loses interest in working.

'Please take your bra off, Rebecca,' he says, his words fart-like and odorous.

'Would you like a dance, Justin?'

'No, no, I just need a moment. I think I might be hammered.'

Thirty seconds pass. A segment of Justin's brain topples out of his left ear and into his drink.

'Take off your bra, Rebecca. I gave you forty quid.'

Rebecca sighs. Bang! He's dead. He didn't survive. For the third time this evening Rebecca reaches her hands round her back and removes her bra.

'How touching, you wish to see my tits,' she says, arching her spine and leaning back. Justin swills his drink, the segment of brain bobs in the milk. This seems natural. His drunk eyes stare across the table at Rebecca; they seem to smoke a thin green gas. He burps again. Speaks: 'Really, Rebecca, you really are as fit as fuck.'

'No, Justin, try not to be so predictable. Try to sober up instead,' she replies.

Justin seems to be drifting in and out of consciousness. Is he drunk or just deep in thought? Rebecca wonders. He sits, slumped and comatose, watching her tits like he's watching television. Her nipples hypnotise like late-night static. She knows that she isn't as fit as fuck. She knows that the alcohol is allowing him to gloss over her lack of height and certain imperfections in her face; imperfections of structure and symmetry.

'I'm sorry,' says Justin, through a gurgle.

It's going wrong for him, too. His drinking has fucked up the plan, wronged the experiment. Oh God, he thinks, I was meant to save us all. Think of all the millions of people across the world, all being denied a happy life of firm sex and expressive, truthful personalities, just because I got too drunk and cocked the experiment up. I should be put in prison.

'OK, listen, Rebecca, put your bra back on.'

'You dickhead.'

'It's fine, I'm sorry.'

Bang! He survived. The squad missed. He survived. I called him a dickhead, thinks Rebecca. I'm fine, thinks Justin. Think of humanity and think of the world. Society. All those sex deaths that should be sex lives. As Rebecca reconstructs her bra, Justin pushes his drink to one side and leans towards her with both his elbows on the table.

'So what's the big idea, Justin?' asks Rebecca, re-assembled once more. Justin smiles a wobbly smile, like a piece of string draped across his face at random. He's speaking.

'One month ago my father died. A week from now I will receive sixty thousand pounds. This, in light of the fact I feel my life will never serve a purpose or last a long time, is a great deal of money. Rebecca, I have lived my life at the sharp end of capitalism. I'm useless. I will serve, and am happy to serve, no purpose.'

Rebecca yawns enormously, like a lioness.

'At the age of fourteen I fucked a farm hand,' she says, 'blah blah blah. Did you know that Dostoevsky survived a firing squad?' she adds, impressed. He's bright, quite funny, too, in a way. Was Dostoevsky funny? Did he crack jokes? What about?

'A farm hand? What do you mean?'

'Nothing, go on.'

'Where was I?'

'Your dad is dead. You are inheriting money and being blunted by capitalism.'

Justin nods, gulps from his drink. The segment of brain seems soured by the milk. Ever so slightly green. No matter. So drunk. No matter.

'I have money and I'm loveless, devoid of affection. Romantically disabled. But the money, that's crucial. I have money. I feel so terrible and powerful, Rebecca. I've never had a proper job, never went to university. I was brought up, schooled and abandoned to all this. And now all I wish is to go down in flames.'

'Perhaps you should try and sleep off the bravery, you look a little pale.'

'Listen to me. I gonna *buy* sexual satisfaction. I'm gonna cut through all the society and the shit and achieve happiness and sexual joy through pure buying power.'

'So you came to the Nude Factory?'

'Well, this is just the beginning. I only had the idea a few hours ago.'

'And a lap dance didn't make you happy?'

Justin seems to visibly rise in his seat, his back straightens and he places both his hands flat on the table, fingers stretched apart. He stares at them for a moment, then says, 'Don't you see how much society could benefit from my experiment?'

This causes Rebecca to start pissing herself. 'Not at all, mate, not at all. I really don't see how we stand to benefit from you fucking a prostitute or two.'

Justin leans closer, his eyes visibly widening and turning battleship grey. Rebecca leans back in response, her cheeks turning red with amusement. Justin continues to speak with what he believes to be world-changing authority.

'I will buy my way through all the mystery and the tricks. I will plough money into sex until all that's left is me: happy or dead, humiliated maybe. But me, an honest representation of my needs and my desires. I will be naked and overjoyed, a beacon, a way forward for everyone else who—'

'I've got an idea too,' interrupts Rebecca. 'It's that men are all subtly fucked up, sexually and socially challenged. I think you might be doomed.'

'No, not doomed, that's just it. I'll save us from the slavery, from damnation. I've got this plan, like a scale, each step of my journey. First here and then to a brothel, a good one, the best. Then fetish. I want to cover a great deal of them. Not the comedy ones, but the ones that have a decent amount of industry behind them. Domination or whatever. And then it gets interesting. Orgies maybe. I'm trying to think of ways in which I could shag a celebrity. Do you see what I mean? I'm gonna buy my way through the myths to see what, if anything, lies behind them.'

'Why?' says Rebecca, more so he'll keep talking and give her time to think. She's scrambling through her silent memories of the compulsory economics course she took last semester. She's wondering whether it's worth her saying her line about how free trade has got fuck all to do with freedom. But instead, she listens, as Justin slams his hands hard down on to the table with a loud smack: 'Because I'm bored and I'm useless and I want to be overjoyed by things.'

Oh, this is the young survivor, thinks Rebecca, as she watches the colour fade from Justin's cheeks. This may indeed be my young survivor. She looks around the club. It's full now, naked girls twisting like pale ribbons above starving men. She takes Justin's drink and takes a large gulp. Is that brain? No, no it can't be.

'You want to understand yourself, understand your mind and your sex?' she asks, wiping a thin line of milk from her top lip. Justin nods, not sure entirely what she means and wrestling with a sudden and overwhelming desire to piss.

'Justin,' Rebecca continues, 'I want to understand your sexual desire.' Registering the lack of reaction on Justin's face, Rebecca leans forward and slaps him lightly across each cheek, whispering, 'I want to know what you think about my tits.'

Rebecca spots her own project at work within Justin's idea. Sexuality, and how the fuck it can be figured out. Is Justin trying to understand how the sexual instinct slots into personality? Is he trying to work out how sex glides into our civilised, considered existence? Perhaps, but he's also jiggling his leg frantically under the table. At length, the lids of his eyes rise. He stares at Rebecca with a look of frightening possibility.

'I don't want a girlfriend,' says Justin.

'I don't want a boyfriend,' says Rebecca.

Am I a prostitute? thinks Rebecca. Is this how it happens? Justin takes out his wallet and hands Rebecca another twenty-pound note. The bar is really filling up, there are no girls loitering about at the back where he's sitting any more, it's just him and Rebecca. He feels extremely tired, as if he's done too much and can't even remember what he's thinking any more.

'What do you reckon? I'll give you my number and you call me when you need me. Then I'll see how I feel about it, see what I can do. For money.' As she's saying this, Rebecca begins to wonder what it is exactly she can do, and why it is she's offering to do anything in the first place. In any case, Justin might be a serial killer. Or this might already be his fetish; getting girls to partake in grand sexual schemes under the banner of social emancipation.

'I won't shit in your mouth, Justin. Really, I won't shit in your mouth,' she says, as a way distancing herself a little, curbing her enthusiasm.

'Yes, I know,' says Justin, wearily, wondering what his mum would make of all this, then eventually deciding she'd be jealous. He watches, his faced scribbled out by drink, as Rebecca writes her name and number down on a piece of paper. She's feeling annoyed and excited by the situation, intrigued by his presence and the potential sorcery she senses in him. But she's infuriated by his fuzzy thinking and by the fact he's fucked.

'Are you Dostoevsky?' she says quietly, more to herself than to him. It's nine-thirty and she has a reasonable stint of nudity to get through. Justin didn't even hear the question, too frozen and pissed. Rebecca feels Marcus's hand on her shoulder. She looks up and he gestures towards a group of bright-red boys in nylon tracksuits of blue and green. Justin has fallen forwards, his forehead glued to the table. Two bouncers take him by each of his arms and lift him out of his chair. As Justin is dragged from the Nude Factory, Rebecca feels fingers the texture of denim drawing circles on her arse. They are just able to hear each other through the loud and terrible atmosphere.

'I like your tits, Rebecca. I really like your tits!' calls Justin.

'OK, handsome. OK!' she replies.

12

Football Mad

IF JOHNNY WAS somehow blessed with magical powers, like if he could see through time and space and be aware of everything, then he'd know that as he watches a football match on TV, Rebecca is walking around a bar in stilettos, panties and bra. But as it is, he's powerless. He's got no idea where Rebecca gets all her money from; how she affords her books, her trips to Moscow, her theatre tickets and her regular restaurant lunches. Maybe she has a job, he thinks. Or just parents, perhaps. Johnny, corpse-like, sits on the couch in his house on Kingswood Road, Fallowfield.

Football is one star in a strange cultural constellation that appears as the sun sets on the twentieth century. It shines brightly. Celebrity, cinema, television, fashion and certain genres of music are united with football to comprise a new and strange cultural constellation. They all shine so brightly you can barely distinguish one star from another. The effect is a powerful and blinding white light; pyrotechnics, special effects.

Most people are kidding themselves. Reality is something that flashes. Disbelief is what makes money. The modern world is utterly unbelievable. It just can't be true. Images of the naked, the happy and the upset float like ghosts in our fields of vision. They are sustained by our blinking eyes. It's like staring straight into the sun and then trying to look at something normal and real. Then finding you can't see it properly because of the bright white light, left by the sun, in front of your eyes.

Johnny isn't the least bit interested in football. He can't detect any beauty in the passing, the movement or the flair. It constantly eludes him. He's shocked and confused when his contemporaries oooh and ahhh at a long shot or a seemingly uncomplicated succession of passes.

'Oh my God, I forgot about the fugging game!'

This is Zakir, Johnny's housemate. He bursts into the living room from the kitchen with an oily fish slice in his hand. Zakir is an exchange student from Delhi, here for a year studying politics and economics. 'What's the fuggin' score, Johnny?' shouts Zakir, waving the fish slice and splashing Johnny with painful drops of hot oil.

'It's nil–nil, Johnny, it's fuggin nil–nil, thank God.'

Zakir sits on the edge of the sofa leaning forward at the television. Johnny estimates that about an inch of Zakir's arse is in touch with the sofa. Incredible. Zakir has the eyes of a B-movie zombie when he watches football. Johnny likes to sit and count how long it takes him to blink, sometimes it's minutes. Apart from believing that it's perfectly OK to say 'fucking', or 'fuggin', in every sentence he says, Zakir is virtually invincible. He doesn't smoke. Doesn't drink. Studies for at least four hours a night. Cooks often and splendidly. Never spends money frivolously. Even manages to work two days a week and send regular letters and gifts back to India.

During the six months that they've shared the house on Kingswood Road, Johnny has watched Zakir like a hawk. It has been his obsession to find weakness in him. Just a moment of melancholy, a hint of despair. A sigh, a tear, a crack. But so far, nothing. He got angry at the news once when it was something to do with Kashmir, but Johnny found no fault in that. It was caring, pleasantly patriotic and it looked cool to get angry at the news. The closest he came to sexual frustration was when he roared Miss India to victory in the Miss World competition. But this was disappointing, too. He did seem to find her attractive, but also seemed to genuinely empathise with her call for peace, global friendship and religious tolerance. 'Very, very clever and beautiful girl, don't you think, Johnny? It is so good for India, too. I'm so proud, really fuggin proud.'

Johnny has come to the conclusion that the English are fucked as a race. Everyone else seems invincible, and the English really do seem ignorant, inane, lazy and obese. He knows that Rebecca agrees with him and blames the impact of American cultural and economic hegemony. The Americanisation of earth and space. Johnny doesn't like to agree. He prefers to take the piss out of the anti-American attitude that dominates the world from the 1970s onwards. It's everywhere by now, rife, a very popular hatred. Most people have issues with the land of the free. Modes of rebellion range from blowing oneself up in public places to experiencing an awkward guilt while watching US comedy.

In the presence of Zakir, Johnny feels weak. The same is true when he's with Germans, Spaniards and Japs. It feels as if their brains aren't bleeding like his does, like ours do.

Like they haven't been damaged by the same attacks of information, colours, pressures and needs. Foreigners aren't great at telling jokes, but they are often laughing. Naturally happy. Slapping each other on the back, having coffee, talking politics in an entire rainbow of languages. Bastards. Why isn't Zakir's brain chasing itself out of his head, like mine is? thinks Johnny. How is he immune to the detritus that owns me? The petty thoughts and obligations: women, youth and happiness?

'Are you OK, Johnny?' asks Zakir, gripping the fish slice, eyes on the pitch.

They haven't really become friends. In the beginning it looked as though they might, but it fizzled. Friendship hit a wall at women, fun and alcohol. They found themselves culturally estranged.

'Yeh, I'm OK. I've got a bit of woman trouble, that's all.'

'Oh I see. Strange fuggin creatures, Johnny, never to be understood.'

Maybe, thinks Johnny, it's all just a question of etiquette and convention. Maybe Zakir thinks it's improper to display any kind of weakness, base emotion or sexual frustration, unlike we who have been tutored in the ways of an open, ugly heart and amplified misery. Zakir's not blind, though. His brain must ripple and react in some way at the sight of Lucy's bust. He must notice the magazines. Something must occur.

'I'm going to get some beers, Zakir. Would you like something from the shop?' Johnny gets up and leaves Zakir glued to the television.

'Oh no, I'm fine thank you, Johnny, fuggin brilliant match.'

Johnny takes his dreadful anorak from a peg in the hall.

He peers through a layer of dust at his reflection in a mirror. Is this it, me? Just remind me, how long is life again? Jesus. The front door slams behind him.

It's dark now, and cold. Johnny walks at speed with his shoulders hunched, overtaking the occasional battalion of boozers that cross his path. They're en route to the bars and clubs of Fallowfield. With each set of girls and boys that Johnny approaches and overtakes, he is more and more struck by the formal agreement that seems to have taken place regarding fabric, cut and shape.

The boys are like toys. Bright, simple clothes. Silly little quiffs gelled into the front of their hair. Each of them subjected to the homogenising forces of money, culture and sport. And the girls, well. Beyond the chronically obese, all girls look beautiful from twenty yards.

Johnny is wearing a fairly decent pair of jeans and a jumper made of thin wool. The collar of his shirt pokes out the neck of his jumper; pale blue and navy blue combine to create something sensible, smart and attractive for the female gaze. It's Johnny's frame that is his undoing, all long limbs and unattractive stooping. He walks down Ladybarn Lane and turns right. He's on his way to a corner shop. I haven't made it clear, because of all the talk about fashion and how it makes people look the same, but Johnny is very sad and feeling a little daring. He's going to do something rather reckless and desperate.

He pushes open the heavy door. The shop is small. The owner is down at the back stacking some new products on to the shelves. 'Hello!' she calls to Johnny. She is small, round and Asian. Her voice has a quiver to it. When she speaks it sounds as if she might be trying to sing.

'Hello,' says Johnny, as he makes the short journey from

99

the doorway to the magazine rack. Lucy's here too, staring out from the cover of the magazine. Fingers over nipples, airbrushed tits, buy me, you bastard, you horny little shit. No, Lucy, thinks Johnny. You're a little too conservative for my and Zakir's needs. I'm afraid we need the kind of kick up the arse that you and your sterile poses simply don't offer. He smiles to himself, he's enjoying this. This really feels like living, he thinks. His eyes scroll up the shelves of bright media to the hardcore pornography on the top shelf.

He's not familiar with the titles, so he's not sure which ones he's going to buy. When his eyes finally register the simple blues, reds and yellows of the pornos, his mouth dries and his nerves begin to fray. He can't make out the words. He can just see sections of women's bodies: arms, tits and face. In the end, he reaches up and grips two magazines at once. Without looking at them and with a techno heart, he takes them over to the counter.

'Just give me one second,' the shopkeeper sings, presumably unaware of the nature of his purchase. I can't wait to see her face, thinks Johnny. Will it be judgemental or simply blasé? She does sell the things, for fuck's sake. I wonder if she has any religious faith. Muslim or whatever. Fantastic. He looks down at the counter and discovers he's bought a magazine called *Razzle* and a magazine called *Just 18*. The cover of the latter has a picture of a young girl wearing what looks like the kind of underwear an adolescent might wear: simple and white. She's also wearing a pair of childish pink socks. Covering up her stomach is a caption that reads, 'I've been naughty, fuck me like a dog and cum on my back.' Johnny genuinely doesn't know whether to laugh or cry. He breathes deeply as he notices, out of the corner of his eye, the shopkeeper clambering to her feet.

Rattle! Yes. There is a rattle behind him, oh God, the door. Johnny's head turns in a flash – something is trying to get through the fucking door. Something's trying to get in the shop. Oh crap. This shop is normally dead. The door opens halfway, then it stops. Whatever this creature is, it must be extremely weak, it can barely push the door open. Shit. This is a nightmare. Johnny wants porn, but not an audience to watch him buy it. He takes a large gasp of air into his lungs; it feels like a drawing pin is being stuck into his Adam's apple.

'Wait there, Mrs . . . wait there, I'm coming.'

Bollocks. The shopkeeper is running towards the door to help the creature into the shop. Why would she do this? I should have fucking advertised this, jokes Johnny to himself, his thoughts oscillating wildly between excruciating embarrassment and a kind of arrogant self-belief. The creature is human. Johnny can just make out a hand and part of an arm. It's an old lady, wow, a very old lady, she might be dying, no, just old. Jesus, she must be at least three hundred years old, thinks Johnny, giddy, drugged by the excitement and the abnormality. The shopkeeper guides the old woman into the shop then squeezes past her on the way to the counter. The old woman's skin looks like beige velvet. It hangs from her like a macabre flesh drape. She looks like the kind of substance that could be scooped and poured.

'How are you, Mrs Stott?' says the shopkeeper as she arrives at the till.

'Oh, I'm fine, dear, thank you,' says the old lady, skin dripping from her wrist like time.

How awful of me, thinks Johnny. I've spoiled this lovely moment of community and charity by bringing a picture of a naked girl to the counter – a girl who wants to be fucked like a dog. What's the old woman thinking? Am I destroying her faith in society? Is this the final straw? Will she think, 'Two magazines? Seems a little excessive,' and lose all her faith in life, humanity and youth? Will she go home and throw herself down the stairs and smash her body to pieces? Johnny looks down at the little old creature; it has clearly noticed the magazines. He stares into her eyes. They look as hard as rock; turned to stone by nearly a century of stimulus.

'Disgusting,' she murmurs. 'Absolutely disgusting.'

Fine. 'Disgusting' I can deal with, thinks Johnny. It *is* disgusting. A girl being fucked like a dog, pretending to be younger than she is, it's tantamount to paedophilia. I agree, he thinks, it is disgusting, fine. He turns to the shopkeeper for judgement. That's what he wants, he's standing by his choices. Fucking judge me. Make up your mind, you shop-keeping cow. *Razzle. Just 18.* How much? How bad? I don't mind. I might just go home and fuck this girl like a dog. I might just decide I want to come on her back – grant her wish. Try and stop me, you silly little Asian woman with your superstitions and your wonderful work ethic. Sell me these fucking magazines!

'Four pounds forty-five please, sir.' The shopkeeper is smiling politely. Johnny hands her a five-pound note. He feels as if blood might be leaking from his ears. 'Would you like a bag?' she asks.

'Yes, please,' says Johnny. The shopkeeper tears a plastic bag from a large stack under the counter. She shakes it open and gestures to Johnny to help her pack his porn: she holds it open wide as he places the two magazines inside. This is like history, thinks Johnny. An *entente cordiale* between the repulsive, sex-obsessed West, and wherever this woman's from. Some little recess in the East. We should go for a drink, thinks Johnny. We could fuck. Yes. You could diet – make your body a little less unfathomable. We could get together, date for a while, talk world peace, age, race, culture. What we need is more harmony. Yes. Pink socks. Help. You could cook curry. Help. Like a dog. On her back. Help. Help, you exotic bitch, I need you, help me. Rebecca?

'Goodbye.'

'Goodbye.'

Johnny walks to the door, his thoughts tripping each other up in his head. The cool air high-fives him, he gasps, back in the land of the living. It feels like freedom, what an adventure, I should be knighted, hahahahaha, oh God, oh God, my mind's on fire, water, water. He walks quickly in the direction of Kingswood Road.

'I'm football crazy, I'm football mad,' sings Johnny, to himself. Delirious. Swinging the carrier bag back and forth in his left hand. You see, he has an idea that may cause Zakir to crack. An idea that might make Zakir angry and turn his brain into a sex milkshake. Johnny's brain is a sex milkshake. And you and me, well, we'd fuck anything that moved, wouldn't we?

'I'm football crazy, I'm football mad, duh duh duh dah, duh dah duh dah duh dah!' sings Johnny, as he passes a gaggle of denim youths.

Johnny has a plan to crack Zakir. If someone else were present on this occasion, you or me, for example, or both of us, we'd probably try to stop him. We'd grab his shoulder and bring him to a stop on the pavement. We'd try to make it clear that Zakir is a clever young man who doubtless has an admirable degree of self-awareness regarding his own sexuality. We'd say that Zakir is probably very much aware of the state of global sexuality in general. We'd make Johnny listen, show him he's being rather inane and insulting, encourage him to use the porno himself, but not to bother Zakir. You need to resolve your feelings for Rebecca, we'd say, presumably that's what's provoking all this. If he wasn't for reasoning with, then eventually, one of us would have to shout: 'For fuck's sake, Johnny, don't even think about putting *Razzle* under Zakir's pillow! Do not do it!'

But sadly, he's on his own and on his way; key in the front door, turning, making straight for the stairs, lest the element of surprise be lost.

'Hey, Johnny, come and watch the match, it's nil–nil, fuggin amazing.'

'Hi, Zakir.' You invincible little shit. You stupid Mr Universe. You boring bastard with your mind of calm and contented thoughts; drones that stand in single file waiting to be used. Ever heard of emotions and agony? thinks Johnny, idiotically, as he silently pushes the door to Zakir's bedroom open and creeps towards the bed. Let's see how this goes down your annoying Indian throat, shall we? Let's see how you handle these girls, Zakir. They'll eat you alive. They'll show you how hard it is to be white, idle, Western and young. They'll tell you what a hero I am, for keeping things together and not buckling under the pressure of sex; its temptresses, creators, doers and sellers. Time to be led into temptation, Zakir. It's time you learned to see in the dark.

The cover photo of *Razzle* is taken from above the girl, as if the cameraman had stood on a chair and pointed the camera down at her. 'Shoot your mess on my tits and face,' says the girl, or that's how the caption reads, at least. She means it, too, thinks Johnny, her cruel eyes looking up at his. He slips the magazine under Zakir's pillow. Wait there, girls, then paint his brain red as he sleeps. Having hidden the porn, Johnny darts into his own room and deposits *Just 18* among the pants and socks in his underwear drawer. I'll leave it there for later. I'll come to bed later and masturbate over my favourite pictures, flicking between the best pages with my left hand. Johnny must think something like this because that's exactly what he does. Later on, in about an hour or so, I think. I think, he must, I think.

Johnny returns to the living room. Zakir is sitting on the floor eating a remarkably well-cooked meal. He shares his attention equally between the television and Edward Said's seminal text, *Orientalism*.

'Hey, man, sit down. It's fuggin tense.' Zakir gestures to the sofa with his left hand, adding a little seasoning to his dinner with his right.

'Who's winning?' enquires Johnny, his mind on nothing but the girl in the pink socks and her desire to be fucked like a dog.

'It's nil–nil. England are fuggin terrible.'

'Right. Are you working tomorrow, Zakir?'

'Not tomorrow, no, Thursday. Tomorrow I'm going to Oldham for a conference on the relationship between British democracy and racial minorities.'

'Oh right, democracy.'

'Yes.'

'Yeh, yeh.'

'Oh my God what a fuggin miss!' On television, a stocky player with a cramped and mischievous face balloons the ball over the bar. He turns and swears loudly at the sky. The camera zooms in. Zakir turns to Johnny with a look of shocked joy smudged all over his cute little face. Johnny makes a mental note: I've become a twat.

If Zakir takes offence, Johnny will claim that he thought he was acting in Zakir's best sexual interests. He will claim that he felt that Zakir had hinted that he might want to look at a porn magazine, that it was all a very unfortunate misunderstanding. A practical joke. They aren't friends, there is nothing to lose. But, nevertheless, Johnny tries to think of ways in which his actions might be considered to be a practical joke. It's unlikely. Zakir will most likely be offended, or, at best, perplexed. One thing is for sure: it is a reckless and cruel decision that has resulted in *Razzle* resting under Zakir's pillow. This house on Kingswood Road will never be the same again.

'Yeeeeeeeessssssssssssss! Yeeeeeeeeeeeeeeessssssssssssss!' screams Zakir, first at the TV and then at Johnny. A goal, a goal, a goal. He goes football crazy, football mad. Neither of them realises that they are, in effect, entering the final minutes of their naff friendship. Zakir dances around the living room. He grabs Johnny by the wrists and tries to lead him in a merry dance. Johnny's brain disconnects from his skull and gets lodged in his neck. Upstairs, under Zakir's pillow, inside the poor porno, the girls wait, pussies prised. Mental note: total twat.

Tonight the porn mag will poison the house with honesty, bad taste and ignorant reality. Nothing will be said, or openly discussed, but the innocent porno will give birth to silence and tension. Pointlessness will reign and Johnny will cower in a bad light. Zakir will discover the glossed pages and flick through them in disbelief. Johnny, he will think, this could only have been Johnny. Tomorrow, Johnny will notice fire in Zakir's eyes. He will fear retribution, an act of domestic terrorism; a toaster in the bath, a knife in the back.

Zakir will leave the house within the month to live with someone else. A kinder, cleverer, more articulate person, he hopes. I imagine.

Johnny is a nobody.

Tonight he will have his first sex with a porno. Dramatic masturbation. Amateur romance.

But Johnny is a nobody.

A story.

Forget it.

13

The Hump

COLIN PLACES HIS beer on the table and takes a seat next to Boy 2, opposite Boy 1. The three of them often meet for drinks after work. When it's sunny, like today, they come to Deansgate Locks, to The Bar, or Revolution. It's nice to sit outside as the sun sets. It's a lovely activity.

The initial motivation for these after-work drinks was an attempt to replicate American leisure. If television is to be believed, which it is, then Americans enjoy carelessly rendezvousing with buddies after work to discuss labour, love and each other. All three lads secretly admire the brightly coloured people on American television. All of them are tied to specific establishments where they're known and can enjoy themselves by bantering with their friends. A coffeehouse, a bar, a bowling alley. Anywhere that a micro-community can be fostered and a sense of optimism and friendship can be allied to the sale of snacks and drinks.

Naturally, the efforts of Boy 2, Boy 1 and Colin never quite achieve the delightful and hilarious heights of American friendships. And, of course, they can hardly compete with relationships depicted on TV, only aspire to them. But they enjoy these moments nonetheless, particularly when the sun is out and they can think of things to talk about.

There is something in Colin's eye. He pulls at the lower lid then plunges his finger right into the corner where a small triangle of red exists. It's gone. He blinks and stares down at the canal which runs alongside the bars and restaurants of Deansgate Locks. He hasn't touched his beer. Boy 1 and Boy 2 discuss the match.

'I only saw the second half.'

'They should have lost. England were fucking shit.'

My God, England is relaxed. It's like the chill-out room of an unfashionable club. Boy 1 and Boy 2 discuss a dubious case of offside in last night's game. Colin drifts. He doesn't listen when Boy 2 claims to have fingered a girl in the pub in which he watched the match. 'Under the table,' Boy 2 explains, 'I finger-fucked her.' But no one ever believes Boy 2. He's a dick.

Around 1992, some scholars suggest that History has come to an end. In 2001, however, the issue of global terror nudged History back to life. Nowadays, it proceeds in unspectacular fairy steps. Political periods come and go, offering crises, war and upheaval, but they lack dynamism and impact. They do nothing to stem the drip-drip of neutered, empty time. We're quietly drowning. Help. Items on the news will always try and garner evidence to the contrary, but it just isn't true. They find evidence of escalating drug abuse, depression, terror, clashes of civilisations and political dissatisfaction, but most viewers are alienated by this culture of doom and gloom. The shiny lives led by the living contrast awkwardly with the forecasting of apocalypse and societal collapse. Nobody sees it coming.

It was in America and Germany from 1890 to 1915 that industrial innovators invented methods aimed at increasing the energy efficiency of their work force. The aim was to make work less tiring and give workers enough energy to approach their leisure time with vigour and imagination. The plan worked. It spread across Europe. As the twenty-first century irons its shirt, checks its hair and prepares to go out pubbing and clubbing, leisure time is the only real time. Very few people break a sweat at work. Most get dangerously bored, but few find themselves lacking in enthusiasm when it comes to charging headlong into a period of leisure. Leisure is what people live for, what people do, how people behave and how they wear themselves out.

'I swear, she let me. My finger stank of fish.'

Take the three gentlemen at this table, sipping expensive lager and twitching self-consciously in response to small changes in their environment. All three watch in silence as new sets of people come and go. They strain to hear the conversations of others around them. They're fascinated, surprisingly ignorant of the ways in which other people pass their time.

For Boys 1 and 2, situations like this still possess a sexual dimension. They starve after the flesh that tenses and perspires around them: the businesswomen in grey suits and shiny shoes. The beautiful girls who come from the salons and boutiques of the city centre in search of eligible men with money, style and good cars. Boy 1 has eyes capable of burning the clothes off passing girls. A one-track mind. Laser lust. A reflex to incorporate these strangers into a thousand fantasies, contort them into innumerable shapes.

For Colin, of course, the situation is different. He stays

alert. His thoughts shudder and shake. His brain threatens to send him spinning round sabotaging these sick, sick women. These dead and buried men. Colin makes do, spends time cautiously, relax, relax.

'I was thinking we should go down the hospital again tomorrow. Get some breakfast. It was a fucking laugh that, wannit?' says Colin, lighting a cigarette. He inhales and watches his friends closely, already irritated by the indifference and surprise he expects his suggestion to be met with. He exhales.

'Yeh, it was fucking funny,' says Boy 2, sniffing the index finger of his right hand.

'Gimme a fag, Colin. Look at that bird,' says Boy 1, reaching over and taking Colin's cigarettes from him. Despite their similar names, Boy 1 and Boy 2 are quite different. Boy 2 is a dick. Whereas Boy 1 is, well, he's more of a bastard. He's currently standing with an unlit fag swinging from his lips, tapping his groin in the direction of a tall girl with extremely short bleached blond hair and a top that reveals a triangle of each of her tits. Colin watches him with disgust. 'I'm not gonna look at the fucking bird, Boy 1.'

'Fuck off, Colin.' Boy 1 stops tapping his crotch. The girl's gone anyway. He pulls a questioning face, his eyes unnaturally wide, prompting Colin to fix him with a squinted stare just long enough for Boy 1 to remember the bad times and what Colin's capable of.

'All right, Col, calm down. I'm up for going to the hospital again. It *was* fucking funny.'

Silence once more. My God this is a quiet affair, surely there must be something to say. The bar sounds like a stream trickling over rocks. It's full of people talking gently about today. I don't know what the date is exactly, but it's summer.

A day. With weather, news, television, tasks, a mood, a place in our hearts.

'It's getting boring. It's just girls-fucking-girls with you, isn't it, Boy 1?' says Colin, vigorously spinning the wheel of his lighter over and over again.

'Well yeh, actually. It *is* just girls, mate.'

Colin is forced to backtrack. He slides the lighter across the table towards Boy 1. The rot must be hidden. The decay must remain unseen; internal, structural. It's only a matter of time before Boy 1 is able to subvert the hierarchy of these three and challenge Colin's leadership. End his reign. Colin is aware of this. Aware that his position is being compromised by his need to stay calm and protect the world from his anger and his smouldering, ignorant unease. He must try to take care of his rage. What might Boy 1 do? wonders Colin. The most logical thing for Boy 1 to do is call Colin a 'total puff'. Total puffs, you understand, as Colin does, don't shag many birds.

Colin swigs from his pint, swallows and coughs deep into his hand. No matter, he thinks, none of this matters.

It's no secret that the Wishing Well and the hospital it feeds are of significance to this tale. It's obvious. It's where Colin's head began to ache. Colin, who is crimson-brained and vital. Tomorrow morning these three boys will return to the café. They will each eat a fried breakfast in the company of victims of cancer and women who are tantalisingly close to giving birth. As they finish their food and one by one position their cutlery in the middle of their plates, Boy 2 will wonder out loud: 'Does your knob prod the kid if you fuck a pregnant bird?'

Of course, Boy 2 is a dick and he will say this too loudly.

A group of women will raise eyebrows and look with disapproval and fear at this strange group of young men. What are three young men doing in the Wishing Well anyway? they will think. Perhaps their relatives are dying. Maybe a mutual friend has taken too many drugs, overdosed, his stomach is being pumped in some other part of the hospital.

'Shut up, Boy 2!' Colin, by now, will be fixated. Fascinated by form. The wide groaning curves of the women: sturdy, delicate, aliens, bearers. These secret miracles, what do they mean? Is it his own ignorance or does society somehow keep the birth of its children a secret? Something to be hidden and not thought about too graphically or realistically? Pregnancy existed on TV, of course, but not like this. Not the calm, musical elegance that these women possess. It's as if their bodies sing gentle, amazing melodies. Their beauty and simplicity mocks the world, which is inane, bawdy and pretentious. Seeing all these pregnant women exerts a power of asphyxiation over Colin. He can't breathe. He can't stop thinking about them. There is something in all this. Those large stomachs. Calm expressions. What is it? Ah, what is it?

For Boy 1, the pregnancies are like flashing lights. Red. Danger. Something to be avoided. Something that happens when recreation fucks up and life bursts with a bang. Bang! Everything changes and you find yourself in deep shit. He'd fuck a pregnant bird, but only for the thrill, only because pregnant or otherwise, it's still a fuck. A conquest, a memory, a victory. He will lean backwards on his chair and push his empty plate to the centre of the cheap table. His mouth will open.

'You have to do it up the arse. Either way it'd be fucked up. Massive nipples, though – bonus.'

'Yeh, I get it, the hump'd get in the way.'

114

'They've all just been fucked by some stupid dickhead anyway. Then after the sprog, they've got bucket fannies, so it's shit.'

Colin will watch in silence, angry at what is being said but unable to see beyond it. He wants to break their logic and find comfort, a way forward. He has seen something new and he does not know what to do.

As the boys carefully retrace their steps down the stony grey stairwell of the hospital, where the air smells of hot water and chemicals, Colin's brain will crank and spit out an idea. Quit your job at the university, Colin, his navy-blue brain will whisper. Why not? Quit your job and work here. Clean. Be a doctor. Work at the café. Anything. Just work here. Dear Colin, Colin who burns alive and has no idea why, his mind fat as fuck with distortion and stupidity, quit your job, dip-shit. Work at the hospital.

But that's not now, that's later, tomorrow. Right now we're still outside The Bar. We're sipping, living, quietly. Colin sits in silence, deep in thought, only pregnancy on his mind. A breeze is sending a shiver through the crowd. Men look up at the sky and consider taking their drinks inside. Might it rain?

14

Financial Times

'IT'S ME.'

The intercom buzzes. The lock on the front entrance is released. Carly pushes at the door with her back, both hands are full of shopping bags. She's not nervous. The foyer to Steve's apartment block is well lit.

She pushes Steve's front door open and walks into the centre of the open-plan living space. Steve is lifting weights in front of a mirror. His elbow rests on his endless knee. A dumb-bell rises and falls. Carly stares into the mirror and catches the reflection of Steve's eye. The TV is tuned to a music channel; classic hits of the 1980s.

'Hey, you,' says Carly.

Steve says nothing. He allows his head to drop and stares downwards at his arm, full of strain.

'Are you mad?' Carly asks, placing the many bags of shopping on to the breakfast bar. 'I mean about the money,' she continues, catching a glimpse of a pink pashmina inside one of the bags, and wincing with affection.

'What did you get?' Words hiss out from between

Steve's gritted teeth. The dumb-bell rises, then pauses, as if the weight itself is intrigued as to what Carly spends money on.

'Clothes.'

Steve puts down the weights and collapses his body on to the sofa to read the *Financial Times*. This is a tactic of basic alienation. Carly doesn't read newspapers. Don't go to the breakfast bar, thinks Steve, if you go to the breakfast bar blow jobs will occur. Stay quiet. She robbed you. Anal is justice.

For a while Carly flits about the flat, unpacking her shopping and pouring herself a drink. She smokes. Pausing occasionally to enjoy a particularly good song from the eighties. Madonna. Michael Jackson. Wham! Steve stares at the pink pages of the *Financial Times*. Pink seems an appropriate colour. Somehow false, deceiving, perfect for pansy investors. Pages one to four are devoted to the Autopen Corporation and the Autopen Relentless Bliss.

'Did you go to Versus?' Steve asks, as he reads yet another account of the unprecedented rise in the Autopen share prices.

'Why would I go there when I've got you?' asks Carly, the slightly flat notes of a lie ruining the pitch of her voice.

Steve says nothing. He turns over another pink leaf.

'Oh, Stevie, don't be mad at me, baby.'

Carly dives on to the sofa, swims under the *Financial Times* and surfaces under Steve's jaw, which she kisses. It's all like a children's story, a simple tale of morality and good behaviour. Carly realises she must be seen to be learning, just as Steve, as the moral centre and judge, realises he must be seen to be teaching. His eyes are fixed like nails on the newspaper. He follows the statistics and the articles purely for show. Purely to show that in some small yet significant way, he's capable of deliberately isolating himself from this girl and the moments of glad, calming ecstasy she is still able to deliver. It feels as if he should sigh then tut, so he sighs then tuts.

'I'm sorry, Stevie, I dunno what I was doing. I can take it all back, I kept the receipts.'

The *Financial Times* is calmly closed, folded and put to one side. Steve is enormous, beautiful, a cherub. He looks at Carly and, with a softening of his eyes, is able to communicate to her his anger, his desire for justice, but also his compassion and his ability to forgive. He watches a wave of comprehension break on her face and becomes aware that for the next hour, at least, he is permitted to behave in accordance with his own real wants. Carly sighs. Steve realises that his life is one of ever diminishing use. The kind of game a child might play.

'Don't fuck about with my money again, Carly.'

Steve's voice is deep, slow and serious. He is a cowboy. A maverick. A loveable villain. All the roles and fantasies usually denied to him by Carly and her neon-lit confidence. He sniffs air hard through his nostrils. He is a Russian assassin, KGB, as capable of thunder and lightning love as he is of exact, businesslike murder. His left hand comes flying in from his side and grips Carly's chin, his right bull-dozes its way under her arm to its pit. Carly finds herself being pushed upwards towards the edge of the sofa, but she always supposed such acts of physical contortion would play a part in her forgiveness.

'Do you understand? I don't want to be fucked about like this ever again,' he says, as if he could clench his fist and immediately punch her hard in the eye. He won't, of course, only dreams of it, but he enjoys reacquainting his demeanour with violence and anger. Enjoys seeing specks of fear in Carly's shining eyes. 'I won't, honey,' she says, 'you know I won't. I love you.'

I LIKE TO MOVE IT MOVE IT, I LIKE TO MOVE IT MOVE IT, I LIKE TO MOVE IT MOVE IT, YOU LIKE TO. MOVE IT. In the control room of whatever music channel is whistling to itself on Steve's television, the eighties end and the classic songs of the early nineties take to the screen. I LIKE TO MOVE IT MOVE IT. The beat drops and Steve leans forward, kissing Carly with aggression to the rhythm of the music. I LIKE TO MOVE IT MOVE IT. Steve feels his thorny chin scraping and rubbing at Carly's skin. This is reconciliation and the kissing must be firm and confrontational, on his part at least. She must accept whatever moods and techniques he chooses to adopt.

The room screws itself up. Beats and melodies of the nineties mingle with the twenty-first-century furnishings and with the bodies and the lips and with the lights, which seem to flash, as Carly brings Steve's hand slamming into her left tit. What fiends we are.

I am Steve and I must not succumb. I must have justice. Anal. Oh God, this is fast. NOW THAT WE'VE FOUND LOVE WHAT ARE WE GONNA DO, WITH IT? The music ploughs into the nineties and Carly's jumper is yanked off her arms and around her neck. But her head's in the way. Steve's on his knees, stripping the jeans from her legs, skinning her alive. He reaches up and wrenches her jumper away, so hard he half expects to take her head off with it, leaving her decapitated but still warm and beautiful. Oh fuck, the clothes, the fucking clothes. Short bouts of desperate undressing cut with increasingly unconvincing moments of mighty, muscular foreplay. Her jeans are off, her jumper too, one massive pull at her bra and the rear connection snaps and her breasts are blinking, startled. WHAT ARE WE GONNA DO, WITH IT?

Carly is adept and marvellous. She hisses, sparks. She's being electrocuted, noises of agony, high-end sonics, entirely staged inflections of lust and enjoyment. Loud guttural groans: where nature and culture meet. She permits her stripping, high-kicks her way out of her knickers, makes herself weightless as Steve drags her crotch towards his. Oh, the anger, the dull, predictable anger of all this, she thinks, perhaps, as she throws her head to one side and squeezes her eyes shut.

By this time, Steve is embarking on several projects of damage limitation. He's thrown his vest off completely, but has left his trousers at his knees. Removing them completely would involve standing up and the loss of mood and momentum. His will is faltering. Maybe anal wasn't such a good idea – fine in theory but, logistically, it now seems rather daunting. His cock, meanwhile, is reassuringly hard, showcasing its impressive width and striking length.

'Come on!' says Steve, to no apparent end.

The thoughts, the bodies and the emotions struggle to maintain this act of redemptive sex. Struggle to create the aesthetics of power and forgiveness. Carly is surprised by Steve's aggression, genuinely rather impressed by it. She thinks of Versus. How she lay between the A-frames of the Relentless Bliss, the handheld operating device, the clit fizzer, the ambient music, the internal vibrating mechanism. She looks down her body to her midriff, watches Steve sculpt her legs high into the air. He is a builder, an artist, the architect of this sky-scraping sexual imagery. Come on then, she thinks, as his cock rises and hovers above the vista of her stomach, the distant valley of her body. Wait a moment.

'Steve, get a johnny!' Carly blurts out suddenly. Yes, get a johnny. You're not a sex machine, so there's still that old-fashioned thing. What's it called? Pregnancy . . . civi . . . yes, civilisation! 'Please, just go and get a johnny,' Carly says again.

Steve grunts, then his face becomes softer, as if heated up by six or seven degrees. 'We don't need one,' he says, running a finger between Carly's buttocks and instantly regretting having done so. 'We don't, I want to try the other . . . way . . .'

'Oh,' says Carly, instinctively clenching her butt cheeks and capturing Steve's subtle little finger in their grip. 'You should have said. Anal? I would have bought the right gels.'

The right gels, thinks Steve, that's right. Life is shit unless you own the appropriate lubricants.

A second happens, then the loud sound of a woman singing. I AM GOING TO LOVE YOU FOREVER. Steve stands and his trousers fall and complete the remainder of their journey to his feet, past his sharp shins. That is that. Carly's feet swoop down from the ceiling, she pulls them up on to the sofa, reaching for her woollen pullover. A ballad is playing and the moment is lost.

'We don't usually do it like that.'

'I wanted to try something different.'

'But it hurts, Stevie.'

'Yes, I know.'

Most women take the contraceptive pill. Don't worry, mate, I'm on the pill, women sometimes say, before shagging a stranger. Carly, however, is extremely paranoid. Never grants sexual asylum to Steve's cock unless it's accompanied by latex and spermicide: the diplomats of progress and civilisation. She demands a condom, a johnny, when having conventional intercourse. Anal is a grey area.

'I don't want to, Stevie, not tonight. Why don't we have a bath?'

'I don't want a bath, Carly, I'm already clean.'

'Then let's do it normal. Get a johnny, then do it normal. Tomorrow night maybe we could do it the other way. I could get the right gel from Versus.'

It's over now, that is that. Steve's standing above Carly, trousers around his ankles, erection falling like the setting sun. Where the fuck does this leave us? he wonders, leaving the room to get away from the girl. And how the fuck did I forget to put a johnny in my back pocket? I should have done just in case. If she said no to anal I could have gone straight in with the alternative. Doggy. It was careless, a badly thought-out plan. Fuck-ups like this cost lives in certain situations. Armies don't forget bullets or helmets, that's why they win wars and succeed in shooting people dead. Fuck. He could always get a condom and go back to the living room. Yeh, I could always go back, he thinks, slip it on, flip her over, fuck her. Fuck it. Too late. I'm losing this war because I forgot the bullets and the helmets, forgot the guns, left them back at the base. Now I'm in some desert surrounded by Arabs with no way to kill any of them.

'Steve?'

Carly appears at the bedroom door, still wearing only her stringy black knickers. The corpse of her broken bra hangs limp in her right hand. Her brown hair falls over her collar bone towards the gentle incline of her breasts.

123

'You know how paranoid I am, baby?'

'It's fine.'

'I want to give you what you want . . . but anal . . .'

'It was just an idea.'

'It's not about the money?'

'How could it possibly be about the money, Carly?'

Carly lingers in the doorway, playing with the dead bra with her fingers. Lifting and rising. She does look like a slice of heavenly ham. Her skin is re-formed meat: generic and artificial but delicious nonetheless. Satisfying. On her face, her features are doing a very good impression of sorrow and guilt. Her eyes are bottomless and her jaw is relaxed. It's even possible that she may feel guilty and sorrowful, but it's hard to say exactly. She approaches the bed and lies down next to Steve. He's leaning on the head-board, she rests her head on his chest. They wait a moment.

'You can do what you like with me,' says Carly, straightening out her body until it looks distinctly medical. 'Really, do what you want with me, I like that. Just with a johnny.'

It's easy to say. This is it, life, England, still and consuming. Show business. The ruthless abandon of individuals and their paper-thin desire to draw breath. People are drying up, are becoming resistant to the visual cultures that nourish them. Their arid innards can no longer play host to the consistencies of this age of imagery. Crimsons, skins and liquids.

Did you ever sit in silence, alone in a room? A kitchen, perhaps. Did you ever assume you were sitting in complete silence, only to find the opposite to be the case? Only to find that the silence was noisy? A thermostat on a fridge turns itself off: suddenly, a previously inaudible humming stops and you realise it hasn't been quiet in the room at all.

You realise that you've been gradually deafened by inaudible buzzing. On such occasions the atmosphere is shocking, dwarfing and uneasy, shot through with shards of revelation. I swear that the years are ticking by and I fucking swear that this is an important metaphor: that the fridge is still buzzing.

This is what must be done. Steve must say something like: 'You know, you should go to Versus, you should go and get the appropriate gels.' Causing Carly to say something like: 'Yeh, OK, I will go to Versus. I will go and buy the appropriate gels.' This will result in Carly going to Versus to purchase the gels necessitated by man's persistent desire to penetrate woman anally. Great stuff. Great shopping. She will come home with a carrier bag on her arm containing the Versus product: a sexual gel called Anomax. Of course, she won't mention the fact that for the second time in forty-eight hours, she paid £9.99 for the pleasure of being powerfully penetrated by an Autopen Relentless Bliss. She won't mention that, so everything'll be pretty cordial between the two of them. Steve will maintain some of his glowing desire for revenge, but on the whole, they will be friendly and even manage to share prolonged moments of eye contact. Suggesting love, future and sexual camaraderie. During one such session of eye contact and having consumed the majority of a bottle of vodka, there will almost certainly be a tacit understanding that they're both sufficiently fucked and free. Both capable of sharing daring acts of physical pleasure. Life is simple and brilliant.

Like all great diplomats, Steve will remove Carly's knickers with his teeth. He will kiss her calves and lick her thighs as an homage to romance. Then, in one almighty celebration of equality and twenty-first-century freedom, he will locate her clitoris with his tongue and lick it with rhythm and tenderness. In the interests of world peace, he will carefully negotiate the entrance to her vagina with his fingers and spend some quality time using them to simulate the presence of his own cock. Carly, to her credit, will pop her mind and considerately enjoy the feeling of Steve's fingers inside her. How lovely, she will think. She will groan appropriately and flights of fancy will make her moist, making his fingers wet and odorous. It's going swimmingly.

In a gentlemanly gesture, Steve will use the moisture from Carly's loins as a natural lubricant. He will gently switch his attention to her buttony anus. Gain access to it with damp digits. Carly, touched by Steve's endeavours, but doubtful of her ability to self-lubricate, will reach over for the Anomax and tap Steve on the head with the tube. A moment of cute humour among the precise infiltration and the orchestrated ecstasy.

In accordance with all reliable guides to anus-orientated intercourse, Carly will have first one, and then two of Steve's fingers introduced to her arse. Her liquid grasp of the theatrics and performative norms of contemporary sex habits will cause her to squeak, wince and finally accommodate. Her colon will loosen up and relax, like it's finding its feet at a house party. Naturally, the polite introduction of Steve's cock to the occasion will bring an element of pain to both participants. Like an enemy bullet to the thigh, the tip of Steve's cock will be squeezed and hurt by Carly's perplexed and disorientated biology. And now, of course, we're fucking. Attention spans working overtime in an age of ignorance and forgetting. This is intense physical enjoyment, no place for the wandering mind. Bang! Bang! Bang!

'Are you OK?'

'Yeh, yeh. Don't stop.'

So, short jabs. Serating sex. A mixture of sandpaper sensation and the memory of kidneys in the windows of butcher's shops. Foreskin agony. A pain in the arse. Anger. A cock stabbing into an anus, making it shabby and devastated, dealing with shit. Keep trying, keep going. Boyfriend and girlfriend. The twenty-first century is getting going and we're fucking for ideas. It stings.

'Euggg euggg euggg euggg.'

This is where we leave. This is where it will end.

'Aueh aueh aueh aueh.'

'Not so hard, Steve.'

'Sorry.'

Savour it, remember. The bedroom walls, Magnolia. The skirting boards of Duck Egg Blue. The decent hi-fi system. Steve has blond hair. The light is shit and bright and the sex is blunt and raging.

'Ouch!'

'I'm sorry.'

This is bruschetta love. Cock wrapped in fajita. Sex on a bed of caramelised red onion. Football romance. The age of lifestyle and hidden agenda. Steve's cock is being squeezed to death and Carly's had better anal in the past. It's all so incredibly humane.

This is when we'll leave. Carly's head will be hammered down sideways into the mattress, hair turning around her neck and over her bony shoulder, like a road to nowhere in particular. Steve will be pasting more Anomax on to his exiting cock. Holding on to Carly's smooth, sensitive sides. He will be staring up at the ceiling, eyes flooded with water, tears of pain and no hope. The girl, oh God, the girl and his life, his decisions. Shouldn't this be hurting less? It fucking kills, bang, bang, bang. He will doubt his ability to ejaculate. I'm never gonna come, bang, bang, bang, I'm never gonna come. It's like punching a wall and I feel dreadful. And then he'll be falling backwards, cock skidding out of her arse. Carly floored and moaning as she must, turning over with her eyes shut and her arms groping for comfort. Steve, his body underworked and energetic, craving exhaustion, a chance to sleep, his cock on fire.

'Was that OK, baby? Was I all right?' Carly will ask.

'Don't, baby, please,' will be Steve's reply.

'Steve? Are you all right?'

'I'm fine, I'm fine.'

'Did you come? Tell me you came, Stevie!'

Heads ache. This is where we leave. Carly panting and wondering. Steve on his knees, not knowing. Breathing and failing. An end of sorts. We're leaving, as we must, but they will be there. The bed, the light, the now. The winds in their veins beginning to howl.

II

Three Months Later

15

THE FACTS FLIT around me like flies, sometimes landing and allowing me to creep at them with a flat palm. And though I bring my hand down with a sudden slap, they get away. They dance above my head as I inspect my fingers for their corpses.

This is draining. This speculative talk of the anus and the cock. I should have anticipated the shame. But with my horror my confidence grows, and so too does the plot. The truth. Running at me like a tit-head with a baton. Preparing to make me with violence.

Again, I'm bullshitting you! I'm blowing smoke directly into your arse. It's only because I need relief. A break from the truth with its dialogues and desires.

Is this pornography?

Please, say that it is not. No, let me rephrase that. Please, let it be so.

I had a visit from my Narrative Health Aid worker this morning. We're all very nameless in here, that's the way it goes. But this woman, whose job it is to monitor my writing and to generally irritate me, I have secretly named Susan. Susan is a simple sort, I've known her most of my life. She's never been a massive fan of my work, but I don't suppose she ever expected me to go this far. To write this . . . this history.

Susan, it transpires, is horrified and astonished. She arrived, her plain clothes billowing around her so as to hide her figure from my eyes. We watched each other silently for a few seconds. I smiled. And oh, dear Susan, she was white faced. She was wondering how the hell I got access to the Evernet system. She paced my room in a panic. She said, you shouldn't be doing this, it's unhealthy. She said, who on earth allowed this to happen? And I was like. I just kept smiling.

She'll be reading this, of course. And for me, that's an exciting thought. Are you well, Susan? I picture you curled up in bed with a mug of hot chocolate, sporting a complicated, lacy underwear affair. Suspenders. Difficult straps on your thighs, cotton flowers decorating the brimming cups of your bra. Oh, forgive me, dear Susan. I'm sure I'm taking the piss. I'm safe, no probs, you needn't be afraid. I've seen the way you look at me.

Susan won't like me talking like this. You don't like it, do you, Susan? She'll return here tomorrow, a cloud of billowing white, shouting, how on earth? How on earth? She'll tell me my learning is killing me. She'll say I'm trying to defend myself when I ought to be writing from my guilty heart. Simple Susan, don't fret. I know more than you imagine.

Enough.

I write because I have discovered a story. And because they only give us words to play with.

Three months later. Justin and Rebecca in a living room. We are going straight back to the facts.

16

The Counter-revolution

JUSTIN'S FOREFINGER WORKS its way up into Rebecca's hair, towards the end of her spine and the southern perimeter of her skull. It begins to massage her head in small, circular movements. It can't be more than two centimetres from her brain.

'Jesus Christ.'

'I know.'

'I've never seen so many people.'

Rebecca and Justin are entwined. They're in the living room of Rebecca's newly acquired flat in Hulme. Watching television in the soft vanilla light of the lounge. The smell that you notice is coming from the last surviving particles of the exquisitely cooked meal they shared this evening. A prawn curry with coriander and sweet potato. Over the next few minutes the smell of quality cuisine will be overwhelmed by the aromas of three thick, scented candles burning on the coffee table: lavender, tea tree, hemp.

'Would you like some more wine, Becca?'

'Yeah, I'll get it.'

'No, you stay there. I'll bring it through.'

Justin withdraws his fingers from Rebecca's hair. She feigns a kind of blissful weightlessness and allows her head to slump backwards on to the cushions. This is a way of showing him that his subtle massaging was a success. A way of showing her appreciation.

'Oh, that was heaven. I'm so tired.'

The wine has been left to chill in the fridge because it would have been spoiled in the warmth of the room. Justin pours it slowly and the sound of cold, trickling liquid merges with the serious voices coming from the television. The television screen is full of protesters. Antiporn has begun.

'Where do they get their energy from, Justin?' Rebecca asks, picking up her wine glass from the coffee table and taking a minuscule sip.

'The same place as us, I expect. Their dismay, or probably just their boredom.' Justin watches the screen with unresolvable anxiety. He finds it hard to watch civilisation fuck up in the face of its participants. So does Rebecca. They both believe in sex. Having replaced her own glass on the coffee table, Rebecca picks up Justin's and hands it to him.

'They'd think we were monsters, wouldn't they?'

'Yes, they would. They'd think we were sick,' says Justin, returning his wine, untouched, to the coffee table.

'Are you warm enough?'

Winter has nailed blackboards to the window frames. Even the streetlights struggle to be noticed. They emit a sheepish yellow glow, scarcely capable of illuminating the tree branches that sway no more than metres from their bulbs. Manchester is under siege from cold and rain as repetitive as breathing or sleep. The city is soaked, and has been for what seems like years. Wet stone. Cars fizzing through roadside puddles. The sound of splashing and the whisperings of winter: how long can this be sustained?

Year after year, Manchester's inhabitants are gobsmacked by the unfaltering resolve of bad weather and its ambition to eat up the year with damp. Its commitment to stealing days. Each year brings the eternal novelty of a dismal climate and its attendant miseries: melancholy, wet socks and foul moods. Summer is remembered as childhood is: a collection of unreal memories and unappreciated joy.

Police reports suggest that there were as many as ten thousand people congregated and cold in and around Albert Square today. Justin and Rebecca watch in disbelief as the crowd huddle and shout on the television screen.

'How many of these people do you think are secretly perverts, paedophiles and submissives?'

'Fuck knows. Countless. Most of them probably.'

The crowd gathers in support of an increasingly popular campaign group lobbying to impose strict constraints on the production and distribution of pornography. Antiporn. The group, led by a retired primary school headmistress, accuses pornographers and specifically the television channels, websites and shops that sell pornography of an open and bloody war on childhood. The idea is that inefficient modes of censure on the visuals of hardcore sex mean that children are being, in effect, parented by pornography. Youth-mutilating images of far-fetched and obscene acts of sex are falling into the wrong minds. Childhood scarcely exists. It has been robbed of its innocence. It is as sick and guilty as the rest of us.

The cheerfully middle-aged news presenter certainly seems surprised by the turnout. He watches as his attractive co-presenter relays the details of the event. She utters the words 'sex habits' and the motions of her mouth seem in sudden slow-motion. A nation of men shift in their seats.

The news item attempts to, and partly succeeds in incorporating the affair into the long and glorious tradition of mass provincial idiocy. But the footage of the protest itself shakes free of constraint and makes an impression on the viewers. Makes them scared and squirming.

The volunteer army of a geriatric nation is out in force, of course. But youth itself is represented, too. Young boys and girls in waterproof clothing hold banners declaring that 'The End of Innocence is Nigh', 'I'm Tired of Being a Porn', 'Rochdale Says No to the Freedom of Pornography'.

When the ex-headmistress takes to a podium and addresses the crowd, the stakes are raised. She is ruthless and determined to shock. 'What,' she implores, 'will happen to these young lives exposed to images of girls blocked up in every conceivable orifice by phalluses? What kind of a role model is a man preoccupied with soullessly enslaving women into sexual malpractice, or a woman whose thirst for semen can never be quenched? We must fight. We must prevent this collapse. Protect youth. Protect the future.'

'Jesus. The pornography of conservatism,' mutters Justin, his lips locked in a small, scared grin.

'Fucking right. Turn it off,' agrees Rebecca, who famously believes that free trade has got fuck all to do with freedom. Has she mentioned this to Justin? She can't remember. Probably.

Justin, whose hair has been growing steadily since the night he first met Rebecca in the Nude Factory, leans forward for the remote and a moment later the TV is quiet. The voices of protest die down.

'Thank God for that.'

Justin drifts back into the slumped position he'd previously been enjoying and is greeted by an affectionate headlock from Rebecca. In a moment of energy, she runs the palm of her free hand vigorously across the top of his head, causing his hair to stand on end in static shock. He hates his hair. He rather resents Rebecca for demanding its growth in the interests of their experiment and in accordance with her deep mistrust of the shaven head. Justin is quick to retaliate. He rotates his body and sends a pointed finger hard into Rebecca's ribs. This is a time-honoured method for causing brief and disabling agony. Rebecca's body blurts and spasms as if she's got fifty thousand volts of electricity searing through her veins. And now they're laughing, hysterically laughing in this warm, medium-sized apartment. Oh, yes, real shrieking laughter. They're feverishly fumbling with each other's bodies, finding numerous ways in which to inflict fleeting and hilarious pain. A knuckle to the knee cap. A swift dead arm. A deadly flick to the ear. What larks, what fun. Rebecca clasps Justin's nose between her thumb and her forefinger and gives it an almighty tweak. Ouch, it wrecks, oh, it hurts like hell, you bitch. Then he's pushed over, his head nestling under the arm of the couch, his hands repairing his nose with their warmth. Oh, the bitch, oh, what friends. Sighs all round, small chuckles in memory of the shrieks, haha, what friends, what friends.

'You're a fucker,' says Justin, still holding his nose with both hands.

'Well, you're a sexual deviant who's spoiling childhood for the kids. Think of the children!'

'Fuck 'em.'

Justin walks over to the window and writes 'Rebecca is a slag' in the condensation with his finger. The lettering is conspicuous against the black of the night. Right on cue, Rebecca skips over and quickly scrubs out her own name and replaces it with Justin's. 'Justin is a slag.' The two young people laugh.

'I should be going,' says Justin.

'Yeah, I've got uni in the morning, I can't be late for my date with Dostoevsky.'

'Fucking student.'

Rebecca is perched on the end of the couch, looking up at Justin. With his hair long, his features seem to soften. In the months since they met, Rebecca has noticed a more general softening in his character, too. He is not the mysteriously pissed punter who praised her tits at the Nude Factory. He is calmer and more calculated. He has become the sexual experimenter he wished to become. Yes, the experiment is everything.

'What do you want to do about Wednesday?' Rebecca asks, following him down the hall to the front door, watching as he selects his coat from the various hooks and prepares to face the cold.

'I want to go to that thing in Cheshire, that "Fuck Power" thing. I wanna have sex with Margaret Thatcher.'

Me too, thinks Rebecca, and doesn't Justin look wonderful in his large winter coat? The type of man that might hold your attention at a dinner party, while modestly explaining his full-time job as a total hero. What am I thinking? she thinks, I must be an idiot. Just as Justin's nodding goodbye and opening the door, she remembers Johnny. When Justin found out that Rebecca knew a twenty-one-year-old virgin, his mind started to formulate plans.

Virgins are useful things when you're experimenting with sex. Good guinea pigs. Yes, indeed, the experiment is everything.

'I'll talk to Johnny this week, too. About the plan.'

'Yeh, make sure you do. That's important.'

'I will. See you later, Justino. Adieu.'

'Goodnight.'

Click. The door closes and Rebecca turns in the direction of the kitchen because she wants to take a cup of tea to bed with her. En route she picks up the glasses of wine and, while the kettle boils, she will carefully decant the contents of both glasses back into the bottle. Her life is as sturdy as ever, as if its feet are spread apart and rooted to the ground, hands outstretched anticipating attack, fists clenched and poised. Not even the whirlwind abnormality of Justin and their society-saving sexual adventure can destabilise her mind, her stripping income, her studies, her thoughtfulness. She continues to sleep soundly and wake with open, interested eyes.

The five thousand pounds that paid for Justin's car virtually leapt out of his bank account. The moment the inheritance registered it all began bursting out, evacuating in the direction of prostitutes, restaurants and, in the case of the car, a second-hand Peugeot dealership in Longsight. It's a modest automobile, no need to splash out on anything too fast or beautiful. It's just a car. Just something to aid the adventure. The project: happiness.

Justin's right hand hangs off the bottom of the steering wheel, nonchalantly negotiating the plodding traffic of south Manchester with a limp wrist. He's been spending Sunday evenings round at Rebecca's since the experiment began, watching films, TV, eating good food. It had happened very naturally. It was surprising to them both that they found this regular and relaxed meeting so helpful. It allowed them to carry out the sexual side of the experiment with such aplomb. The Sunday evenings together instil a sense of unity. They never experiment on a Sunday. Never screw. This gives the more unsavoury dimensions of their alliance credibility and generally makes their investigations more fun and, perhaps, more moral.

But they're yet to find anything, happiness or whatever. They've had some fun, of course, but the fact is, they're fifteen thousand pounds down and still no closer to finding any answers.

17

The Parcel

CARLY HAS BEEN considering opening the parcel by the front door for over an hour. Perhaps, if she had a job, the parcel wouldn't be so fascinating and inviting, but she doesn't, she's bored. She was aware that it had been delivered early this morning. She had heard Steve lugging it in and had wondered what the fuck it was. The parcel is large and covered in about half a dozen stickers, some with Japanese writing and others in English. It came from overseas and is addressed to Steve.

On the breakfast bar, however, there is an envelope with Carly's name on it. She lifts herself up on to one of the three high stools and leans in towards the letter. 'Carly,' she reads, written in Steve's handsome handwriting. It feels a little like romance. She sits alone in this attractive flat, cigarette in one hand, burning grey smoke into white morning light, a note from her loved one directly in front of her. This is my life, she thinks. 'Carly.'

The envelope contains two hundred pounds and no note. She eventually discovers that on the back of the envelope

Steve has written 'Back Wednesday'. As an afterthought, she guesses. Or perhaps out of guilt: the result of some sudden and arresting fit of morality. She counts the money three times, tens and twenties, two hundred pounds for the two and half days that Steve will be away at his parents'. Two hundred pounds, but no note.

Around the time that Carly appeared at the Magistrates' Court, she and Steve attempted to separate. It was all very amicable. As if they both realised they didn't have the depth or closeness to negotiate her trial for ABH together. They even made jokes about it: we'll try a trial separation for the period of the trial. Ha. Goodbye. See ya. Carly went to live with her mum and Steve didn't even attend court. He just waited for the phone call – they let her off. By which time Steve was getting lonely at home, tapping his foot to his mid-tempo desire to fuck her. They reunited and were smiling and together once more.

The attack on the girl was Carly's first offence. She got a warning, if she fucks up again she'll face prison. It was clear that the judge couldn't bear to punish Carly too severely. She looked so beautiful in the dock. How could he send her to prison? She might be spoilt or damaged in some way. The judge didn't want that kind of guilt. Didn't want such beautiful blood all over his hands.

For Carly, the trial was testing. No more violence, she decided. She lost her job at the shoe shop. She now spends every single day alone in the house watching TV. She jokes about learning to cook but is yet to bother trying. Fuck that, she reasons. Each evening Steve comes home with a take-away. They eat and their days fade softly to sleep. These are TV times.

It's in the context of this boring televisual period in

Carly's life that the parcel arrived, bringing with it promise and excitement. Carly grinds out her cigarette and stares across the room to the front door, where the parcel seems to pulsate with possibility. A Trojan horse. She's so bored. The parcel is an attack on her sweet, red heart, which beats faithfully in accordance with the television schedule. It must be opened.

The bread knife makes short work of the box, it shreds the lid quickly, the sound of cardboard tearing like a motor-bike revving up. Let's go. She pulls away some polystyrene and registers the smell of technology. Wires and plastic. Oh, technology. She removes the remainder of the lid with her hands. The parcel contains loads of wires, mostly yellow and red. They're attached to half a dozen white pads. They look a bit like knee pads, I guess. There are lots of black straps, too, like seat belts. On top of all this equipment is a letter.

Steve,

Everything is going well. This is the only bit of kit I've managed to get so far. It's a prototype, pretty basic, they're hoping for much more. You wouldn't believe it.

Anyway, my friend, look after it until I return, maybe let Carly have a play! I'll know a lot more when I get back. It would help if I spoke Japanese!

Regards,

Frank

Besides the electronic equipment and the letter, Carly digs out a thick booklet, presumably an instruction manual, written entirely in Japanese. The details of Steve's financial interests and his investment projects are completely unknown to Carly. They stopped discussing them because it usually meant epically dull speeches from Steve on market fluctuations and innovations in Internet trading. Still ignorant as to the nature and purpose of all this equipment, Carly takes the manual over to the sofa and turns on the television. She lights another cigarette. This is a busy day.

On page three, a crude rendition of a human being is sporting the electronic device. It looks a little like a suicide bomber, a suicide bomber lying down, its loins decorated with Semtex. Two thick seat-belt-like straps go round the human's back, over its shoulders and then meet and connect just above the midriff. A third goes between the legs, like a gusset, eventually joining up with the other two at the stomach. Two of the white pads are stationed in between the third strap and the line drawing's loins. Two others appear to be attached to each nipple. The whereabouts of the other pads is a mystery.

There is, of course, no need to pretend that we don't know what's happening here. Although Carly's brain is yet to calculate the correct sums, to put two and two together, we know that sitting in the corner of the room is one of the most advanced devices for sexual gratification that humans and their societies have ever invented. We know other things, too. Yes, we do. We know that the proximity of this machine to Carly is almost like fate. It's faintly romantic. We know that if she knew the precise purpose and workings of this machine, the two of them would, in all likelihood, fall in love with one another. The machine would poison her against Steve and the Autopen Relentless Bliss. It would sweep her off her feet, buy her chocolates and take her walking in the cold and under-gardened parks of Manchester.

We know a little more, too, if you think about it. A few bits and pieces. We know that the Japanese plug can't possibly agree with the English sockets that appear at useful intervals around the walls of Steve's flat. This is a disappointment. It's particularly disappointing if, like me, you were kind of hoping she might have sex with the machine right now. Like, perhaps, she sees the diagram in the manual and suddenly her brain is full of pennies dropping, pennies from heaven. It's four, of course, she thinks, two plus two equals four, not five: a sex toy – I get it. Then maybe she'd leap from the sofa and swoop in the direction of the box and the Japanese sex machine. I understand you, she would say, cradling it in her arms and beginning to work out the straps and where precisely she's going to attach the pads. How could I ever have misunderstood you? You want to pleasure me, don't you? Oh, how wonderful. Quick, quick, you must be attached to me.

But no, she's not going to do that now. It's partly because of the plug problem, I admit that's a big issue. But also because, believe it or not, the idea that Steve is somehow involved in the mechanical sex industry is ludicrous to Carly. She can't convince her mind that the drawing in the manual is what she thinks it is – a sex machine. But, as I say, the machine won't plug into the English sockets, so don't get excited. But don't be naive, I'm sure the penny will drop in time. She'll get it in the end.

So now she's just relaxing into the rock-ribbed and carefully mediocre structure of her day. The TV is discussing the problems of various individuals, families and friends. You know the sort of thing. Dads who beat wives and slap children. Boys who fuck the friends of their girlfriends. Friends who fuck the boyfriends of their friends. Teenagers who do drugs and avoid school. Mums who drink too much and forget they're meant to be mums as well as alcoholics. The sounds of silly debate and of society seemingly falling down to the ground. We could stay and watch it with her, I suppose, but it might be a little slow and tedious.

In any case, better things happened last night. Better things happened than Rebecca and Justin laughing and joking on a sofa, or Steve and Carly eating take-away food and having blank paper sex before sleep. Yes, last night Colin was working at the hospital, his new job, where he has made friends with a naughty nurse.

18

Exit Wounds

AT NIGHT, THE hospital's quieter wards take on the atmosphere of a morgue. As if patients don't sleep, but steal six hours of death. We can hear the sound of whispering men.

'Ssshhhh.'

'All right.'

'Seriously, Colin, you've got to be quiet.'

Colin and his new friend, Deaks, edge into the dark of the maternity ward. The room is large and contains twelve beds, which in turn contain twelve pregnant women. It is lit by just a few emergency lights; green boxes above the doorways with the word EXIT displayed on them.

Colin met Deaks a week ago. They got talking about women. They got on, found it easy to talk. Both single men, relatively bored, both strangely bowled over by the sight of heavily pregnant women. Deaks is thirty years old. He has matted brown hair like twisted thread and has been corrupting the maternity ward for five years.

This room is surely colder than it should be. The air is fresh and lacks the chemical scent of death that exists in most wards of the hospital. Colin's been working as a cleaner here for three months: Deaks is his only friend. Colin looks to Deaks for guidance, as this is his first expedition into the ward at night. Deaks is breathing heavily, his vital organs sloshing about in randy panic. If you were to shave Deaks's head and remove a small square of skull, then you could peer through and view a brain of the richest crimson.

'Which beds have agreed?' whispers Colin, his bowels loose because of the nerves, a light fart creeping silently from his arse.

'That one there, and the third one along from the far wall.' Deaks points a finger towards the end of the ward. In the bed in front of him, a sleeping woman snorts and adjusts her position. He and Colin hold their breath, then exhale as the woman begins to purr once more. The women are fast asleep.

There is a peaceful humming sound coming from certain pieces of medical equipment, just enough to drown out the soft whispering of the two men and the sound of their careful footsteps. If we'd met Deaks earlier, we'd know a little more about him. We could have shaved his head, cut his skull and perved on his brain. Yeh, it would've been ace. But we didn't meet him earlier. It's my fault, forgive me.

These secretive missions in the dead of night are not new for Deaks. They have been happening on a regular basis for years. They're usually undertaken alone, but, occasionally, he'll invite a like-minded person along, like he's done tonight with Colin. Deaks has become adept at befriending the frightened women of the Antenatal Ward. Women whose pregnancies have become problematic and difficult to predict. Women for whom the prospect of completing their pregnancies in the outside world would be too risky. They must be monitored, looked after and kept safe.

'The one at the end's young. Better for you, Colin.'

'Fine.'

Over the past five years, Deaks has successfully decoded the emotional compositions of these fearful women. He can earn their trust with a few carefully turned phrases. He can put them at ease and share the burden of their uncertainty and excitement. When he's confident they trust him, he begins to articulate his plans. He offers to visit them late at night, to comfort them. He describes it as an effective form of therapy, a helpful way of getting them through these knife-edge days. He says it's not strictly allowed, but, if they wish, he will visit them and perform a secret and sensuous massage. Only occasionally do they agree. Certain women take to the idea, find it quite exciting and surprisingly therapeutic. Deaks believes the women need him. He is a carer. A Florence Nightingale. A sensible and giving man – a fully qualified nurse. Right now, he's silently drawing a thin white curtain around one of the beds. Out of the corner of his eye, he monitors Colin, as he makes his way down the ward to do the same.

For Colin, this night could not have come sooner. Deaks approached him last week, having noticed the look in his eye and his religious devotion to the sweeping and mopping of the Antenatal Ward. His decision to cut down his hours at the university office and apply for cleaning work at the hospital was starting to make sense. For the past three months he has diligently swept the floors, made it clean for the ladies. He has marvelled at their large stomachs and tricky, spitty breathing. When Deaks proposed he join him on a night-time voyage to meet and soothe the women, his brain warmed in its bloody sauce. He felt like weeping. Salty tears seeping from within his dried white mind. He felt like he was thawing slightly, coming back to life.

One, two, three. Colin counts the beds from the far wall. He admires how the bedclothes have been dragged over the curved shapes of the patients. So this one's mine, he thinks, staring at a sleeping girl through the thin light of the room. A few strands of blond hair dangle out from within the covers. But no face as yet. He wonders how her face will seem. He walks silently along the side of her bed, noticing a pale, porcelain hand leaking out from under the covers. He unties the curtain and slowly guides it along the rail and around the bed. They're alone.

This is the first time Colin has been alone with a woman in over a year. His hands and knees are shaking nervously. She's still asleep. How will I wake her? he thinks. Should I rock her gently until she's awake? Say hello? Will she be expecting Deaks? This is absolutely incredible.

He moves closer and peels back the top of the duvet. The girl turns gently in her sleep. Her head's pointing directly upwards. Flower petal eyelids. Colin is frozen, his heart feeling like a fire alarm. The girl is nice looking, incredibly young, maybe seventeen. Jesus. He touches her hair. The poor girl. Her eyes: they're opening. Fuck. Her eyes are opening. Petals wilting. They're staring right at his. Am I an awful man that should be killed?

'Hello,' says the girl, yawning, her whole body flexing and coming to terms with itself. The small child is in her womb, chilling perhaps, or sleeping. She's so young. Shouldn't she have had an abortion? Was she raped? No, she's smiling slightly, it can't have been rape. She's at peace with her situation, more likely it was just an accident. An experiment with a silly boy at a house party. It went wrong, but then she wanted it. I wanna keep it, she thought, I'm not too young. Maybe her parents backed the idea, said they would help her out financially. Shit, shit, shit. Colin is still rooted to the spot like some guy visiting a terminally ill friend and not knowing quite what to say. You're going to die. What to say? You're going to die. How's the food?

'Deaks said he couldn't make it tonight,' she whispers. Thank fuck, she knows, thinks Colin, wondering if he'll be able to get away with saying nothing at all. He just wants to feel her, touch her skin with his hands. Is that so bad? Ha, he wants to eat her in delicate little bits. Dilute himself and be happy and wet and touched.

'Well?' says the girl, rising slightly and supporting herself on her elbows. She's wearing no make-up, but her features are young enough to be naturally defined. They're yet to be threatened by gangs of wrinkles and burst blood vessels. Fifteen, she could be fifteen. For a second, Colin sees the moment when her child was conceived. A black-eyed boy on top of her, pus beating round the pimples of his cheeks. Ah, he flinches and the memory falls, down his windpipe, sliding through his veins and landing with a splat among the contents of his stomach. Relax. Relax.

'Colin.'

'Sorry?'

'My name is Colin. I'm a cleaner.'

'Oh right, not a nurse? My name is Melissa.'

Colin steps forward as if flames all over his body are beginning to catch, fire up and lick at his chin. His skin's melting and he's loving it, loving the heat and the feeling of finally burning down. Fuck. He feeds both his hands under the cover where it's incredibly humid. Like a rain forest, his fingers walking the terrain, the ruffles in the bedsheet, the cleanness, Jesus, the heat. A few inches in and he hits torso, wrapped in cotton. A thigh. A hip. He touches it, the thin, second-skin fabric heated by her body. Knicker elastic; keep calm.

'Deaks just massages, strokes me gently.'

'I know, it's fine.'

Under the covers, Colin begins to drag Melissa's nightie up her body, passing it from hand to hand until he reaches the seam and drags it up over her belly and discards it. His right knee is up on the bed for support. His arms have elevated the bed covers well above her body. His hands hover above what he knows to be her naked and bloated stomach. Like a conjurer, a healer. His fingers fall slowly, quivering, like a helicopter landing, waiting to touch down. When will it come? Her skin, her hot skin. What does the foetus make of this? wonders Colin. The child, what's the child thinking? Nothing, it can't know, surely, it's asleep. It's way past its bed time.

'They've said it's a girl,' says Melissa, her suspicions growing as Colin's eyes shut with desire. He waits for touch down. Seconds happen. 'I was really hoping for a little boy,' she says.

But Colin can't hear. There should be an almighty hiss as his hands connect with her belly, but there isn't. No sound at all. The palms of his hands. Her body. The baby girl. Melissa's stomach is like an African drum: a bongo, pig skin pulled taut across wood. But hot, hot and wet. A greenhouse in summer. Colin circulates both his hands around her stomach, fingers erect and stretched apart, adapting to the contours of this stack of skin, sliding every-where in her sweat.

His hands move all over her because they must. They must know every part of this flesh. Around her extruded belly button, around the seams of her stomach where the stretched skin disappears and the soft, silk-like sensation begins. Colin's fingers reach the summit of her belly, then come skiing down, right to where her body levels out and his wrists scrape along the prickly waistband of her underwear. Then down, further, down, of course. Colin, who doesn't touch women, runs his fingers lightly over Melissa's knickers, feeling the tendony, featherlike contents. Then back up, over the belly and down to her breasts which seem muscular and strained. He kneads them until they feel free and mobile. The charity. The healer.

His eyes stare down at the ground, then directly at Melissa's face which appears more alert than at ease. For Colin, all this can never be enough. He brings his leg down from the bed, pauses for a second then bows forward, head first under the covers. Hot air is gassing his mouth, like he's not breathing at all but suffocating. It's pitch black and steamy. He pushes his cheek up against Melissa's body, skids his lips around and around her stomach, wetting his entire face in her perspiration. Drinking it. This is it, something; a feeling, hot flesh, a lovely feeling. Desire. Confusion. He wants this, wants this magic for ever. He is gasping with pleasure.

'Colin, stop.'

A muffled noise. A voice from outside the covers, not Melissa's. Shit. And oh fuck. Colin pauses, closing his eyes, pressing their lids against stretched skin.

'Colin, stop.'

Colin edges out slowly, lifting the cover back over his head and placing it down by Melissa's side. His eyes are reddening. His hair is disturbed and sticks out in strange directions. His mouth is open, lips rendered indistinct by perspiration.

'Get the fuck out of here,' whispers Deaks, as if he'd rather be shouting at the top of his voice. What have I done wrong? thinks Colin, despairing. He'd massaged her, that's all, that's what she wanted. What the fuck is he complaining about?

'Get out of here, Colin. I'll deal with it,' says Deaks, touching Melissa on the shoulder and gesturing towards the glowing EXIT sign above the door. Colin ignores him and stares at Melissa. She's fucking fine. What is his problem? He half expects Melissa to leap to his defence, say she was enjoying it and ask Deaks what the fuck his problem is. But she doesn't. She's just staring at Deaks, a look on her face like she's just been dunked by bastards into an ice-cold swimming pool. Colin leaves in silence.

It's five minutes before the text message from Deaks comes in. It tells Colin to meet him at the Wishing Well. Neutral territory, away from the doctors and their large and effective ears. It's another five minutes until Deaks is sitting down in the Wishing Well opposite Colin. No food or drink. What the fuck is his problem?

'Well, what was that about, Colin?' says Deaks, tapping an unlit fag on to the grey tabletop. Colin says nothing. 'She said you felt her fucking tits. Do you have any idea how careful I have to be? How much trouble we'd be in if a woman complained?' Again, Colin elects not to reply. He's thinking about his school days in Stretford; the relentless bollockings, the speechless lust, rushing home to wank into a sports sock. Ha, his innards crease into a smile. The pretty-shitness of life. The painted veil. He looks up at Deaks, who exhales melodrama: 'She said you tried to finger her.'

'She's lying,' Colin replies, leaning back on his chair, looking around the cafeteria. A few tired people wait for news of life or death. It's a grey area: Deaks massages the women, helps them but also helps himself. He needs the women and they need him. It's convenient. But, of course, he can't take it as far as he'd like. He can't fuck them or wank over them directly. He sticks within certain boundaries, so as to make it all last: his life, his sanity, his caring sessions with the women.

At an adjacent table, a gingernut in a yellow dressing gown burps horrendously. Colin and Deaks share a glance, then listen as she spews a pink mess on to the table. There's a commotion involving endless reams of paper towels and the drip-drip of sick on to the floor. The mood changes and Deaks leans in towards Colin sympathetically.

'You have to take what you can get in this life, Colin. If you can't fuck pregnant women, then you do the next best thing: you touch them and care for them.'

'I don't want to have sex with them,' says Colin, watching the sickly gingernut being led away at snail's pace. It's true, he doesn't want to have sex with a pregnant woman. It's fascination, only fascination.

But Deaks is not convinced: 'Bullshit,' he barks. 'I saw you under the covers. The feeling of fucking the already fucked is the feeling that has changed my life.'

Colin flicks his head violently to one side and performs an exaggerated swallow. Deaks smiles an unhappy smile.

'They let me do it sometimes, you know? Once a year or

155

so, a woman comes along who wants it. Imagine that. I can't afford to lose my chance. That's why you messing around tonight is so serious.'

An enormous tea urn blows steam from its loose-fitting lid. There is a smell of old food. Colin notices a few drops of pink vomit that the sleepy staff neglected to clean up. He can't imagine having sex with a heavily pregnant woman. Partly because he's unimaginative, and partly because the prospect of such pointless touching makes his lips scrunch with upset terror. 'Why?' he says. 'Why do you fuck them, Deaks?'

Deaks's smile widens. His teeth are bared. 'Because I really, really want to,' he begins. 'It's a feeling I have. A desire. The same reason your hair is dripping in that girl's sweat.'

Instinctively, Colin spikes his hair with his hand. It stands on end. His eyes are open wide and bright. It's uncommon for Colin to speak to anyone and he feels unusual, like a new person. He even feels a little more normal, despite the fact he's in a hospital cafeteria discussing the merits of sex with pregnant women. Deaks continues to persuade.

'Everybody has their fetish, Colin. Chances are you're beginning to find your own.'

'No,' Colin replies. He stares at the cheap tabletop and senses that, deep down, he'd rather be dead. Better to be dead than staring at this tabletop. He slams his hands down and stands up. Deaks's head bows and Colin fights the temptation to bring many plates smashing down on to his crown. Colin grimaces and breathes. Words drop from his mouth like a slow strand of thick spit.

'I feel . . . that it's not sex . . . It's like I've just discovered

the origin of myself and the rest of us . . . and it was innocent . . . and I'm surprised.'

It's three-thirty on Monday morning and this is a black
and sooty world. The lights of the cafeteria appear to
be locked in a process of dimming. Getting darker
and darker. This plastic room contains not a single drop
of natural light. It's just a space that humans have locked
themselves in to eat, drink and wait on news of the
sick. The air isn't air at all, but a liquid that we bob about
in.

Colin, who is certain he doesn't wish to make love to a
pregnant woman, but is nonetheless fascinated by their
concept, is leaving the hospital. He's working his way down
flights and flights of steps. Outside, the air is iced glass;
splintering slowly and dramatically all around. There is the
possibility of snowfall, Colin stamps his stone feet on
the stone ground, searching for the light of traffic and the
bus home.

And, of course, the early morning lights of the city begin
to glow and nudge at the blacked-out windows of the bus.
And, of course, the bus contains people. Tired ones, for
whom the scrolling red and blue lights of Rusholme are
like a dream; the types of shapes and colours you see when
you shut your eyes.

Colin's pale-blue bedroom is almost certainly both
cold and odorous. But, in truth, it seems to simply stink
of a disgusting coldness. Like it's entirely unified, bound
by frost and sharp ice. He picks his way across the
warzone floor. It's no man's land at Christmas; cheerful
and still, but bloodstained by battle. His wet bedsheets
work against the warming instincts of his body. Oh, it's
winter and it's always so cold. He brings his legs up into

his body so his knees are resting just below his chin. He shivers, remembering the warmth of Melissa's belly, picturing her lying in that hospital bed. He falls into her sleep.

19

Drinking Formaldehyde

SHE WON'T COME, thinks Johnny. There's no way she'll come. He's sitting in one of Withington's fashionable bars, frequented by second-year students and reluctant estate agents. The walls of the bar have had large planks of dark wood grafted on to them. They're decorated in memorabilia: old football pennants, photos of forgotten movie stars, oil paintings of an older world. Or rather, a younger world. Yes, a younger world, of course. We are an ancient civilisation, the eldest and weariest society. Johnny feels old and indifferent.

It's a terrible sign that Rebecca is already fifteen minutes late. It's a terrible sign that Johnny has already finished the cup of tea he ordered on arrival. The waitress, who seems simplistic and happy, is eyeing him carefully. Does he require more tea? Johnny hasn't met Rebecca in a while. After that day at the park, they saw less and less of each other. He phoned her, but she was always busy with university or whatever. In the three months that have passed, Johnny has lost his grip on the society of enjoyment, casual coffee and laughter. He's so upset.

She should come, thinks Johnny, she really should come. She'd texted him yesterday, they'd agreed to meet here. The text came as a surprise to Johnny, a pleasant one: is it finally time to forgive? He takes a moment to arrange the empty mug, the miniature teapot and the jug of milk neatly to one side of the table. There is a rose in a sleek glass vase. There is an old and cold chip.

'Would you like another cup of tea?'

'No thanks, I'm fine for the moment.'

'Would you like to see a menu?'

'No.'

Since the incident with the porn mag and Zakir's hasty departure, Johnny has been entirely alone. Thinking back, his life casually fell to pieces in a matter of hours. Two jokes, one about a twat and the other involving a surprise porno, were all it took to make him alone and pessimistic about the fifty or sixty years that may indeed be ahead of him. A birthday had passed by, his twenty-first. His mother had sent a card: the only evidence of his getting older and older.

One thing stands between Johnny and an undeniably gloomy life: pornography. The helpfulness of pornography cannot be exaggerated; it has temporarily saved him. During a phase in his life when time threatened to pass out at the steering wheel, Johnny has been able to keep up with himself through the frequent purchase and enjoyment of porn. He has become a wanker. Pornography makes his life exciting. It fills his evenings with tension, glory and imagination. It is a reason to wake up and move about the city, to compile sexual data, attend lectures, shop. Pornography entirely makes up for the absence of friends.

Johnny's virginity is largely self-imposed, not by religion or anything foolish, it's simply a biological thing. Puberty made a scarcely perceptible imprint on his brain. It half-heartedly decorated his body in wiry, insectile hair. But that was all. It failed to jerk his brain to life and fill it with the necessary shit. So for so long, girls had not been an issue. He'd not been strangled into sex like most of his peers, he had been a carefree and content young man. But this is no longer the case.

Since coming to university and being subjected to the finest and most nubile configurations of flesh and fabric, Johnny is a wreck. He's gasping for breath. His lack of experience with women and the untimely collapse of his relationship with Rebecca has left him lost for words. Pornography was the only route open to him and he has compiled quite a collection. To the Asian shopkeeper, he has become a phenomenal source of business and profit. At more light-hearted moments, he likes to imagine how her quality of life must have improved considerably since he began to purchase seven pornos a week from her. Perhaps she has a picture of him on her mantelpiece. Maybe her and her family thank him in prayer before each meal. He's paying their fucking rent; putting trainers on their feet and making them rich and happy. Johnny is great business.

Besides rejoicing in the seemingly endless line of girls who appear only too happy to remove their clothes and be photographed in a variety of poses, Johnny has become smitten with the activity of phone sex. Of course, it costs him a fortune in phone bills, but his diminished responsibility to lifestyle makes it affordable. Barely a day goes by when he doesn't find himself crouched over his magazines, phone in hand, wanking at speed. But wait – Rebecca.

'Sorry I'm late.'

'Rebecca.'

'The bus was a nightmare, sorry. How are you?'

Rebecca's arrived and her face is glowing, a red traffic light on each cheek. She takes down her hood with its fake fur trim, removes her coat completely and sighs. Winter has stabbed her to life. She's breathless and glowing, eyes scanning the bar. Alert, clean and cold, she rubs her hands together vigorously and stares into Johnny's eyes.

'It's been ages. What have you been up to?' she asks, taking a seat and examining the miniature teapot for signs of tea. Johnny begins fumbling around with the mug, convinced that, once again, he will inappropriately refer to a twat. Or a cunt.

'Oh, this and that, killing time. Zakir's left so I'm living on my own at the moment.' Johnny's voice oscillates with agitation. Platitudes in the key of panic.

'Is that not a bit lonely?'

'Yes, it is.'

A clear code of conduct exists between human beings who have got to know each other, spoken and spent time together. The streets, squares and rooms of England are often quiet and unfriendly; strangers rarely speak. But if, for some reason, you've come into contact with another person, then you're obliged to try and make it work and attempt to maintain your ties. This is why we are here, in this bar. This is why the room has been gently heated and decorated. Why Johnny is hovering above Rebecca, gesturing manically – he wants to buy her a drink.

'What would you like to drink?'

'A cappuccino.'

This is why coffee beans were grown and why machines that brew coffee and froth milk were researched, invented and perfected. Because people clouted together by instinct, accident or desire, must be bound to one another. We must try. This is friendship and morality. It has little to do with phone sex, and more to do with the widely held belief that loneliness is shit.

The cappuccino arrives in a dull thud of glory. Chocolate sprinklings. A ginger light. Johnny repetitively rubs his right cheek. It's as if he's persecuted by some unfortunate neuroses, brought about by an awareness that life, and the things we do, are all a little crap. He's not, of course, he's simply riddled with nerves. He can't believe she's actually here, and so beautiful. This glorious moment must be taken advantage of. His personality must be articulated at pace, like a character in a short film, or one of those apartment blocks which secretly construct themselves overnight.

'You know, Rebecca, I'm sorry about what I said that day. I didn't mean to offend you, when I said I wanted to do that.'

'Do what?' says Rebecca, searching through her bag.

'Hammer away at a twat,' says Johnny, half covering his mouth with his hand.

'Oh, yeh, of course, it's fine. Don't worry about it.'

Prejudices, hatreds, grudges and opinions are not expected to be maintained. The standards imposed on the thoughts that people think are very lax. Opinions, like disco lights, can flash on and off, like most things they can be forgotten. So Rebecca feels no inclination to maintain her largely feigned outrage at Johnny's use of the word twat. It was ages ago. Three months. Forget it. She leans in. She's all smiles, health and just a glimpse of cleavage, a perspective on death.

'So, go on, Johnny, it's been ages, tell me about things.'

'There's nothing to tell.'

'Why did Zakir leave?'

'I've honestly got no idea, he just did.'

'He probably realised what a retard you are. Ha.'

'Yeh. Listen, Rebecca, I really wish we saw each other more often, like we used to.'

Even boys like Johnny are capable of cutting to the chase once in a while. Course they are, how else would any of us get anywhere? So it is that he's demanded more of Rebecca's time, rather abruptly and out of the blue. When your life is akin to holding your breath for unnatural lengths of time, you're likely to gasp loudly when you finally open your mouth and breathe. Johnny is brimming with pent-up society. Months of phone sex and isolated living and wanking are blowing from his jaws.

'Looking back, Rebecca, you were pretty much my best mate. Offending you was a really big mistake. I didn't mean to, I regret it.'

'Oh, Johnny, you're a sweetheart.' Rebecca studies Johnny and thanks God she met Justin.

'I think my life might be really shite,' continues Johnny, enjoying the sensation of words passing his lips and admiring the two lines of cleavage that descend into Rebecca's blue top, towards happiness. 'It's mostly shite in really big ways. I have no friends, no interests, no ambition, no love. I really—'

Rebecca, who can't stop thinking about Justin and how fucking brilliant he is, interrupts unconvincingly: 'What about mates off your course?'

'I blew it,' confesses Johnny. 'Things go so fast and I just missed out. Honestly, please, what do you do with your time, Rebecca?'

The coffee machine coughs and a plate is placed on an

adjacent table, stacked high with focaccia and fries. Eyes widen and the door clatters and vibrates in its effort to repel the cold. The bar's rammed with civilisation and its pendulous moods; its absurd and twisting periods of emotion, event and despair. We have arrived at some poorly signposted junction in Earth's existence, when people can do little but pay their rent and sit at tables, order drinks and chew Italian bread to mush. Who is remembering all this?

'I've met this lad.'

'A lad?'

'Yes. Actually, Johnny, there's something I've been meaning to talk to you about.'

Johnny leans forward so far he could comfortably dribble spit into Rebecca's cappuccino. He doesn't. But he imagines that glorious moment when Rebecca decided there was something that she wanted to talk to him about. How is he manifested in her brain? he wonders. A cloud of dust, perhaps, a drop of fluid, a ghost. How he would love to be exactly who Rebecca thinks he is, even if it were bad, at least he would be simple and still.

'Justin and I,' Rebecca begins, her voice betraying enthusiasm for the first time, 'we're experimenting, trying to find better sex. As a virgin, and a person who clearly has had few sexual opportunities, you'd be really useful to us.'

Johnny feels certain traits of his personality evaporate and exit with a hiss from each of his ears. I shall never be funny again, he confirms with a smirk. 'I'm not a virgin,' he suggests, causing Rebecca to erupt with self-interest.

'Yes, Johnny, you are. Don't be ashamed. We're trying to liberate ourselves from these dire sexual shackles binding everyone nowadays. We're finding out where we'd be and what we'd be like if we actually did what culture is daring us to do.'

'What is culture daring us to do, Rebecca?'

Rebecca bows her head and looks up, her pupils peeping at Johnny from underneath her forehead and the plucked ridges of her eyebrows.

'Culture, Johnny,' she says, the mug poised at her lips, 'is daring us to do what the fuck we like.'

She sips from her drink and glances over to an area by a window where it's lighter and people are laughing and enjoying themselves. She is unrecognisable from the girl Johnny first fell in love with. She is on a mission. She behaves as if her head is stacked with secrets that she must never share but only allude to charismatically. She blinks and her eyes return to Johnny's. 'I could fuck you for instance, Johnny. Justin could just watch, or, we could have a threesome. We take it very seriously, we've even got a website.'

'You could fuck me?' says Johnny, confused by the smut his beautiful friend is spouting. She leans towards him, displaying the sort of faux-importance that only a lifetime spent in front of a television can generate.

'We're amassing experience. Me fucking a virgin would be one such experience. I may find that I adore the feeling, you just never know. You should visit the website.' Rebecca takes out a piece of paper and a pen from her bag. She jots down the address of Justin's website: newsex.biz. This is a very common activity. Lately, if you don't have a website then you're basically a total tit. Johnny speaks, but Rebecca doesn't listen. This is common, too. Although even if you don't listen, you can still be fairly cool.

'But you'd be with me. I really like you, Rebecca,' says

Johnny, one eye on his personality, as it disappears into an airvent. But no, Rebecca finishes writing down the address and then slides it over to Johnny, reaching for her cappuccino as she does so.

Oh, they talk. Naturally, they blah-blah for a bit. This and that. On and on. Yes, in reality (ha, what a fate!), they talk for a little while longer. But who remembers? Really? Who remembers? I do not.

For your own benefit, try to imagine that after this exchange time mysteriously accelerates, life fast-forwards itself to the moment when Johnny and Rebecca separate outside the bar. In reality, yes, they talk for half an hour. But the topics they cover are fairly dull. The whole occasion lives in the shadow of Rebecca's suggestion that she takes Johnny's virginity as part of an elaborate and fairly vague social experiment.

Johnny, in particular, fails to make much sense of the occasion after listening to Rebecca's proposal. His eyes glaze as she talks about a French writer she's recently developed an interest in, Michel Something or other. Johnny can't believe what she has just suggested. He can't believe how vulgar love can be. Because he does love Rebecca, sexual experiment or not. He loves like we all love. But he's disgusted by her proposal, by the whole idea of the experiment. Who is this lad anyway? This Justin? How can Johnny's mind churn out affection for this repulsive girl? Jesus, love is like drinking formaldehyde, or dipping your scalp in water that will soon turn to ice. How can I cope with this? thinks Johnny.

They separate outside the bar. Rebecca skips in the direction of a braking bus, arm outstretched and hailing. She's off to God knows where; to fuck a horse, to shag a corpse. Johnny's got no idea. He's on Wilmslow Road, roughly grappling with a series of contradictions in his head. Of course, he's seen films. I know what romance is, he thinks. And it's got nothing to do with experiments or virgins, horses, chains or piss. Yes, I know what romance is and I want it. His brain bellows towards the south of his body, echoing around his torso and down his acoustic ribcage. His eyes go wide. I need to be in love.

In light of Johnny's belief in romance and his faith in the idea that other people, specifically girls, are capable of being tear-jerkingly wonderful, it's annoying that Rebecca has soiled her image by propositioning him. If this was a film, and the two of them were facing each other on a moonlit coastal veranda, then Johnny might say this:

'You were everything to me, Rebecca, you know? I would have done anything to be . . . to be . . . to be with you.'

But this isn't a film and Rebecca's nowhere near the sea. She's on a bus heading north up Wilmslow Road. Johnny's on Egerton Road, trapped in the suburbs, wondering whether the fact he's been alive for twenty-one years qualifies him as an adult. Were his parents in love? Did their eyes well up with tears at the thought of making a child and spending their lives together? Did they love the idea of buying a house, partaking in daily rituals, nights of passion, looking after each other? Is my lanky frame capable of letting me live and be happy? I'm so tall, thinks Johnny. My face is not right, somebody got me wrong, made me badly. Will I really live to be sixty or seventy years old? I just don't see how. God? It makes no sense. I want a fire to sit by. A rug. A hot drink. A conversation. A girl to devote myself to, please, this is so ugly and I'm so lonely. She wants to have sex with me because I'm a virgin. She wants to take me, guide me. Would we kiss?

I won't do it, thinks Johnny, as the front door shuts and the throaty desire to wank fizzes up his cock, over his chest, and up his spine to his mind. Lonely and desperate as I am, I won't do it. She is lost, but I have a brain and I'm not disabled. I can find my way out of this dark winter. I'll find my way to beautiful, expansive terrain, where people discover shared interests. Where people are perplexed by an immediate and tacit attraction to one another. Where people make love and make the most of each other. I just want love.

Johnny walks down the hall and removes the cordless phone from its cradle. It has been charging, conserving energy. He's climbing the stairs, stooping because he's tall and depressed. He feels that Rebecca has got it all wrong, feels her whole project sounds a little trendy and political. Love, that's what will remove us from this culture of sex, mindless masturbation and slavery. He removes the two most recent pornos from his underwear drawer and throws them on to his unmade bed. They're bright and new. Love is the answer. Thank God for pornography.

He begins to turn the pages, kneeling by his bed like a child preparing to pray. There is a foolproof formula for the photographing of women for the purposes of male masturbation. Each photograph must refer clearly to a specific mode of intercourse or foreplay. A crouch and a gaping mouth says blow job, naturally. An arched back and a protruding rear says doggy or anal. It's child's play. The necessary nudges and prompts for a primitive and electric imagination. Johnny skips calmly from page to page until each magazine is catering for the majority of his sexual desires. A black girl's pussy stares at the camera, this takes care of race and doggy. There's a blonde with a glint of oral sex in her eye. A brunette's face suggests personality and gentleness. In addition, her legs are open wide and her breasts are huge. Finally, Johnny locates a good tit-bra – his favourite pose. A tit-bra occurs when two girls touch their tits together, meaning that each set of tits is supported by the other. Yes, I love a good tit-bra, thinks Johnny. At last, the age of the tit-bra is here. Ha, you don't believe it, but it's true. This is it. Monsters. Monsters.

Johnny has his preferred sex line on speed dial. A flick of the finger and it's ringing. Flies lowered, cock hard, love and life, love and life, hurrah, hurrah. Not too fast, now: you'll come before you hear her voice.

'Hello,' says a voice, female and cracked.

'Hello,' says Johnny.

'Who's that?'

'It's . . . er . . . Dave.'

'Hello, honey, how you doing?'

'Fine, fine, I'm OK. How are you?'

'I'm OK. How old are you, Dave baby?'

'Twenty-three.'

'Do you work, Dave?'

'Yes! I . . . er . . . work in a Boots.'

'Oooh, I love Boots. The chemist, right?'

'Yeah!'

It is not yet evening, but the light outside suggests that somebody has attached a lampshade to the sun. Phone sex is a popular form of sex. It plays second fiddle to the Internet, but it's still a widely enjoyed romance. It is a laceration through a lonely world; past all the lines, the airs and the barriers. Past the bullshit that prevents easy and impromptu dialogue between people. These girls are paid to talk. These men, oh, these men. Their hearts will smudge and be destroyed if they're denied the sound of a woman speaking.

'Well, Dave, I'm nineteen, I'm 34-24-36, I'm wearing a black lacy bra and matching knickers and suspenders. I'm fingering myself.'

Johnny begins massaging the root of his penis with his left hand. This is romance, too; it slows down the process, improves the conversation. The girl stops talking; Johnny knows this silence well. He must describe himself to the sex-worker.

'OK. I'm tall with brown hair. I'm wearing jeans and a mustard polo shirt and . . . er . . . I've got my cock out.'

'How big's that, then, Dave?'

'It's, it's about seven inches.'

'Oooh nice, do you wanna give it a rub for me?'

'Yes, I do.'

The love that doesn't know its name. A fuck-awful bedroom in Manchester. A winter. A vital act. The absolute need to put a knitting needle into your brain. Johnny can't afford to gently caress, so he rubs vigorously. Friction. Pleasure. Onwards. Thoughts crash like cymbals in his head. Rebecca sucks his cock. The Asian shopkeeper probes his anus. Certain girls glimpsed in streets push their tits into his eyes. Thank God for this, for the heavenly humanity of the wank. The lovely speed of his hands and the feeling of his elbow on the bed sheet. His breath held. The colourful pornography. The years he will spend alive. Quick, civilisation, quick.

'I'll lick your balls slowly.'

'Yeah.'

'I'll wrap my tits around your cock.'
'Yeah.'
'I'll dip my cunt on your tongue.'
'Yeah.'
'I'll scream like a baby.'
'Yeah.'
'Fuck me, Dave.'
'OK.'
'Put your length up my twat.'
'Your twat?'
'Yeah, now my arse.'
'OK.'
'Harder.'
'Yeah.'
'Harder!'
'OK.'
'Fucking harder, you prick!'
'Yes.'
'Harder!'
'Yeah, yeah?'
'Now spray it in my face.'

There is a light groan. Love is loveless. Sex is sexless. The line goes dead. Exhale.

20

The Glass Coffee Table

YOU GROW WEAK. I sense it. I grow weak. My pen is snapped. I need a replacement. I want to get out of here. No, let me rephrase that: I have to stay. Though I'd dearly love to snort a line of dog dirt from my desk, start sniffing like a villain. But I don't. No, the story must go on. The facts gather around me like guests at a party. They rest their hands on my back and duck down to see what I'm up to. And you, you're still with me, right? I'll continue. Hesitation is for pricks. I am not a prick. I always carry a spare pen. Remember Steve?

Steve made a decision to sacrifice himself to the mainstream. He offered himself to everything that is simple and inane. He is a goat. A lamb. A toast to boring failure, champagne, cheers. The story is this: a boy who was political and motivated makes a decision to be a lifter of weights, a dyer of hair, a getter of girls, a small nothing like the rest of us. That is the story, certainly, entirely believable and important. He made the decision. His mind is fucked.

Steve is standing with his father in a pub car park in Southport. Dusk is everywhere. The air is paper and the light is sandstone. You remember that he went to visit his parents for the weekend, leaving Carly in the flat alone? Well here we are. His father is tall and was born in 1947. He wears a large, billowing suede jacket. It's brown and covered in zips. Yes, he's middle-aged. Awful trousers. Glasses. Shoes with solid soles.

'I'm very proud of you, Steve,' says Steve's dad, fiddling with one his jacket's many zips.

His father is called Michael. Michael seems suddenly overcome by a massive and belated desire to be alive. To be a human. His arm fires out of his body, his hand comes to rest on Steve's shoulder. Like an Olympic swimmer with a perfected front crawl, Steve leans left and brings his right arm arching over his father's shoulder and around his back. Embrace. Tighter. OK, enough, let each other go now, and speak, speak . . .

'Son, you're making money and Carly is a lovely girl; beautiful and kind. You've made me and your mother so proud. You've made us happy.'

The two men exchange an odd look. They hold each other's blue eyes. Steve's gelled, bleached hair remains still and unmoving as a strong breeze wreaks havoc on his father's scalp. Michael pulls his large suede jacket around his body and looks at his son. Can you really be my son? he wonders.

Steve is dressed in distressed denim, ripped at the knees. He reeks of perfume. Stiff styled hair, coloured at considerable expense. He's of a different generation; represents

174

a totally different way of being alive. Can you really be my son? wonders Michael again.

'Are you gay, Steve?' Michael asks, after a short silence. Because he recognises nothing in his son's appearance and behaviour, he simply can't relate to any of it. Sure, thinks Michael, my son makes money. But look what he does with it. All this style. He asks again: 'Are you gay, Steve?'

Steve chooses not to reply. They stand in silence. Michael eyeing his son, entirely perplexed by his appearance. What happened, and when did it happen? Why does my son look so fancy and incredible? Is he famous? I don't think so. Is he a style icon? A designer? No, he is not. What is this, high capitalism? A purchased look? A purchased personality? Michael is bewildered by change.

Steve isn't bewildered. He knows. He remembers deciding to become this. He abandoned his brains and signed up for a shit and delicious life. Now he's standing in a car park saying goodbye to his father.

'No, Dad, I'm not gay. Goodbye.'

'I'm glad to hear it. Goodbye, son.'

Steve turns on his heels and strides in the direction of his Audi TT. It's five o'clock. His strides are long. He reaches the car in good time, keys in hand. The atmosphere in the car is tense. The air is plastic and scented with petrol and vanilla. Steve is thinking about Carly, about the choices he's made regarding his future. Lies are told: I love you. Questions are asked: how are you? Sooner or later you're on the wire, twisting and flinching, unified; the sum of all those things you said that were untrue. An anthology of lazy, navy blue lies.

When the car gets on to the motorway, it accelerates. Steve puts his foot down. What is this like? Oh, I don't know. No doubt you've been in a fast car before, just remember what that was like. Steve puts on the radio. There is music. Concentrate.

It's ten past six by the time Steve drives the car into the basement of his apartment block. It's a short skip though the black trappings of winter to the entrance of his apartment block. As he arrives at the door, he can already hear, faintly, the sound of a woman screaming.

'Aaaaaahhiiaahiiiaiaiiaiaiaiaiaiagggh.'

He swipes his access card and pushes at the door. As he enters the building, the screaming is instantly louder, as if some cosy act of domestic genocide is unfolding in one of the apartments above. A door on the ground floor opens and a middle-aged man comes out into the foyer. His chin is coated in shaving foam. He peers up the stairwell at the screams, annoyed and disturbed.

'Aaaaaaaaaaahhhhhiiiiiiiiiaiaiaggh.'

The screams are constant. The sound is so incredibly sharp and long. Steve begins to climb the stairs, above him he can hear doors opening and slamming, footsteps running up stairs and along corridors. Someone is being murdered, surely. This must be one of those unfortunate moments when a group of people are indiscriminately murdered by a madman acting mad.

'What's happening?'

'She sounds like she's in pain.'

'What number is it, who is it?'

'Break the door down!'

Around fifteen residents are gathered outside Steve's apartment on the second floor. Steve arrives and joins the back of the crowd. He can't see his front door because it's entirely surrounded by people. A tall man with a thick, black beard and round, black eyes sends a beady gaze over the congregation. The man pauses and waits for the latest high-pitched scream to subside. Then speaks: 'Could everyone acknowledge that the door is locked? I think the woman is in danger. I'm going to break the door down. OK?'

A wave of approval breaks within the crowd. Steve looks down at his door key, then places it inside his pocket. He stands aside to give the bearded man a sufficient run-up; these doors are new and difficult to break down.

This is my life, Steve confirms in his mind. No doubt about it. I'm assisting in the break-in to my own home. Why is Carly screaming? Why is she making these large and anti-social sounds? What will I do if she's being killed? he wonders.

Steve closes his right eye and rubs it with his right hand. His head bows and he briefly examines his outfit of distressed denim and expensive white brogues. He breathes in his affluent aroma and runs his finger though the exposed wires of his designer haircut. Please stop screaming, Carly. Steve's mouth opens. It says: 'Mate, use a fire extinguisher.'

'Good idea, mate. Give me a hand,' says the bearded guy.

Within moments, Steve and the bearded guy are exchanging reassuring glances and preparing to bring a fire extinguisher smashing into the front door of Steve's apartment. There's another terrible scream, like a pin into the wrist, an injection into the eye. Steve bends his knees and his trousers pull tight; the shape of the house key in his pocket is briefly outlined. Then smash. Again. Smash. Again. Smash. The lock is beginning to break.

'Aaaaaaaaiiiiiiiigghhhhhh.'

'Keep going,' says a supportive onlooker, desperate to know the source of the screaming. Steve ought to be laughing; he's laughing inside. How has it come to this? Were my choices really so bad? Is breaking into my own flat while the key is in my pocket really the logical extension of everything I've done? This is a key moment in my life, I suppose, hahaha – a key moment, ha, is this madness? Why is Carly still screaming? She can surely hear the banging. It must be murder, oh dear, I shall need a new lover. I should use the keys, this is manslaughter. Guilty. I'm a liar.

There is one final bang as the man with the small black eyes kicks in the remainder of the door. The crowd spills into the apartment, led by Steve.

'Aaaaaaaaaaaiiiiiiiiiigggggghhhh.'

You'd think it would be quiet now, but it isn't. Carly screams still. It's louder than ever. Steve watches the crowd: jaws drop. He watches the shock register on their faces. Their eyeballs suck smoke. He follows their burning gaze across the room, to Carly, who may or may not be about to die.

'Aaaaaaaaaaaiiiiiiiiiigggggghh.'

Carly is lying naked in broken glass, squirming about in the splintered remains of a lovely coffee table. Why won't she stop? She's cutting herself to ribbons. There is dark red blood, ripped skin. There is white light, she continues to scream. She's entirely naked, apart from a strange contraption that binds her body. Seat-belt-like straps. Strange pads. There is a loud buzzing coming from Carly. How bad is this?

The bearded man pushes Steve to one side and strides purposefully across the room. He passes Carly, who screams. He walks over to a socket and pulls out a plug. Carly's body goes limp. Her head drops down on to the carpet of glass. Her knees bend and the soft sound of her weeping is faded gently into this dreadful occasion.

'Call an ambulance,' says Beardy. He bears a striking resemblance to Che Guevara. With the plug in one hand, he lifts Carly and her contraption and carries them into the bedroom. Steve follows him in.

'She's OK, I think. The cuts aren't too bad.'

The man removes the contraption so quickly, you'd be forgiven for thinking that he spends his life dealing with complex sex machines from the Far East. Steve comes over to the bed and begins to pick shards of glass from Carly's body. She's coated in cuts. Leaking blood like a sieve. Skin falling off her everywhere, flapping and ripping.

'What were you doing, baby?' says Steve, removing a fingernail of glass from Carly's collarbone.

'Steve?' says Carly, her voice scratched and paper thin.

The beardy guy shoots a stern glance at Steve. There's a chance he thought he and Carly might have a future together, after his act of bravery, after the wounds heal. When he realises she's already Steve's, he gets up and leaves the bedroom, muttering something about an ambulance. So Steve and Carly are alone. Young love.

'It's Frank's machine, isn't it? A sex machine from Japan. Jesus, Carly, you stupid, stupid bitch. What were you thinking?'

Carly says nothing, her eyes float in blood and her lacerated back is disposing of it at either side of her body. The sheets are drenched. Steve stamps his right foot on the soft carpet, barely making a sound. 'Am I not enough for you, Carly?'

She croaks then replies, gurgling unnatural concoctions of fluid in her throat as she speaks. 'You used to be,' she says. 'But things have changed now.' Though weak, her voice remains charged with the steely resolve that powers her incredible, metallic life. So she's covered in blood, half dead, yet in some significant way, she really doesn't give a shit.

'How did you get it working? Why did you open my mail?' demands Steve, still stamping inaudibly on to the carpet.

'I . . . ouch . . . I bought a Japanese plug adapter from Dixons.'

'Right, OK, a Japanese adapter. Good. Dixons. Where's the fucking ambulance?'

Steve goes to the door. In the living room the beardy guy is whispering to a red-faced brunette of about thirty. They're probably discussing why Steve didn't have a key. Why he helped to break down his own front door.

'The ambulance is on its way, mate. It'll be a couple more minutes.'

Steve turns to the bedroom again, to Carly drowning in red. Jesus. He goes over to the Sex Machine, which is slumped in the corner, spattered in tiny crimson tears. Suddenly, Steve's heart slows down to crawling pace. He watches as the Sex Machine becomes alive and stares back at him with a fixed grin. It props itself up against the bedroom wall. Wow.

'How do you do?' says the Sex Machine.

'You speak English?' asks Steve, edging backwards away from the machine, until he's leaning against the bed.

'Yes, yes indeed I do, I have a basic grasp,' exclaims the Sex Machine, his voice plump with pride. The Sex Machine has a suave demeanour which is rather intimidating.

Steve sighs.

'What did you do to Carly, my girlfriend?' he asks.

At this, the Sex Machine appears to blush. No, no it can't possibly blush. It muddles its straps for a moment, as if deep in awkward thought. It taps at the skirting board with one of its white pleasure pads. It's slightly ashamed.

'Yes, yes I'm sorry about that,' says the machine, finally, turning to face Steve. 'She's a lovely girl, my first love. My first love, indeed. Oooh, my goodness, that must sound too far-fetched, me a machine and whatnot. That must sound sick to someone who is indeed alive. Of course, I'm a machine.' The Sex Machine jangles its various components for a second, as if confirming to itself that it is, indeed, a machine.

'Why is she bleeding?'

'She's bleeding because, when we were making love, we fell into the coffee table. Do you realise that your coffee table is made entirely of glass? It's rather tasteless.'

The machine corrects its posture properly now. It rearranges its straps and its pleasure pads so its appearance becomes much more refined. Steve sits cross-legged and stares down at his red palms, ignoring the groans and whimpering coming from Carly's bloody mouth. He cups his hands around his mouth and nose then points his eyeballs at the Sex Machine. Which smiles.

'Do you have any questions?' says the Sex Machine, striding about now, jauntily swinging its pads and straps. It walks like a 1930s homosexual: reserved but with great rhythm. It's self-assured. Worse: the Sex Machine is cool. Steve can't bear to watch. Questions, he thinks, what can I ask a Sex Machine?

'Well, what did you do to her?' he says at last, causing

the Sex Machine to pivot on the tips of its pleasure pad and walk in his direction.

'I electrocuted her mildly in a number of key areas, her nipples and . . . er . . . downstairs, if you get my meaning, haha.'

The machine chuckles. Oh God. It's overexcited, dancing like a chorus girl. All it needs is a cane or a large pink feather. 'In addition,' continues the machine, 'I vibrate. Very powerfully. Small spheres in these pads of mine vibrate so intensely you can't actually tell they're moving at all. The human eye is too lazy and slow, but your skin and your sexual zones, well, they are perfect for me. Don't thank me.'

'I wasn't going to.'

'So be it, my friend,' says the machine, turning once more and prancing wistfully along the skirting board towards the wardrobe. Steve uncrosses his legs and crawls panther-like to where the Sex Machine is admiring itself in the wardrobe's mirror. The machine catches Steve's reflection coming towards it, and sighs.

'You raped my girlfriend, you bloodied her,' whispers Steve, holding the machine's gaze in the mirror.

'Haha!' the machine guffaws, turning to face the crouching Steve.

'Do not laugh, you machine,' whimpers Steve, recoiling from the machine's manic grin.

'Your girlfriend strapped me to her body and switched me on. She loved me. She loves me still.'

Steve's handsome features shape as if to burst with rage, but then they relax into an expression of sad surprise. Like an arresting officer has just tapped him on the shoulder. The game's up. The Sex Machine registers Steve's melancholy. It moves cautiously towards him and gently strokes his knee with one of its pleasure pads. There there, man, thinks the machine, there there. Steve removes the machine's pad from his knee and gets to his feet.

'Please, could you just fuck off?' says Steve.

'Yes, yes, I suppose I could,' says the Sex Machine.

The machine calmly and carelessly fucks off, collapsing gently on to the floor. It won't be returning, it won't be speaking again. Steve turns again to Carly, she looks as if she's lost consciousness. Poor girl. She's lost so much blood, the bed seems as if it's covered in a plush velvet tablecloth. Her eyes open, like nuts cracking, they flicker in the direction of Steve, her lover: 'Steve . . . there are things I like about you . . . ouch . . . of course there are.'

Steve looks at his lover with total disgust. Machine, he thinks, you shagged that bastard machine.

'I thought I could change the world once, you know?' he says, standing, groping self-consciously at his acutely fashionable shirt. 'I thought I could pick holes in its policies, the way it tricks and trades.' Steve's voice is scarcely audible. He wills tears to his eyes, but he's as dry as a bone.

He walks to the doorway and is greeted gloomily by the man with black beady eyes. Che Guevara. Beady eyes tells Steve that the ambulance has arrived. The living room is illuminated by paramedics, a well-washed man and a well-washed woman in green outfits. Steve beckons them into the bedroom, the paramedic with the thin hair and the creased face addresses Steve, asking, 'Thank you, sir. Are you the boyfriend?'

In the interests of consistent human behaviour and because he understands English, Steve says, 'Yes.' Then watches as the paramedic rushes to Carly's aid.

'Hello, Carly, my name's Jonathan, I'm a paramedic.

We're gonna get you in the ambulance as quickly as we can, OK? Jesus, what happened here, mate?' The paramedic turns to Steve, noticing the extent of Carly's injuries.

Steve shrugs and expels a breath of air: 'She was having sex with a machine and they fell into my glass coffee table. It broke. It's really ruined.'

Carly's shredded body is wrapped in plastic and lifted on to a stretcher. Steve gathers some of Carly's clothes and takes them out to the ambulance. On the way back, he passes Carly and the paramedics on the stairs. He stands and watches as she's carried to the rear of the vehicle and put into place. Carly, so beautiful and strong, even when she's covered in cuts and blood. Oh Carly, Steve runs out to the ambulance. Carly, Carly, my love.

'Will she be OK, mate?' he says, tugging at the green uniform of the paramedic.

'She'll be fine. Are you coming, mate?' A door slams.

'No, I'll follow in the car. It's an Audi TT. Carly's my girlfriend. She's fit, isn't she?'

The paramedic places a hand on Steve's shoulder and looks seriously at his face: 'Yes, mate, she's fucking fit.'

Steve opens the ambulance door and ventures in, crouching over Carly's beautiful face. He runs his hands through her matted hair. He looks at her eyes in such a way as to suggest that, in this instance, forgiveness is possible without recourse to anal sex. It's romance, it has to be. After all, she only shagged a machine, it's an unfortunate accident, that's all. He leans in and kisses a bloodless portion of her forehead. The seal of her mouth breaks, she speaks.

'Steve?'

'Yes, my love?'

'Keep the machine safe.'

'What? But . . .'

'I mean it, Steve. Keep the machine safe. Clean it.'

'What?'

Carly's thin eyes, shot and crisp with blood, spear Steve with a stare. Slowly and carefully she says, 'It is incredible. So please, clean it and keep it safe.'

Steve edges out of the ambulance, a door slams, within seconds his brain is floating in the sound of sirens. In his mouth there are sirens, in his eyes, too. The evening falls down to earth. A bad light. Silent cars smudge the streets. Steve climbs the stairs, enters his flat and closes what remains of his door. She chose this device over me, he thinks, sitting on the bed, prodding the excellent Sex Machine with an outstretched toe.

21

Another Tremendous
Moment in Time

THERE IS A click, then there is a flame, it is bright against the night. Sheltering it carefully, Justin guides the lighter towards Rebecca's mouth and the cigarette is lit. He sees to his own, inhales, exhales, and laughs.

The motorway lay-by is bathed in heavy orange light. Cars go by at speed, lorries too, like shots from a futuristic firearm. Colours painted on black, quick streaks of light. Rebecca leans on the bonnet of the car, seemingly indifferent to her hair, which is airborne and circling her scalp, dancing wildly with the wind. It's as if neither of them is quite enough, neither is able to be larger than their surroundings. Neither can outdo the atmospheres and the subtle boredoms with exceptional living. Having begun an experiment and having taken risks, Rebecca and Justin reacquaint themselves with a sinking sensation. Like weak children in quicksand. Sinking. They experience a deepening despair. Shit, they think, once again we're dwarfed.

Justin edges towards the road and blows smoke at the cars and their loud sounds. You only have to stand by a motorway to realise how precarious our situation is, how easily we are fooled and what tightropes we walk.

'It was another failure, wasn't it, my love?'

A few shards of Justin's question are blown into Rebecca's ears, just enough. There is a sense. She understands.

'Yes. It was another failure,' she shouts back. Shit. Rebecca turns and scrapes the soles of her shoes through the grit of the hard shoulder, irritated that she's having to shout to make herself heard. On top of everything else that has disappointed and malfunctioned, she is forced to shout in order to be heard. Sensing irritation, Justin turns from the road to find Rebecca strutting and angry by the rear spoiler. He traps her against the cold car. The traffic rages at superhuman speeds. Life is cinema.

'I suppose we should try something different, think more carefully and be more discerning about who we deal with,' says Justin, a hand on each of Rebecca's shoulders.

'But it has to be fun, Justin, it must be enjoyable, in some ways at least. What happened tonight felt like fucking rape. Bill Clinton was trying to get up my arse and Thatcher was really chewing at my tits. It felt like fucking rape.'

'I know, I know.'

'Gandhi refused to wear a fucking condom.'

It is unheard of for Justin and Rebecca to kiss, except as part of the experiment, when they're working and researching. But they kiss now. Justin's right hand journeys from her fringe over her head and down her back to where her hair stops. He leans in and so does she. Now they're kissing by the motorway with gentle, dry lips. Rebecca melts a hand into Justin's chest, another reaches up and kneads his cheek, his neck, his hair. There is a growing warmth, a defeating of the wind and the cold air.

'So how did it feel?' asks Justin, pulling away and framing Rebecca's face like a rather twee painting; an all too real-istic portrait of a breaking youth. 'So how did what feel?' Rebecca replies, disappointed that the kiss is already ended.

'When you thought you were being raped, was it good? Is it an answer?'

'Oh, Jus, you don't really believe that we're saving the world, do you?'

'Yes, I do. I want to know if it felt good. If it did, then we could orchestrate a rape, somehow I'm sure. How did it feel, Rebecca? Because if you want we could—'

'No good, Justin,' she interrupts. 'It felt no good.'

Rebecca escapes under Justin's arm and makes for the door of the car. A light rain begins to fall, introducing new sounds to the atmosphere; slimmer sounds. A thin hissing that slides under the clatters of the traffic.

'You are a beautiful and wonderful girl, Rebecca. I'm glad that I met you,' Justin shouts through the weather. A handful of seconds fall silently to the ground.

'I don't want a boyfriend.'

'I don't want a girlfriend.'

'We should get back on the motorway.'

They spent the evening at an event called 'Fuck Power' hosted by an eccentric group of people from Cheshire. 'Fuck Power' invites people to come along and partake in protracted orgies consisting of people dressed up as major political figures of the past and present. It's billed as a way of venting frustration, political as well as sexual, getting your own back. But it turned out to be about a dozen people, all in possession of a dense desire for aggressive sex.

Thatcher, Clinton and Gandhi were there. Tony Blair, of course. Nelson Mandela, Churchill, the Queen, Nixon, Princess Diana, Lenin. Bushes Snr and Jnr (they 69ed, in fact). But the masks were poor and the likenesses implausible. Motivation was also lacking. Mandela's mask came off at one stage, mid-screw, and he didn't even bother to put it back on. He just kept hammering away at the Queen. He wasn't even black.

Rebecca and Justin were not required to dress up. They played themselves, as usual. They were simply meant to take the opportunity to have sex with world leaders, to fuck power. Jesus, the whole situation was dreadful. I suppose the dominating desires of the politicians should have been expected. It was unlikely that Blair was ever going to be submissive. He was always going to bend Rebecca over, was always going to hold her in place while Thatcher probed.

So the experience was a failure. No answers. Still no closer to sexual happiness and self-knowing. The problem with most of these fetish groups is that the participants rarely possess much in the way of taste. They rarely live in exquisitely lit apartments or grand mansions. It's all very well being granted the opportunity of sex with Richard Nixon, but if you have to wait in a narrow, brightly lit corridor watching Gandhi wank himself hard beforehand, then it hardly seems worth it. Fuck Power took place in an atrociously furnished bungalow in Chapel-en-le-Frith. Lenin and Nixon discussed the hazards of applying creosote to their rotting garden fences. Churchill offered

Bombay mix and miniature gherkins to those about to fuck. Where do all the brilliant moments occur? Please, where?

There is hope on the horizon, however; a gloriously smudged sun full of purples, yellows and blues. The hope relates to Justin's firm belief that he can meet, seduce and shag a celebrity. Rebecca is coming round to the idea, too. She's beginning to realise what an enormous goal it is. What the possibilities and the potential findings might be. Incredible. Shagging a celebrity is like shagging a unicorn, or shagging Helen of Troy or Zeus. It's like shagging the Virgin Mary, Joseph, Jesus, God. It would be glorious, a biblical gang-bang.

Rebecca and Justin don't exchange words on the way home. The heater is on full; it's incredibly stuffy. They arrive back at Rebecca's flat at about eleven thirty. As they approach the front door, the sound of a warm and gentle sobbing can be heard, like a mouse singing softly. They follow the sound. It's coming from a pile of clothes and body that has been deposited on the doorstep of Rebecca's flat. The pile of clothes and body is drenched in rain and flinches intermittently.

'Who the fuck is this?' asks Justin, delivering a light kick to the wet bundle.

'It's Johnny, Justin, this is Johnny,' says Rebecca.

Yes, it is Johnny, and he's hammered. He rolls clumsily on to his back and stares up at Justin, like an unarmed character in a film preparing to be riddled with point-blank bullets. His face is wet and red, as if he's not made of skin and bone but of a more malleable solution. Silicone or blubber, milky porridge. His eyes are dots, drawn quickly with a Biro.

'Hell . . . o.' Johnny's Biro eyes disappear, recoiling swiftly into the mush of his face.

'He's drunk, let's get him inside.'

Johnny doesn't notice being picked up. He's not aware of being lifted in Justin's arms and carried to the living room. He feels the warmth of the house, the gold light, the soft furnishings, the distant sound of Rebecca's deep, concerned voice. But his thoughts are of childhood games: hide and seek, ping pong, tig.

'Nice house,' slurs Johnny, as crystals of yellow and red rotate before his eyes. He's fucked. He spent the afternoon sipping lager in his bedroom, spent the evening sipping vodka in numerous hideous bars.

'Where's the experiment? Where is the sex?' he demands, because he wants to have sex and wants to know about the experiment. He is a small piece of paper, dropped from a balcony on a windless day. He flutters and turns like a quickly winking eye, slowly making his way down through stationary air. Then he lands. Content. Then he is violently sick all over his chest.

'Fuck this, Rebecca. I'm not cleaning him up. I'm going to make a call.'

Justin watches Rebecca as she begins to scrape and scoop at the sick on Johnny's jacket. He runs his hands through his hair and suddenly wishes it was shaved again. Can you imagine a simple life? he asks himself. Basic actions. Solid sex. Interesting thoughts. Energy. What a joke. He watches as Johnny embarks on an untimely squirm; vomit runs on to the upholstery, eager to stain.

In the hall, Justin picks up the telephone and punches in a number. In the living room, Rebecca and Johnny play about with sick, half listening to half a conversation.

'Hello? . . . All right, mate, you know that film premiere

you're working on? . . . No, no, it's cool. I'm not bothered about the film, but who's going to be at the after party? . . . Which celebrities? Anyone famous? . . . Really? . . . Fuck . . . You've gotta get me some tickets, I may need as many as six . . .'

Johnny's clothes are almost clean. What little vomit remains will grow crusty overnight and be brushed off in the morning. Rebecca removes his jacket. His mustard polo shirt is full of rainwater and must be removed as well.

'Johnny, stand up, I need to get you out of your clothes,' she says, tugging at his top.

'Oh, finally, Rebecca . . . finally . . . it's happiness, isn't it?'

'No, no, Johnny, it's just that you'll catch cold.'

'Oh, finally . . . happiness and Rebecca.'

Rebecca shrugs, her eyeballs do a loop-the-loop. She could swear that for a second she was staring through the darkness of her skull at her own brain, and that it looked rather fed up. She pulls Johnny's shirt off his back and undoes his belt with a click of her fingers. A sharp pull and his trousers are removed too. She's about to place the garments on the radiator when she notices the scent of urine and semen crawling like an exotic insect from Johnny's underpants. Her nostrils flare.

'Jesus, Johnny. You stink.'

'Just be gentle with me, Rebecca, go slow, please go slow.'

This is another tremendous moment in time. Johnny stands in the centre of the room, swaying as if under the influence of a mysterious indoor wind. Wearing only his boxer shorts, the ungodly nature of his body is revealed in all its spotted, stooping glory. His endless legs, crooked and splattered in entirely random hedges of horrible black hair. His chest is concaved like a half-dug swimming pool, abandoned due to sudden and shocking bankruptcy. His poor feet. His thin arms. His regrettable face.

Justin appears in the doorway. 'What are you doing, Rebecca?' he asks.

'We're going to make love, you stupid Justin,' says Johnny, bending at the knees and waving a poorly clenched fist at Justin. 'We shall make true love . . . Rebecca and I . . . true love!'

Justin ignores Johnny completely and looks at Rebecca. 'Are you going to shag Johnny, Rebecca?' he asks.

'No, I am not,' shouts Rebecca. 'I'm trying to dry his clothes.'

'Are you sure?'

'Yes,' she says, holding up the wet bundle.

'Then why has he got an erection?'

'He hasn't.'

'He has,' says Justin, pointing at Johnny, 'look!'

Rebecca follows Justin's finger to the jumbled contents of Johnny's underpants which have indeed stiffened. 'Oh, yeh, so he has.'

Tears leak from Johnny's eyes. His entire face is water-logged, fit to burst. His cock tents his kecks, points at thin air. A melancholy erection, dwarfed by the room and the moment. The three people stand in silence as the world composes itself. Time, once again, spares the blushes of humanity by passing. Johnny speaks.

'Who was it that called life life? And couldn't they have called it something else, like shit?'

Rebecca places a hand on Johnny's mossy back. Poor Johnny. She guides him upstairs to bed and tucks him in carefully, brushing the last dried-up molecules of sick from his lips and his cheek. The lids of his eyes droop slowly, like blankets being draped over particularly unsightly corpses. Johnny fumbles a glimpse of Rebecca in her underwear before sleep takes hold irresistibly, like the ending of some world.

Rebecca secretly squirts Johnny's groin and chest with perfume. There is a brief battle between the scent of pissy semen and the scent of roses. The scent of roses wins, assisted by unknown chemical compounds invented to make women smell more like women.

Rebecca lies beside Johnny, wide awake, listening to the noises of Justin downstairs; the dull thumps and the clicks. She remembers the motorway lay-by and how he'd called her beautiful and wonderful. But where do words come from? And how much do people truly care for their meanings? We must take care of the meanings of words, thinks Rebecca, control them if we can. Beautiful and wonderful. Personality. Sexuality. Justin. Perhaps he is honest, his frank ambition to explore the mythology of sex, perhaps this is what honesty looks like. But what of love?

She stares straight up at the ceiling. She imagines the night sky filled entirely with stars, no darkness whatsoever, just millions and millions of distant suns shining next to one another. Would such a situation fill the world with romance? Would we all give in to the apparent beauty of the blinding natural light, and somehow desire to love? No, she concludes with a quick blink of her eyes, we'd probably continue to fight. I think, she thinks, that Justin is beautiful and wonderful.

Time elapses quietly out of respect for those who wish to sleep. It's approaching one o'clock when Justin slinks into the bedroom and begins to remove his clothes. He is close to being a completely silent human. There's just the sound of the mattress groaning as Justin gets into bed beside Johnny. Who gurgles distantly. Then there is the sound of whispering, as hushed electrical currents travel between the boy and the girl.

'Rebecca?' whispers Justin.

'Yeah?' she replies.

'We're sleeping with Johnny tonight, then?'

'So it seems.'

'What's that smell?'

'It's a mixture of perfume, semen, urine, me and you.'

'OK.'

Justin carefully liberates a pillow from under Johnny's head and turns over so his eyes look out at the wall, away from the smells.

'Justin?' whispers Rebecca.

'Yeh?'

'Are you OK?'

'I'm OK. Are you OK?'

'I'm OK.'

In a daring act of nocturnal manipulation, Rebecca climbs over Johnny and nudges him over to the side of the bed she had just occupied. 'Can you hold me tight?' she asks, placing a hand on Justin's stomach. Justin embraces Rebecca. His arms collar her neck. Her face is ground into his chest. His whispering is a soft, warm breeze.

'I checked the website just now,' he says. 'A guy's gone on suggesting a new idea. It might be a pregnancy fetish, I'm not sure. His name's Colin and he's left a number.'

'Will you call?'

'Dunno, maybe. I need to concentrate on the celebrity project, we're halfway there I think. There's a few TV stars going to this premiere next week. I can get us in, but after that I'm not sure. I might need to rent out some of the girls from the Nude Factory.'

'They'd be up for it,' says Rebecca, wishing that each moment of intimacy didn't have to include the discussion of some laborious sexual mission. 'Hold me tight,' she demands, mid-yawn.

Their breathing slows down and Justin's arm begins to go dead. Memories of his old girlfriends can-can through his head. All the girls that he's lain beside. The rituals that are repeated without ever acknowledging the fact that it's been done before, intimately, with someone else, in almost exactly the same ways. Is it a lie or simply what human beings need and do? Is it wrong that we so expertly remember to forget, and allow the ancient to masquerade as the new?

'I don't want a girlfriend,' whispers Justin, his voice note-less, just breath, like the sound of two different airs passing though each other.

'Yes, I know,' says Rebecca, buried to her nose in sleep. Then a silence, a silence which seems to promote the idea of more noise, of more whispering. But there is no more noise, just sleep. Three young people, out like lights. Justin is the last to fall.

22

Figures of Eight

'LET'S WALK,' SAYS Frank, his tanned cheeks lifting into a smile like two large, brown drapes. He's back from Japan and fatter than ever. He is a boat, a schooner. His blazer comprises enormous expanses of grey fabric.

'Doesn't winter happen in Japan, Frank?' enquires Steve, envious of his colleague's tanned skin.

'Oh, yes, my boy, it was freezing. My tan is fake. That whorehouse down in Burnage has just got a sunbed – it's a regular little country club.'

Steve and Frank turn off Whitworth Street and on to Oxford Road. It's been three days since Carly's accident and they're off to the hospital to pay her a visit. Steve sports the most contemporary elements of his wardrobe: a red tweed flat cap, a pair of white moccasins and a fitted denim jacket. There is no chance that his decisions can be reversed; he will not return to his studies, he will not stop lifting weights and the beautiful girl must always be his. So this morning he visited a salon and had his hair coloured and cut into fantastical geometric proportions. After all, the

Sex Machine doesn't have a fashionable haircut. How could it? Nor can it be fashionably attired, because it can't go shopping and the clothes won't fit. Ha, he thinks, as a passing brunette catches his eye. I shall win Carly back. I shall. The machine will lose to me, to man, to fashion.

'So let me get this straight in my head,' begins Frank, stuffing a circular mint into his mouth. 'Carly was using the machine when she fell into the coffee table in some kind of fit of ecstasy, right?'

'So it seems.'

'Brilliant news, Steve, my boy. We're rich. And that table wasn't very tasteful now, was it?'

It's noon and the air tastes like freshly squeezed orange juice. A white light winter day. No wind whatsoever. Frank can't help rubbing his hands together like a cartoon million-aire. His trip to Japan appears to have yielded results.

'Autopen sales are already beginning to level out. The clit thing isn't to everybody's taste, what's it called? The clit fizzer, that's it. Apparently it's a bit feeble, not as good as most vibrators. And the repetitive penetration is just a novelty, certainly not a great source of pleasure. It's purely a replacement for men, and it seems we're hardly worth replacing, haha.'

Steve tuts, his lips vibrate as if he's just jettisoned an invisible jet of saliva on to the pavement in front of him. It's fine for Frank, he's a fat bastard who only screws pros-titutes. Steve likes to think of himself as a sexual athlete of Olympic proportions. That's the main reason he changed his life: for the sex and for the fit-as-fuck girls.

Frank is brimming with delight: 'If Carly's reaction proves to be anything like the norm then I don't see why we can't get to work right away. We can import the things ourselves. Sell to Versus, Shirley Rivers, sell the things ourselves over the Internet. We just need more evidence, and then we shall need a great deal of publicity.'

Steve begins to feel faintly ridiculous. As if the red cap he purchased this morning might already have drifted out of fashion, and been replaced by something newer and entirely different. Are people laughing? thinks Steve. Must I really make the Sex Machine famous? Must I really be its pimp? That machine. That fucker.

As Frank and Steve enter Carly's ward, Frank speeds off ahead in the direction of the poor victim of his incredible machine. The fat bastard can't contain his excitement; his jacket flaps about him as if he might be in danger of flight. He pours himself over Carly. Smiling, pointed, questioning eyes.

'How are you, my sweet, sweet child?' says the terribly fat bastard.

'I'm fine, Frank,' says Carly, the victim of the sex machine's love.

'You're a naughty girl opening Steve's post like that. What were you thinking?'

'I was bored, Frank, you know, I'm always so bored.'

Steve appears at the end of the bed. This isn't the first time he's visited, of course, but they're yet to have a proper conversation. He stares at Carly until her eyes are forced to wander from Frank's face and meet his own yellow gaze.

'Nice hat, Steve,' shrieks Carly, an unfortunate mania affecting her voice.

Steve blinks nervously. He's so anxious about his clothes. They must be in fashion, he reassures himself, I only bought them this morning. He composes a smile, a cool one that alludes to his financial brain and able cock. He takes a deep breath: 'Carly, do you really like my hat?'

But Carly doesn't answer. Her healed and healthy hand leaps from the bed in the direction of Frank's. Frank's hands look like cow's udders. 'Listen to me, Frank,' Carly shrieks again, 'where did you get that machine? It's better than the Relentless Bliss.'

'I hadn't realised you were a connoisseur.' Frank smiles, the sort of smile that businessmen perform when a punter has fallen for their product. 'Let me guess, you didn't like the clit fizzer?'

'Well, I liked it, of course, but it was nothing compared to your machine!'

At the end of the bed, Steve's heart leaks down into his stomach then onwards into his bowels. It continues though his intestine, then drips down the bones and ligaments of his right leg and into his feet, and then to his shoes. It seeps though the rubber soles of his moccasins, and finally comes to rest, bloody and beating on the hospital floor. Someone ought to call a doctor.

'Well, you'll be pleased to know, my dear, that your boyfriend and I stand to make a great deal of money from that machine. Do you suppose all girls will like it as much as you?'

'I love it. It will be loved.' Carly pauses and looks down at her body, still wrapped in bandages, but mending, healing calmly, returning to perfection. She turns to Steve, who's staring at the floor, to where his broken heart still beats. 'Steve,' asks Carly, 'have you cleaned the machine yet? Like I asked.'

'No,' says Steve, nudging his heart self-consciously with his shoe. 'No, it's still covered in your blood.'

Steve removes his cap and prods his hair into a heart-stoppingly fashionable shape. But something is dying. A way of life is being stretched and tortured. He holds his cap as if in mourning. His hair and his distressed jeans are suddenly a source of shame, his status is being flushed down the toilet, is circling round and round in dirty water, preparing itself for the sewers.

'He's so precious, is he not, Carly?' Frank interjects. 'He can't bear the idea of a machine doing a better job than he himself.'

'I used to think I could change the world,' says Steve, for the second time this week. Frank looks at Steve with sympathy, sensing that society may well be changing and that Steve may well be a casualty of this change. He attempts but fails to change the subject.

'What do you know of this website, newsex.biz? Some guy and his girlfriend are documenting their efforts to partake in every single kind of sex. It's the talk of every brothel in the city. I thought the girl could be a useful guinea pig, what with her refined tastes.'

Carly's and Steve's faces are blank. Almost featureless.

'I mean I could offer the machine to my whore friends,' continues Frank, 'but they're all so numb to new experience and sceptical of orgasm. Unless it's with their dreadful boyfriends . . . "Sorry, Frank," they say to me, "I save my arse for my boyfriend." My God, the times I've heard that sentence. Will they never relinquish their cherubic arsehole, uncork it like a fine wine . . . ?'

Frank trails off, distracted by some invisible object that seems to be hovering inches from his fat nose; an invisible arse, perhaps. Steve takes this opportunity to walk round the bed and kneel at Carly's side.

'Will you be coming back to the flat, Carly?'

Carly shuffles awkwardly, turning to meet the gaze of her fashionable boyfriend. 'They let me out tomorrow. I guess I'll come back, I'll need to see the machine for one.' As she says this, the colour of Steve's skin seems to fade, as if he's shedding the top layers of his bogus tan.

'And me for two, right?' he says.

'Yeah, yeah.'

Would anyone care, wonders Steve, if I was to pinch a scalpel and slice Carly's face off with it? Would anyone really care, if I was exceptionally quick? Then I could stab her a thousand times in the heart, the thousandth lunge as committed and lethal as the first. I want to spill my beautiful lover's guts, pound her until she's a revolting stain.

The invisible arse in front of Frank's nose disappears and he comes to his senses like a flock of seagulls flapping into flight.

'Come, come, my sweets, don't argue. Steve, I do need you to clean the machine. No girl will try it if it's covered in Carly's blood. I need to get it to this girl at newsex.biz. She's local, it won't be difficult.'

'Would you just shut the fuck up, Frank?' asks Steve, back at the end of the bed, stuffing his heart back into place.

'Oh, Steve. How unkind. You look unwell, rather grey. Let's leave. Carly, I wish you a speedy recovery, I will send your regards to the machine.'

'Make sure you do, Frank . . . and Frank – thank you.'

Steve is a house built too close to the sea. Year after year, the waves work away at the cliff beneath him, burrowing into the rock. It takes time, but eventually the house falls; the ground gives way and the house slumps downwards, bricks and masonry falling into the sea. No one dies. The inhabitants are warned and leave in good time. Steve is doomed, vacated, preparing to drop.

Along the corridor from Carly's ward a mop moves about the beige floor in slow figures of eight, steered by Colin. He looks up from his work and notices a fat man and a tall, attractive guy making for the lift. Colin must try to take care of his rage.

News travels fast among the emergency services and quickly works its way down to the hospital cleaners. Carly, the girl who almost died from mechanical sex, has become quite a celebrity among the doctors, nurses and the lesser staff of the hospital. Colin mops his way carefully along the corridor to view the beast.

Colin hasn't seen Boy 1 or Boy 2 in a while. Last he heard of Boy 1 was that he'd split his foreskin shagging his sofa, but that remains unconfirmed. Colin has been in his room, liaising with the rat and perfecting his sexual needs. He thinks often of what Deaks said to him that night in the Wishing Well, about the feeling of fucking the already fucked. He hadn't spoken to him since. He'd seen him around the Antenatal Ward and noticed the knowing glances he exchanged with the women, but that was it. Melissa gave birth a week or so ago. Colin spoke to one of the doctors about her, enquired about her health. She was fine and so was her kid.

After that night with Melissa, everything changed. Colin has discovered new and minimal ways of surviving on his part-time wage from the hospital. He has given up drinking, no longer goes out. He buys what clothes he still needs from charity shops. His time is spent in his room, which continues to rot. The rodents have multiplied. They have heard of his hospitality, scurried in for the winter and taken up residence amid the decay. Colin lives entirely on rice and peas. He never smokes, never masturbates. There is a calm about him. There is an unnerved subsistence, and a sense that he is preparing for chaos.

The volume has finally been turned down. The motion slowed. The women of winter are of little distraction, wrapped as they are in thick coats, fake furs and wool. But no, in truth, women don't concern Colin at all, because they are already lost. Men, too. Lost at birth.

Colin refuses to iron his clothes because smooth clothes are not necessary. He refuses to kick balls or throw stones and he refuses to run. Colin refuses to smile, refuses to cry or be angry, refuses to wank his cock, to say hello. He refuses the media, refuses to crane his neck, refuses women and men, refuses to thank the helpful or punish the rude. He refuses to be questioned or answer, to consume, refuses his phone and his mail, refuses his friends, his past, refuses to hear the drunken singing in the night, the gossip in the streets, the sirens and the laughs. Colin categorically refuses to die.

Colin has only one ambition: he wishes to make secret, unseen lives. He wants to make minuscule hearts beat unheard in vacuumed spaces. He wants to create uninter-rupted biological constructions; secret configurations of nature that operate unbeknownst to people and their dismal working-out of things. Put simply, he wants to impregnate women and abort the child.

He mops to the doorway of Carly's ward and peers cautiously through the open door. The room is too white, like an unused plate. Carly lies spotlit flicking through a magazine, nails painted nosebleed red.

Colin can just make out the colour of skin on the front cover of Carly's magazine, airbrushed and eggshell-like. Belonging to some famous person, a life turned professional. It's not a photograph of a person, it can't be. It is a photograph of a photograph of a photograph of a photograph of a photograph; an endless regression of captured images that continues infinitely, until the subject of the first photo is no longer understood, and seems devoid of humanity and sense. Something arbitrary, something forgotten.

Colin stares at Carly, watching the slight changes of direction in her eyes as she scans the different pages. She spends only moments on each page, like she's blessed with superhuman reading skills and is hurrying through some great work, just so she can say she's read it. The girl with painted nails who was ripped to shreds by a sex machine. The girl who tied her hair into a ponytail before she spoke to her visitors. Breaking a personal silence of what must be days, Colin steps into the doorway and speaks in a thick Mancunian accent.

'What do you remember, girl?' he says, his eyes like marbles containing small strips of white ribbon.

'What?' says Carly, bending the pages of her magazine to one side.

'What kinds of things do you remember?'

'Get lost,' blares Carly, her mouth a drunken circle of soft, purple lip. By the door, Colin winces and places a hand into his brown, overgrown hair.

'I remember nothing,' he says. 'I've just mopped a floor, I must have – why else would I be holding a mop?'

'Can you fucking believe this?' Carly appeals to an elderly lady in an adjacent bed. As she does so, Colin disappears, begins mopping the remainder of the corridor in slow figures of eight.

It's late by the time Colin returns home to the rats and the room of dark dirt. But what of time? He heats some rice and peas in a pan and takes it to the bedroom, greeted by the familiar sound of small claws scratching at wood. This is a situation, no question it is. A room infested with rodents and debris, lit by a solitary bulb which hangs from the ceiling like a noose. And Colin is in transit, as humans are. He inhabits a succession of moments that alter him and help him to understand the precise nature of his regrets. He lifts a forkful of rice to his mouth, and bites.

The night with Melissa helped to reveal the more precise characteristics of his sexual desires. It wasn't the form of the pregnant women that was so captivating, he realised in retrospect. The large bellies and the manner in which they are carried is all incidental, all part of a far greater beauty which he has been unable to forget: the beauty of a life that has barely been interfered with at all. A life that never sees the light of day. Foetuses do not paint their nails. They do not speak shit or think shit. They don't go to bars and fight and drink too much. They float, alone. A foetus has never been spotted propping up a bar, reading a magazine, sipping Bacardi and Coke through a straw.

So what if human life never saw the light of day? thinks Colin. It would be perfect. It would be brief, of course, a matter of weeks or months, but at least it would be untouched by the withering boredoms and the dull dangers of society. This idea has draped itself over Colin's brain like a hot towel. Finally, a meaning to sex, a meaning at last. The creation of short, perfect life.

It's been four days since he posted the message on Justin's site – newsex.biz. He's yet to hear any reply. But he needs help, needs conspirators, fellow believers. Women who will agree.

A rat is lured out from underneath the wardrobe by the smell of steamed rice and peas. It noses the corner of a pizza box for a moment before staring up at Colin through the blue light. Colin stares into the rat's small black face. Vermin, he thinks, I'll be happy at last.

23

Invisible American Footballs

MEMORY LOSS IS a terrible thing. Particularly if it coincides with waking up in an unknown environment and being told extremely large lies. As Johnny's eyes open there is a brief moment of calm and something vaguely akin to happiness. Memory loss does this to you. Your lack of any concrete idea of what happened the previous night somehow gives you the impression that you were happy and did something worthwhile. But this feeling quickly fades. It fades as Johnny tries to work out why there is a copy of *Crime and Punishment* on his bedside table, then a little more when he realises that neither it, the bed nor the table beside it actually belong to him.

That's when your brain notices what a state it's in. It notices the shattered glass, the strange stains and the empty bottles that are littered all about your skull. That's when the guilt strikes, the massive fear. What the fuck happened? Johnny rolls over and sees Justin and Rebecca sleeping in each other's arms beside him. Oh, what? What the fuck happened?

At this stage the memoryless brain begins to behave like a teenager who's hosted a house party in their parents' absence. Frantically, and still rather drunkenly, it runs about tidying and searching for clues. There must be something here that can tell me what happened. After a few minutes of careful thought, Johnny happens upon the broken vase of his memory and kneels down to pick up the pieces. The guilt, shit, the guilt. He remembers clearly buying lager and pornography from the corner shop. He remembers the phone sex and then he remembers going out to the pub and ordering vodka at the bar. But then the production values on his memory deteriorate rapidly, like a secret celebrity sex video; grainy and inconclusive. He'd gone to a few bars and then . . . his brain pulsates and he begins panting for air.

'Good morning, Johnny lad,' says Justin in a friendly voice laced with the unmistakable and sonorous sound of mocking. It was Justin's idea to convince Johnny he'd shagged Rebecca. They had awoken in the night and he'd suggested that it might be fun. It might. Rebecca had agreed, not anticipating how convincing the two of them would be.

'Morning, Johnny,' purrs Rebecca, stirring from feigned sleep and flashing a glazed and sultry gaze at Johnny's jumbled features. At this stage, Johnny locates a couple more shards of memory. He picks them up. He remembers the doorstep, the living room. Had he been sick? The memories cut his fingers. He sucks at the blood and succumbs to the fact that certain events from the previous night will be lost to him for ever.

'Well, how do you feel? Any different? It was quite a night,' Justin continues, looking intently at Johnny.

'But who are you?' Johnny mutters, the desire to vomit running up and down his neck pipes like a bastard. 'What are you talking about?'

'I'm Justin, Johnny, you must remember. I'm talking about your virginity, and, more precisely, about your losing it in the early hours of this morning to fair, fair Rebecca.'

The look on Johnny's face suggests that a mysterious fourth party has just placed a knife into his back. His eyes seem to anticipate imminent death. His mouth looks as though it should dribble blood at any moment. Surely, he reasons, I couldn't possibly have shagged Rebecca. My virginity, it can't possibly be lost.

'Surely I didn't,' says Johnny. 'I can't remember a thing.'

'Well, you most certainly did,' says Justin. 'I viewed the proceedings from that wicker chair in the corner. It was quite a spectacle.'

Guilt takes hold of Justin at this stage, like his throat is suddenly zipped up. But you can never back down, not when someone is being so comprehensively fooled. Rebecca, too, is suddenly slapped about the cheeks by shame and regret. Poor Johnny, she thinks, and how wonderfully convincing Justin is. Johnny waits patiently for the effects of the knife in the back to kill him. Where's the blood? Where are the white lights? Heaven's gates? He sits up in bed and begins fidgeting about, trying to slow the tides of vomit rising from his gut.

'Rebecca . . . I'm so sorry . . . I can't remember a thing. I rarely drink at all and, I suppose . . . shit, forgive me.'

'Don't worry about it, Johnny. I enjoyed it.'

Rebecca gets out of bed and goes for a shower, a laughter bomb preparing to explode in her mouth. By the time she returns Johnny has left. She enters the bedroom with a towel around her waist. Justin lies on the bed, his lips arranged in a ludicrous smile. She goes to him.

But, Jesus, it gets worse for Johnny. He leaves Rebecca's house and walks back to Fallowfield through Hulme and Moss Side. It takes an hour and a half. He is thinking desperately. But you can only rack a brain so much. In the end it begins to resent being overworked and refuses to give out any information at all. By the time he arrives home he can barely remember his name. He throws up then watches TV.

By mid-afternoon and still having no better purchase on the events of the previous night, he just resigns himself to it. I fucked her, he concludes, as the children's programmes begin. He vaguely remembers a girl pulling off his trousers, Rebecca, he supposes, it must be true. Virginity; another loss.

Not surprisingly, several hours later Johnny finds himself sitting alone on a scarlet sofa in Fallowfield's leading massage parlour. Waiting for sex. His virginity having been lost, Johnny finds what all boys find at some stage; an insatiable appetite for more. It doesn't matter that he has no recollection of the sex itself. The gate has been opened, never mind that he was guarding it drunk. He gets a sense of power, progress and victory. Like a nineteenth-century imperialist preparing to scramble for Africa. More countries, more pillage, more sex.

So at around half past twelve that night he goes along to the brothel. It's only a short walk. He pays the cash and is watching football highlights on a small television when the parlour door opens and a familiar-sounding voice begins negotiating sex.

'Yeah, I just want it straight, no messin', a quick fugg, that's all.'

At this precise moment, Johnny remembers how much he likes life deep down, and why. Because life is perfectly hilarious. Zakir ghosts into the waiting room, pausing by the doorway when he clocks Johnny on the sofa. He doesn't seem to recognise him at first. It's as if he's trying to identify him from thousands of metres away, through squinted eyes. Finally, the penny drops. Zakir remembers.

'Fuggin hell . . . Johnny.'

'Zakir. How are you?'

'Oh, fugg.'

'It's OK, mate. Look, there's football on TV!'

Oh, thank every single god ever, thinks Johnny, as coincidence erupts in his favour. He imagines earth from space, all the countries moving about and forming an enormous grinning face. Thank God for global failure, for the irresistible attacks of Western sex. Civilisation shivers, as if cold. Then a noise: a death rattle.

Zakir takes a seat next to Johnny on the sofa, the smell of whisky smoking from his lips. What had happened? Maybe the brief glimpse at the porno under the pillow had been enough: the gates of shit burst open and his brain got swamped. Or maybe this is how Zakir has always coped. Maybe there were no conferences on British democracy and all along he'd been emptying his ballsacks into Mancunian prostitutes. No, thinks Johnny, looking at Zakir's wasted face, this is a fall, this is classic human collapse. Eventually Johnny speaks.

'Is this my fault, Zakir? It's just that you never seemed like the sort.'

Zakir turns to Johnny, his features spoiled, muddled by the booze.

'Ha . . . whose fuggin' fault? No, not yours, not yours,

but the girls at the university . . . yes, Miss fuggin' India . . . Whose fuggin fault? Oh mine . . . mine.'

Just as Johnny realises quite how hammered Zakir is, a young brunette dressed in red underwear appears above them and speaks Johnny's name.

'Johnny? Oh hello, Zakir, you back again? We must be doing something right. I'll be with you in a minute.'

And she is, in a sense. Johnny doesn't take long to process. He enters a dark red room where the air is talcum powder and the walls warp inwards towards a low ceiling. It is nothing. He reaches for a small breast. He marvels at the economy of the girl's actions: not a muscle or a movement wasted. She rocks on top of him for around forty-five seconds, working her hips vigorously when she detects the puny pulsations in Johnny's cock. The sex reminds Johnny of one of those primary school rhythm orchestras. It reminds him of figuring out the use of some strange percussive instrument, then failing to play in time.

He passes Zakir on the way out and nods farewell. They will never meet again, but at least they have shared something. End of story.

Yes, I digress. All this happened days ago, last week perhaps. It was just too good not to share. At present we're with Justin. He's standing in Exchange Square staring at his mobile phone, waiting for it to ring. It's approaching nine o'clock. A large television screen relays footage of a natural disaster to a few uninterested passers-by. Justin stares at his phone. It's high time he seduced a celebrity.

He spent this morning and much of this afternoon shopping for dresses with Rebecca. They bought six at considerable expense, one for each of the strippers he's rented for the night. In order to seduce a celebrity, one needs to be in possession of certain capital, ways of rewarding the celebrity for its love. Fame, of course, is the most obvious and the most lucrative; a celebrity likes nothing better than loving one of their own, combining their values and holding hands as they are captured by the cameras. But money is a close second: in the eyes of the wealthy, a celebrity recognises a mutual concern, a shared love, the confident glint of cash. Appearing to be rich is Justin's only hope. If the celebrity is to be lured, then the promise of cash must appear entirely genuine. The celebrity could bolt at the slightest sniff of reality. They mustn't suspect a thing.

A neat side parting has been combed into Justin's hair by Rebecca. There is a nuance of the 1930s gentleman about him, the playboy, the cad. His suit is purest white and instead of a shirt he wears a black vest that lightly traces the contours of his toned chest. He is modern yet traditional, old money combined with contemporary style, he is perfect. Stains are his only concern: if a drink gets spilled on the suit, then he might be screwed. Celebrities shy away from mistake and mild humiliation. They don't like it. But there are always risks, particularly when hunting a celebrity; there is always peril and the possibility of failure.

Finally his phone rings. It does so twice, then stops. This is code. It means that Rebecca and the other girls are in position, they're at the party and are awaiting his arrival. Justin places his phone in his inside pocket and breathes deeply.

As he leaves Exchange Square and heads towards Papparazzi, the night club where the party is being thrown, Justin identifies the first possible flaw in his plan. He has no idea what the film is about. All the celebrities will have just attended its premiere and Justin has no clue what the themes and plot of the thing are. As he reaches Papparazzi, however, his fears melt away. Above the entrance on a large canvas awning the film is being advertised. He pauses to figure it out.

The film is called *The Blood of the Flag*. Justin sighs with relief as he realises the film is total shit. A young man stares out across the poster with stern, longing eyes. He's dressed in the green felt uniform of a Second World War Allied soldier. The soldier's gaze is met on the other side of the poster by a woman with sky-blue eyes and blond ringlets of hair dangling like springs from her scalp. She is beautiful, dressed in a long silk summer dress decorated with roses of yellow, pink and red. Justin clasps his neck with his hand, his eyes squint. The question is simple: does the young man get gunned down or does the couple's love survive the experience of war? Justin pulls out a cigarette from his top pocket and lights it with a gold Zippo. He smokes and watches the poster, examining the gazes of the two young leads. Only popped corn is missing from this cinematic experience.

After a few seconds it all becomes clear. The young boy meets the young girl in about 1941. The war is in full swing, but they're Texans and feel kind of out of it and invincible. They're worried, of course, but not enough to resist embarking on a combative love affair of overblown romance, tactile teasing and finally explosive, meaningful sex. They get married and you suspect she might be pregnant. Then one day they're smooching in a barn when the radio relays the Japanese attack on Pearl Harbor. Shit, says the young man, I've got to go to war. Don't, says the young girl, I don't want you getting hurt. Don't worry, says the young man, I'm an integral part of this film, it's unlikely I'll die. So he looks smart in his uniform and kisses her goodbye. As he leaves, she drops the bombshell that she's pregnant. Fuck, he's overjoyed, but goes to war all the same. While fighting in Iwo Jima he sees a few things that fuck him over and a really good mate dies in his arms. Meanwhile, she's at home making bullets and discovering her independence, telling her son how great his dad is. Finally, just when she's assumed he's been killed in some much publicised and futile offensive, he walks into a room and catches her doing something mega wholesome like mending the kid's pullover. They're reunited, thank God, and fuck. For a while, though, it's not great; they struggle to communicate, he's troubled, she's grown up and whatever. Their son wonders why his dad is so sad and nothing like the stories. But, in the end, the young woman goes downstairs one night to find the soldier sitting at the kitchen table with a gun and she's like, what's up? and for a moment the young soldier says nothing, then he just cries and cries and cries. They embrace frantically. Then everything is OK and there's a lovely musical score to their lives. The two young people truly enjoy the 1950s together, he goes into plastics and they have a second child, a girl.

Shit film, thinks Justin, as he drops his cigarette and walks towards the entrance of Papparazzi.

Justin meets Rebecca at the main bar, a short distance from the VIP area where the party's taking place. She looks incredible, high-heeled and heavenly. Elongated by expert tailoring, a green silk dress giving the impression of an entirely new body. She smiles and Justin stares at her subtle bust.

'Well, the good news is the celebs have arrived and the girls are already mingling. They're saying you invested in the film, in *The Blood of the Flag,* that's what you do, you invest in the arts, right?'

'Right.'

'Have you got the coke?'

'Yes, just now.'

'Good, they'll expect it if you get back to the hotel.'

The club is electrified by the rumour that fame is present. Girls and boys hover by the VIP area, flashing pushed tits and painted eyes at the bouncer, believing, perhaps, that if they stare hard enough the thick red curtain will become transparent and they'll see celebrity with their own actual eyes. Justin orders two White Russians for Rebecca and himself. It's red velvet, you fools. It will never be transparent. Only reminiscent of bloody murder.

'You don't have a chance with the cast,' says Rebecca. 'They've got lines of people waiting to talk to them, even the minor characters.'

'OK.'

'But there are still loads to choose from, TV stars mostly. I think some have done film but I couldn't tell you which. I guess it'll only work if you see one you like. Just don't waste time with the cast, we're not going to blow this chance, right? All right, Justin?'

Rebecca is demonstrating that manic and babbling bogus enthusiasm for which women are famous. She refuses to catch Justin's eye, just stares at the neckline of his vest and occasionally at his shoulder or his hair. Justin can only make out the meaning of Rebecca's eyes if he really tries. She loves him. In an adjacent world, he loves her. Yes. On the other side of life, these two are lovers. They are choosing ingredients in a bright supermarket. They are meeting each other's parents and sharing a bank account. But not on this side. On this side they are personalities in the dark. Blinkered experimenters. Justin looks at Rebecca as he might a fading photograph.

'Are you OK, Rebecca?'

'Are you sure you want to do this?'

Justin pauses, sucks liquid through a straw. You can only love once or twice, he maintains. In any case, love is the great Western lie, a white one perhaps, but a lie all the same. He glares. Love is banal, safe. Please let it be so.

'I hate society, you know? I hate almost everything about it,' he says.

'I don't want a boyfriend. Haha.'

'No, listen to me. I hate society.' Justin throws a fag into his mouth and watches impatiently as Rebecca's eyes begin to plead.

'Please don't do this, Justin. Please,' she says. 'Let's go home. Don't do it.'

1, 2, 3, 4.

'I have to.'

He walks forward past her exposed shoulder, which seems dissected by the thin green strap of her dress. As he passes by, he notices, out of the corner of his eye, Rebecca's head, bowing slowly towards the ground. Too much cinema, he thinks, way too much cinema in the world. Love is the white lie of the West, he chants, love is the white lie of the West. He places a hand on the shoulder of the bouncer and assembles a devastating smile. He produces his ticket and is shepherded into the VIP area, to the astonishment of the herd.

As he enters, the six strippers prick their ears, their eyes suck like syringes. Justin pauses and smiles. He arches his neck slightly, then sips at his drink. That was a good sip, elegant and controlled. Great sip, great start. As planned, Sidney is the first girl to approach. He watches as she carefully avoids the gropes of a group of middle-aged men and makes her way over to him.

'Oh my God, Rudolf de la Hooting, it's an honour to meet you. I loved the film.'

She leans in and kisses the air either side of his face. The name is a bad one. Justin realised this as soon as Sidney said it. Nobody is called de la Hooting. But what do celebrities know? The two of them move to the bar, where Justin pays four hundred pounds for a bottle of 1986 Margaux. There is a commotion as the wine is sought. A cellar door slams. One by one, the incognito strippers congregate around Justin. The minor celebrities begin to stare.

The celebrity is, in essence, a gentle species. Doomed to teeter on the perimeters of reality, about which little is known for sure. The celebrity walks a tightrope. On one side lies the valley of mortality, where the living dwell. On the other lies a steep ravine, immortality, where the dead scramble at the rocky slopes and are eternally known.

Justin pays attention to each of the strippers, nodding and smiling calm asymmetrical smiles. In this comparatively overdressed state, the girls are a delight, convincing beauties. At least two, Sidney included, are so fit that they actually deserve to be real celebrities, seriously, they do.

'So what do you reckon, de la Hooting? Seen a celeb you like the look of?' Sidney whispers into Justin's ear, the blubbered curves of her fake tits sighing into her dress.

'I don't know. Did Rebecca come in?'

'She's angry with you.'

'Why? Because I'm going to shag someone famous?'

Towards the back of the room there is a round of crap laughter, like children imitating Gatling gunfire. Justin's eyes scan the room, searching for a face he recognises, a face that has sneaked into his mind and pissed on the carpet. Eventually he spots the victim, located just across the room, no more than ten feet away. She's standing at a slight angle, looking up at a black man in sunglasses. That's her, he thinks, she's fit and I know her face.

'Got one,' he says, moving Sidney to one side in order to get a better look at his prey. Sidney's been talking, whispering into Justin's ear about Rebecca, how she's not sure about the experiment any more and feels she might be falling in love with Justin. But what of such nonsense? Love is the white lie of the West. Justin scrawls the words on the inside of his eyelids in lines of light. He blinks, then stares at the celebrity. Are her tits real?

If the company of the famous is to be kept, then new senses are required. It's an entirely novel mode of being alive. There is no use in smelling and hearing; seeing is secondary. Never make the mistake of trusting your senses in the presence of the known. It is a culture of awareness and appreciation. Everybody can be seen, not everybody can be famous. The air is battery acid, energetic but reliant on successful currents, introductions, charmed hellos, chains and buzzing circuits of power. These people don't pay, don't listen or give a shit. They tell stories, they brag, laud, frightfully anticipate the next new thing.

'Shriek, girls, everybody shriek with laughter, like I'm funny.'

Justin whispers the order to his congregation. The strippers shriek as if Justin has told the greatest joke ever told.

Sidney bends double as if she might be sick into her wine. Jesus, that was funny. Men look over at the hysterical beauties, wishing they could tell jokes of that calibre. That must have been a great joke, they think, wishing to be exactly like Justin.

It works. Her eye is caught. Justin holds tight to it. He's gliding through the crowd of laughing strippers and striding purposefully towards the celebrity. There's nothing like laughter for drawing attention to yourself; it's an advert for happiness. The celebrity glances briefly towards Justin and his entourage, away from the black guy in sunglasses. That's all it takes, one look, eye contact, hope, the nature of the beast.

Justin's walking across the room. The celebrity knows he's coming already. She's composing herself and talking to the black guy with a renewed and exaggerated vigour. The question is, who the fuck is she? Certainly Justin has no idea of the celebrity's name; he doesn't even know her character's name. He suspects she acts in a soap opera, a Merseyside soap opera; that would make sense.

Her hair is brown and shoulder length, touched by faint strips of yellow dye. Her figure is full, breasts peeping out of her maroon dress like targets at a firing range. The celebrity has a delightful face, round eyes, soft nose, comfy pink lips. As Justin smiles at her, he recalls more precisely the nature of her fame. She appears on an early evening soap opera. Her character is sexually manipulative, but capable of love. She supplements her income with modelling, underwear shoots for lad's magazines. She may have even made the front cover. Ha, the bitch, the famous bitch.

'Hello there, and who might you be?' says Justin, his washed face beaming.

'I could ask you the same question,' replies the celebrity, its black heart beating.

'Oh, I'm nobody.'

'I find that hard to believe.'

'Perhaps. May I buy you a drink?'

Justin is concise and charming, the glass of wine hangs loose in his finger and his voice swims breast stroke through the air. God. The celebrity spoke. Who would believe it?

As Justin begins his manoeuvres, the black man removes his sunglasses. His eyes are dark brown with a thread of bright white woven around his pupils. He clearly has his own designs on the celebrity. He eyes Justin with irritation. But she is for Justin, that's the way it must be. Justin is suave and detailed, devastating and brave, the experimenter, the winner.

'My name is Davine, and this is Claude.'

Justin turns to the black guy, Claude, they shake hands and Justin stabs his large head with a shining, sharp, go-fuck-yourself smile.

'Rudolf. My name is Rudolf. Come and join me at the bar.'

You're beaten, you great big bastard, thinks Justin. Put your sunglasses on and fuck off. Justin places a hand around the celebrity. She draws breath and her chest expands, imprisoning air in her ribcage. Another smile from Justin and Claude is defeated. He retreats, the glass of champagne threatening to shatter between his sausage-meat fingers.

'Claude choreographed a lot of the battle scenes, you know?'

The celebrity pirouettes, causing Justin's hand to slide around her body, skin speeding over maroon silk, to the top of her arse.

'No, I didn't know that,' says Justin. 'To tell you the truth, I haven't seen the film yet.'

'Oh, so you weren't involved?'

'Well, not directly, although I paid for most of it.'

Back at the bar, the strippers continue to vie for Justin's attention. At one point, Sidney seems to almost square up to the celebrity. The effect is charming, the celebrity is won. The bottle of wine is finished, another is ordered. The celebrity watches the fifty-pound notes pass over the bar. The celebrity is distracted and vulnerable.

'Fine wine, my only joy,' jokes Justin as he nimbly avoids the gaping grins of the strippers. They're drunk now and their behaviour is becoming over the top. Justin moves the celebrity to a table, refills its glass and sits down opposite. He offers it a fag, which is accepted. They both smoke. All around the room, biologies begin to give in to the complimentary champagne; the embarrassment of tomorrow is foreshadowed. A woman at the bar impersonates a dog. She barks and bends over, woof, woof. A drink is spilled and an idiot mouths along to the music.

It's not long before Justin is able to negotiate a fairly swift departure. The major celebrities have already left in search of a secret and more elite occasion. The crowd is thinning and the glamour of the event is virtually extinct. But Justin's celebrity still seems interested. It's talking. In fact, it won't be quiet. This is certainly a good sign. Her eyes are animated, probing Justin's face in that way that people do, to demonstrate their interest. Approximately every five minutes she puts both her hands into her hair as if she might be about to peel off her face. This manoeuvre affords Justin about two seconds to spend working out the finer points of her breasts. They are everything you would expect from famous tits. Hairless and highly marketable, they seem almost laminated for the purpose of masturbation. They glow – a real feature. Maybe, wonders Justin, evolution will work in the same way. Maybe the great tits of the future will develop a kind of laminate, wipe clean finish on them, like skin but even smoother, more like plastic. Bums, too, perhaps. Indeed. People ejaculate on bums all the time. Men. Perspex skin. Finally—

'Rudolf?'

'What?'

'Are you OK?'

The celebrity hasn't shut up in half an hour. The expensive wine is in her blood and making her talk and talk and talk. The alcohol simplifies her, breaks her up into her component parts, pixelates her. Justin imagines her as a viscous puddle on the chair, a gloopy collection of beautiful eyes, lips, tits and rear. If he doesn't do something soon, she will surely talk herself into some kind of mood. Women can do this if allowed to speak for too long while drunk. She'll talk some problem into her head, some melancholy. She must be stopped.

'Would you be prepared to leave? I find these parties rather dull, don't you?'

She says yes, ha, I promise she does. Yes, says the celebrity, finishing her drink and looking in the direction of the cloakroom. Of course, she says yes. I promise.

Then comes the silence.

Justin and the celebrity sit in the taxi. It is completely silent, although for some reason the celebrity's mouth is moving. In fact, the celebrity is talking. And yet there is only silence. There is no sound in the car, neither the sound of a celebrity's voice, nor the sound of Justin shifting in his leather seat. Justin burps. Silent. A whiff of wine, but nothing else. The car makes no sound, nor does its driver. Nothing in the street is making any noise either. People shout, but it's as if they're just swallowing large objects, invisible American footballs. The wind is inaudible, the rain too. Absolutely everything makes no sound.

Whatever the celebrity is trying to say, it seems rather dull – no, wait, not dull, erotic perhaps, sultry. Her lips nibble at the air. Perhaps she's talking about sex, or maybe about the misery of her former lovers. An arm drops between her legs, causing her dress to ride up her thighs. She's leaning in towards Justin's face, still mumbling something, mouthing the end of some sentence, trailing off midway perhaps, like lovers sometimes do.

The kiss, too, is silent. Justin waits for that sticky sound as their lips separate, like air being released from sealed Tupperware. But it doesn't come, there is no noise, just the sight of the celebrity adjusting her posture and half-heartedly attempting to straddle him. Justin runs both his hands up her stomach and cups her breasts from below. There is that magical moment as she permits him: yes, it is allowed, my breasts can be yours. And Justin's hands, oh the hands of men, childish and meek, as if all they ever wanted to be was a bra and all the punches and the strangulations were all tragically incidental.

Where is the tapping? This is serious: where is the sound of tapping? In the bridal suite of the hotel the sound of tapping cannot be heard, and it ought to be. Justin is cutting up lines of cocaine on the coffee table. Tapping at the larger blocks with his credit card until they break up, sweeping the powder into neat lines. The celebrity is reclined on the bed. Still talking, Justin imagines. Although, to be sure, he'd have to turn round and check, to see if her lips are moving.

And of course the healthy snorting sound that should accompany the taking of cocaine fails to materialise. Justin and his celebrity crouch over the powder and draw it up their nostrils. There is a silent gasp, like watching wind. The celebrity rocks back to lean on the bed, her lips flicker, silent words. You moved your lips without saying that, thinks Justin, as he crawls towards her fame and kisses at her numb gums.

Shit, the dreadful routine of life, thinks Justin, as he performs all his tired moves on the celebrity; a kiss to the neck, a finger gently circling the haunted regions of her inner thigh, the curdled flesh of her loins. This is celebrity in my hands, this is famous skin, this is fantasy and my world-weary foreplay has no place here. Justin wrings out his brain, desperate for a drop of inspiration. The drug begins to take hold.

The time is probably something odd like 1:27 a.m. when Justin stands the celebrity up in the middle of the room and begins to circle her slowly. The silence remains intact.

He kneels down at her feet and removes her black high-heeled shoes. He reaches up into her dress and pulls down her tights. He places the sagged fabric to one side. Her legs and her feet are naked, her face is candle wax, features pressed by thumbs into the warm substance. Justin dims the light slightly.

He goes round the back of the celebrity and takes down the zip of her dress. He frees her shoulders and the dress drops to the ground, maroon silk at her feet. Still standing behind her, he unfixes her bra and casts it forward, sensing the relieved lurch of her tits as they're freed. On his knees again he pulls down her knickers of black cotton. They feel like a spider's web. She's completely naked now, silent, standing still. Justin fights the urge to run his tongue over the celebrity's anus.

He stands, facing her. Periodically her lips move but there is no sound; it's all swallowed by the silence. His eyes watch every section of her body. Her large feet, muscled thighs, her patchy sprouting pubes, the dip of her hips, her praying tits, collarbone, neck, whatever else. Slowly, and with complete self-assurance, he approaches the celebrity and carefully removes her left arm. There is no blood and, of course, there is no noise.

Having arranged the arm neatly on the hotel bed, he returns for the other. It detaches as easily as the first; the celebrity is entirely bloodless. Next go the nipples, then the breasts themselves, eased off her chest and placed on to the bed beside the two arms. The features of her face provide the biggest challenge. It's with a steady hand that Justin peels off the eyes, nose and mouth of the celebrity and places them in an unused ashtray next to the bed.

Now he's able to really get to work on her body. The legs are easy, a modest yank and they drop off. But they're heavy, because of the fat in the thighs. Justin lugs them over to the bed, then pauses, breathless, running fingers over her severed calves. Next is the arse, which he dismantles buttock by buttock. Then the midriff, which drifts away from her back when pulled. Finally he's just left with the little fiddly bits: feet, vagina, ears, hair. It takes about fifteen minutes, but it's certainly worth it. As he pours himself a whisky and Coke, Justin can't remember the last time he saw a celebrity so expertly taken to bits. He wishes Rebecca could see what he's done. She'd be proud of him.

They could have played games with the different parts of the celebrity, fucked amongst them.

How big is this silence anyway? wonders Justin as he slaps one of the separated buttocks to no audible effect. Is it all over Manchester? If Rebecca is caught up in it, she will certainly be frustrated. She'll be dying to say something about free trade, how it's got nothing to do with freedom, how the silence is the silence of protest and dissent, how we've been dumbed, senses dulled by senseless lives. But, of course, if the silence has got her, then she'll have to keep quiet and just waggle her lips at the world.

Using the celebrity's midriff as a pillow, Justin begins to drift off to sleep on the bed, surrounded by bits of body, thinking about the celebrity and the silence. A green light on the dehumidifier illuminates. I suppose the air must have changed a little.

Then finally a noise, a sniff, Justin's nostrils hiss, snot gurgles, then the distant sound of a woman's voice. Shit. Oh God, thinks Justin. His pulped brain bubbles inside its papier mâché skull. Shit. He's dribbled gozz into the midriff's belly button. He turns round, knocking a hand on to the floor with his leg. Where's the voice coming from?

His head feels like someone's been sick into it. The celebrity's going to kill him for this. Time has passed. He scrambles over to the coffee table and sips from his whisky. The experiment is fucking up, he's wronging society, playing games with the sexual fates of others. And still the woman's voice, tiny and delicate: where is it coming from and what is it saying?

Justin crawls towards the bedside table, following the sound of the speaking. The voice is minute and sounds like footsteps creeping on gravel. He peers into the ashtray at the facial features of the celebrity. The mouth is leaning against the two eyes; the pink lips move like splintering wood.

'Put me back together, you prick.'

Oh shit, thinks Justin, I should never have taken her to pieces in the first place. He runs to the bed, picks up a hand and tries to stick it to an arm. Is that right? Yes, hands and arms, classic, legs on feet, where the fuck is her back? Shut up. Shut up.

'Who the fuck do you think you are? Taking me to pieces, what did you think you were doing?'

The lips are back on her face now and talking loudly. Justin positions the hair on top of her head. She's beautiful again, and furious.

'What about my stomach?'

'I know, just give me a second.'

Justin picks up the midriff and squirms his index finger around the belly button. There is a sound – a faint squelch.

'What's that?' asks the celebrity.

'Nothing.'

'It's spit.'

'It's dribble.'

'Give it back.'

Justin hands the toned midriff to the celebrity and she puts it back into place, wiping the remainder of the spit from her belly button with her finger. He hands her a drink. She's drinking. Thank God she still works. She lies naked on the bed, gulping at the glass, the seams between her body parts fading. Suddenly she begins to laugh, then she just can't stop, she's lying there just laughing out loud.

'Hahahahahahahaha.'

'What's the matter?'

The celebrity can't reply, something is as funny as fuck, surely. Her oinking laughter is causing her body to fold; her stomach shudders and curves. Her eyes are squeezed shut, just creased skin leading to nothing. Justin panics, has he assembled her correctly? Yes, yes, it's fine; her eyes are on her face, and her anus is in place. Justin is fretting.

'Erm . . . how is your acting career going? Have you thought about film?' he says.

The celebrity explodes once more, squirming about on the bed, laughing uncontrollably, messing up the sheets, clutching her stomach. 'Hahahahahahahaha.'

'The progression from TV to film can be made,' continues Justin. 'Look at Robin Williams, or George Clooney.'

'Hahahahahahahaha.'

Justin sits down on the bed beside the celebrity. He places a hand on her shoulder, which rocks and vibrates along with her cackling mouth. 'Please, celebrity,' he says, his voice anxious and containing the untuned note of defeat.

'Sorry,' the celebrity replies, hands on each of its red cheeks, bracketing its gasping mouth.

'What's so funny?' asks Justin, causing the celebrity to speak cautiously through her lingering laughter.

'I didn't like the way you took me to pieces. I have a past, you know?'

'Yes, of course you do. Of course you have a past.'

'You shouldn't have done it. You made me look like a right tit.'

'I agree. But all I wanted was to seduce and have sex with you. I wasn't being political, I promise.'

'I believe you. I feel sorry for us both.'

The celebrity pulls the duvet over its body. Justin

discovers that his face has frozen into a hideously pulled and uncomfortable grimace. Like a smiling doll, fixed and nasty. He is trying to relax, jittering about on the spot, knees bending, bowels loosening. The poor, poor celebrity speaks.

'Get undressed, Rudolf. Join me.'

'Actually, my name is Justin.'

'It's all lies, of course, isn't it?'

'Yes, it's all lies.'

Justin gets undressed in a kind of crouching position, with a surprising sense of shame. As he slips under the duvet he's confident that the celebrity would have been incapable of glimpsing his cock. Once in bed, Davine puts her arm around him and directs his head into her chest. Justin's face finds comfort between her stone collarbone and the soft beginnings of her breasts.

'Is that your . . . ?'

'Yeah, I'm afraid it is.'

'Weird,' says Davine, lifting up the bedsheets and peering down. 'I didn't think you'd be turned on.'

She can feel Justin's erection tapping at her kneecap, although it doesn't feel like a cock. It feels more like an object mislaid within the sheets, a mobile phone perhaps, or a vibrator.

'The fact is, Davine, I can't help but get hard. You're naked and I'm such a boring boy.'

'I understand. I'm famous, after all. And, of course, I have a vagina, or rather, *but* of course I have a vagina. And a childhood. I don't know. I feel terrible.'

Justin places his fingers into the glued loins of Davine. There is a smell of sickly chemical, then the sound of a celebrity laughing uncontrollably, preparing to make love.

24

Rape Games

FRANK AND STEVE left Justin's apartment about ten minutes ago. God knows why Steve came, the guy's a wreck, he's in no state to be conducting business. He is convinced that fashion is conspiring against him. That designers and retailers are creating and distributing clothes so fast that he's drifting and drowning way out of fashion. He's spending hundreds of pounds a day and his eyes are bloodshot. He can't escape the feeling that he is faintly ridiculous, constantly behind the times, no matter how many new garments he buys.

He and Frank came round to Justin's to collect the sex machine from Rebecca and to collect a ten-thousand-pound investment from Justin. After about an hour of deliberation, Steve chose to wear a trilby with red feathers in it and a T-shirt with the phrase 'Rape Games' written in geometric text across its front. The trilby is surely a classic piece of clothing and the fact that it has been relaunched by a leading male fashion house put his mind at ease. I'll be in fashion all day with this hat, he reasoned. The T-shirt, he had hoped, would appear rather controversial. The words 'Rape Games' ought to suggest to the viewer that Steve is a hardcore and deeply brave young man. A man keen to buck social convention and reorganise the meanings of dangerous words. Steve left the house confident that he was in fashion.

But he can't walk down a street nowadays without a giddy sense of unease. He's scared to turn corners or cross roads, for fear that the act may trigger some hasty cycle of fashion. For fear he'll find himself looking ridiculous. Frank had to reassure him at every step. 'You look fine,' he kept saying, as Steve dismantled the faces of passers-by, searching for signs of amusement.

They arrived at Justin's at half past four; the transaction was fairly swift. Frank had met with Justin and Rebecca two days earlier and handed over the sex machine. He'd also discovered that Justin had money and had outlined his business plan for the sex machine. Justin agreed to invest, pending Rebecca's opinion on the machine.

Rebecca was meant to keep the machine for a week, so she could really get to grips with it and see how it fitted into her life and her daily routines. But within hours of having the machine confiscated, Carly became irritable and began to shake. She'd been using it constantly since being discharged from hospital. After a day without it, she wouldn't leave her room and started to sweat profusely. Last night she was crying and screaming for hours, calling out for the machine until the sun rose and she passed out through exhaustion. She is addicted to its love and cold turkey was impossible. There was nothing Steve or Frank could do to reassure her. So they came round to get it back, to apologise, to get the money.

'So, how about my hat?' said Steve the moment Justin

opened the front door. The guy's a wreck, he'd never even met Justin before. Justin stood at the door confused, thinking that the hat looked kind of poncey. A little gay.

'The hat, the trilby? What do you think about it?' Steve said again, pointing to it with a tense hand.

'My name is Justin.'

Still confused, Justin held out his hand expecting to have it shaken. But instead Steve quickly undid the buttons on his jacket then removed it completely to reveal his T-shirt.

'Rape Games,' Steve said, pointing this time at the words displayed across his T-shirt.

'Sorry?'

'I've got "Rape Games" written on my T-shirt. Look, "Rape Games". Don't be alarmed, I'm hardcore.'

Steve was staring down at the text on his T-shirt, his mouth slightly open, the tip of his tongue visible like a dying dog. At this stage Frank interrupted; he squeezed his body around Steve and grabbed Justin by the hand.

'Let me apologise for my business partner here; he's having a few relationship difficulties.'

So anyway, the transaction went fine. Steve kept quiet as Frank got the ten thousand quid off Justin and had a private discussion with Rebecca about the sex machine. They left ten minutes ago. Right now Justin is giving Rebecca a scalp massage. He's sitting on the edge of the sofa, she's sitting on the floor between his legs, describing the machine.

'The word to describe it is "fierce", or I guess you might call it a "white orgasm", or a wall of orgasm, or like being set in orgasm cement.'

'Frank is a sleazebag and his partner's insane,' says Justin, kneading half-heartedly at Rebecca's scalp. Rebecca is experiencing one of her confident days. She secretes self-esteem from all orifices. Words process along the conveyor belt of her tongue.

'The most appropriate analogy is pain, it's a lot like pain. At least, in its consistency and intensity. Imagine every bone in your body being broken extremely slowly, but it's somehow enjoyable, extremely enjoyable. A disorientating pleasure that you can't find your way out of, but you don't mind.'

'My hands are tired. Is this helping?'

'Yeh, it's heaven, keep going.'

Rebecca used the sex machine three times in the twenty-four hours she had it. On one occasion, Justin had been present, watching but not wanking. It was as he watched her squirm and scream around the bedroom that he became certain that he should invest in the product. But Rebecca is adamant that the machine does not mark the end of their sexual experiment. She maintains that it's not the answer.

'I'm not even sure I'd buy one,' she says. 'It's too much insofar as it's too much pleasure, and too little insofar as it seems to have nothing to do with happiness. Even when it's on and you want to scream with pleasure.'

The sex machine sorted out the problems Justin and Rebecca had been experiencing since his night with the celebrity. It made them equal, brought them back together as experimenters in sex. It's only now, after Rebecca's affair with the machine, that calm has been restored. He had a celebrity and she had a machine. One all.

Justin described the sex with the celebrity in the only way he could. He spoke rather vaguely about how it was like shagging a void. Fucking a myth. Discovering the vulgar truth behind the constructed beauty. It didn't matter that it wasn't at all like shagging a void or fucking a myth. It didn't matter that it had been quite nice in the end, if a little emotional. But the fact is celebrity-shagging isn't an answer, so Justin felt he should reassure Rebecca by pretending the sex had been shallow.

Justin stops massaging. He gets up from the sofa and walks to the window. It has been clear for a long time that Rebecca is falling in love with him. There is an unavoidable atmosphere when they're together. It's awkward. She'd attempted to make him jealous by flirting with the sex machine, but it hadn't worked. Of course, he thinks Rebecca is beautiful and wonderful. In another world, he keeps thinking, we are lovers. If he stares hard at her living room walls, he can almost see beyond to where their doubles are making real life plans on the sofa. But the experiment is everything. The other worlds are just the other worlds.

'I think we should go to the Antiporn rally on Saturday,' says Rebecca, joining Justin by the window and trying to get him to give her a piggyback. 'We should get that headmistress on her own and proposition her. If we could threesome with the leader of Antiporn, that'd be amazing.'

'Would it?' says Justin, refusing to grab her under her knees and bearing her weight with his shoulders instead.

'Wouldn't it?' says Rebecca, sliding slowly down his back to the floor.

The two of them reconvene on the sofa where Rebecca demands that the massaging continues. Justin agrees, thumbing her neck with force. Rebecca's sexual suggestions are increasingly unconvincing. They sound like ideas she's had for the sake of it rather than for the sake of global joy. Justin has recognised this and is disappointed. He'd tried to hold her in place and protect her from love. But sadly, people love love. And Rebecca has wriggled free from Justin's lovelessness. She wants a boyfriend. She is falling in love with him.

Justin turns his attention to Rebecca's hair. This is love, he thinks. If love is anything, it's running your fingers across chemical scalps.

'We're not going to try and fuck the headmistress, Rebecca. We're going to go with Colin's idea.'

'Colin's idea is ridiculous,' says Rebecca, suddenly angry. She's been arguing against Colin's suggestion since it appeared on the site. Justin says nothing, just continues making small circles on her scalp with each of his fingers. 'So, what?' says Rebecca, her voice tinny with irritation. 'You expect me to have a kid?'

'I expect you to get pregnant and I expect you to have an abortion. I expect you to at least give it a try,' says Justin softly, killing her with calmness. He feels the added blood pulsing through the veins of Rebecca's head, it's noticeably warmer. He stops massaging. Rebecca's head drops back into his lap so he can stare right into the depths of her nostrils and at the extremities of her eyeballs, where they become red.

'With you, Justin? Are *you* going to make me pregnant?' she says, with the stretched and tortured eyes of a ghoul.

'No, my love,' he replies. 'Colin is.'

25

Bleep Bleep Bleep

A DAY LATER, in the grim light of the Nude Factory, Johnny's face is performing a foul grimace. The rolls of skin on his cheeks and forehead cast unfortunate shadows down his face. How did it come to this? For the third time in a minute, he demands confirmation that he lost his virginity to a prostitute. Rebecca adjusts the straps of her bra. Her breasts seem to titter within their satin cups. For the third time in a minute, she says: 'All I'm saying, Johnny, is that you didn't sleep with me that night. That me and Justin tricked you.'

'Right, OK.'

'Have you been using prostitutes, Johnny? Please say you haven't.'

'Well, how long have you been a stripper?'

'A year. Have you been sleeping with prostitutes?'

'I can't say, Rebecca.'

It seemed perfectly normal to Johnny when he recognised the ring on the girl's finger, as he handed her the Nude Token. It was a plastic emerald thing, exactly the same as the ring Rebecca often wears. His eyes scanned up her arm and over her shoulder. It came as no surprise when he found himself staring at Rebecca's face. Oh, he thought, my friend.

He'd come into central Manchester for the afternoon. He'd woken up with this strange desire to buy a DVD and put his life back on track. He didn't know what DVD he wanted; a film perhaps, or the complete series of a television comedy. But before he could even locate a shop he felt himself gravitating towards the Nude Factory. It felt like a ton weight was hanging from his cock. He got an erection. Had to put fists into his trouser pockets to hide it. He walked into the Nude Factory at about two o'clock, and it wasn't long before he discovered that Rebecca worked there. But as I say, this seemed normal. Every attempt Johnny makes to enjoy an episode of illicit erotica seems to culminate in embarrassment. Usually when he encounters someone he knows.

So in the grained atmosphere of the strip club a few revelations are revealed. Johnny hadn't slept with Rebecca. Johnny had indeed lost his virginity to a prostitute and Rebecca works part time as a stripper. But, of course, *we* knew all this already.

Rebecca doesn't even entertain the idea of lap dancing for Johnny. His unexpected arrival at the Nude Factory is yet more evidence of man's cloudy and horrendous imagination. The mystery of sexuality and personality, she thinks, as she rests her thighs on the stale banquette beside Johnny. Jesus, men are melted tar.

'Look, Johnny, if you want to talk you'll have to pay me. I'll get bollocked otherwise,' she says, folding her arms to block his view of her breasts.

Johnny hands Rebecca a handful of change, about five

quid. He turns his body towards her and wonders what life was like in the sixteenth century.

'So you tricked me,' he says. 'We never slept together?'

Rebecca nods with irritation. The manager, Marcus, is gesturing to her from beyond Johnny's left shoulder. He wants her to unfold her arms. She does so reluctantly, then watches as Johnny's gaze journeys down from her face, over her collarbone to her breasts. She sighs. So does Johnny. The two young people sigh.

'You know, I came into town to buy a DVD,' says Johnny. 'I wasn't certain what I wanted, but I felt sure that I could stand in front of the displays, look at the different products on offer and make a decision. I even felt sure that I could go home and watch it, put it in the DVD player and sit in front of it for a while, until it ended, I suppose.'

Johnny runs his finger over the space on his face where he wishes sideburns grew. But they don't. He can feel the uneven texture of a pointless rash and the presence of a few wiry and isolated hairs. Staring at Rebecca's boobs is no fun either; they remind him of crying. Her skin looks like clothing, her breasts simply accessories.

'But I haven't bought anything,' he continues. 'Apart from you, I suppose. I was hoping for a lap dance, or maybe not, maybe I wasn't. I was hoping to get this thick cement out of my mind.'

'Cement?'

Johnny seems to fall uncontrollably towards Rebecca, but then halts decisively inches from her smirking cleavage. His eyes trace the arched journey of her bra. To be a bra, he thinks, yes, what a divine fate. The concept of happiness flits quickly through his mind, causing him to laugh, speak and long to weep.

'I feel that if I were to sneeze, I might disappear into thin air. I feel like I'll never be happy, just crap and frustrated. And, of course, I love you.'

'Don't cry, Johnny,' says Rebecca, trying desperately to relate to Johnny's puddle-like destiny. She puts a hand to his cheek, but he spasms and her fingers return to her knees. Johnny speaks again, his voice a weak squeal.

'I shouldn't be here,' he says. 'Earth, I mean. I shouldn't be here. I don't matter, that's the way it is . . . Look at my thin wrists, do you ever look at my thin wrists?'

'You've got lovely wrists.'

Quite suddenly, Johnny is up like a shot. As if he didn't really want to leave but suddenly found his body propelling him towards the door and up the stairs, like the dregs of a drink being sucked up a straw. Rebecca gets to her feet and calls after him, but he's gone. She can hardly run after him in her underwear.

So yes, Johnny runs. He's running. He exits the Nude Factory and heads east away from Castlefield in the direction of Market Street. As he flies past a large toyshop, a huge woman staggers out holding an enormous wooden doll's house. She laughs, at him? Surely not. He passes a pub (there are always pubs). The sound of football. Beery cheers and groans. Johnny carries on running. The streets are packed. He changes direction with each skip, avoiding collision. In the back of his mind he hopes Rebecca might be following him, chasing at full speed in her knickers and her high heels, screaming his name. That's impossible, though; run on.

He tears up King Street. A man dressed in leather seems to have oil for hair. A woman with large teeth and the thatched head of a scarecrow pauses as he runs by, tibia conspicuous inside her suede calf. On Cross Street a bus drives by, containing a pinch of people.

At the southern end of Market Street a space exists. In another city it might be a pleasing piazza buzzing with atmosphere, but not in Manchester. It's just uneven tarmac, argumentative architecture; bad maths. Johnny arrives and a pigeon leaves. The droves of people continue to move, not noticing the speedy arrival of the young man.

Are my clothes too baggy? wonders Johnny, marvelling at the plastic bags that bulge from the people's wrists. Can I do anything at all? He's stops and stares, people revolve around him like he's the central spear of an ancient merry-go-round. They bob up and down and round, like brightly coloured plastic horses with gaping mouths and fixed expressions.

'Can I do anything at all?' he says out loud, trying to catch the eye of an old man who limps past supported by a wooden stick. Pigeons circle overhead, they're enjoying this.

'Can I do anything at all?' he says again, to himself. Can I run back to the Nude Factory and demand that Rebecca gyrates on my lap for a while? Can I run to her and cover her exposed flesh in a large blanket? Can I tell her that everything will be fine and that I'm getting her out of stripping and building us a new and better life? Can I rescue anything? Johnny's thoughts tumble out of his brain, landing on the Tarmac with a wet thump. He screams at the top of his voice: 'What am I meant to be doing?'

He's running again, prompted by the grim glances that turned to him as he screamed. He's running up Market Street, fumbling with his phone. He hardly recognises any of the names in his phonebook: Andy, Anka, Ben. The names of people he's lost touch with, an entire alphabet of failure. He slips off Market Street and runs a little further down a quiet pedestrianised road. He comes to rest outside a pub called The Shakespeare. He's panting heavily as he taps in the telephone number of the sex line.

In this situation, what would Shakespeare do? Write a play about it probably. A girl, a guy, rejection, sexual experimentation, trickery, farce. But this is not the age of Shakespeare. For a moment Johnny considers entering the pub and buying a pint of Coke, but then his call connects.

'Hello, who's that?' the girl's voice, unknown but familiar. Just like the rest.

'It's me,' says Johnny, pacing frantically, staring up at Shakespeare's portrait. Which swings on a sign overhead.

'Who's me, darlin'?' says the girl. Bless her, bless the girl. How long does she wait by her phone? And has she just sipped from a beaker of gravel? Her voice is ragged.

'It's me. Johnny,' says Johnny, using his real name for the first time on this line. 'I need your help. Do you know what I'm meant to be doing?'

'Sorry?' comes the crackled reply.

'What am I meant to be doing?'

Johnny kicks an invisible football from his feet and senses tears conspiring in his eyes. Against him, of course. He listens to his phone; the girl's confused. Why won't she speak? What am I meant to be doing? Wait – she's speaking.

'Well, Johnny, usually guys just choose a fantasy, then wank as I talk 'em through it.'

'Really? But everything is going wrong.'

'You know, like doggy? Or anal?'

Johnny is tall with thin brown hair. The sky is blue. At

246

the end of the road a lorry reverses slowly away from a building site. Bleep, bleep, bleep.

'Please, I need some guidance.'

'Blow job? Tit-fuck?'

'Help me.'

Out of desperation, Johnny takes the handset from his ear and watches as the lorry works backwards towards him. He thinks about dying, then about God. Does God have personal problems? Surely he must. Johnny decides quickly that he definitely believes in God, just to give himself an outside chance of meeting the fucker. He brings the handset back to his ear, the tone of the girl's voice has changed completely. Shit.

'Are you outside?' she asks, her voice missing its previous eroticism. 'You're fucking outside, aren't ya?'

Johnny feels tears sneak across the southern borders of his eyes.

'Yes,' he says. 'I'm outside, help me, please!'

'You're a fucking pervert!'

The line goes dead. The crackled voice of the girl is replaced by a warm monotone. The reversing lorry continues towards Johnny, its bleeping getting louder and louder. In an ideal world, Johnny could just stand still and be slowly crushed by the reversing vehicle. In a perfect world he would be flattened like a pancake by the lorry's heavy wheels, then folded up like a cartoon fatality and posted to his parents. But naturally, this is not a perfect world. This is a world where lorries bleep when placed into reverse, allowing people to step on to pavements out of the way and be safe. Johnny leans on the sandwich board at the entrance to The Shakespeare: cold lager, homemade sandwiches, steak and ale pie, bangers, mash.

In his head he begins to count silently to himself, one, two, three and so on. He pauses at twenty-one: his age. Two decades and one year. God knows how many days. Certainly he can't recall any specific ones offhand. Life: blue sky, red blood, grey streets, bleep, bleep.

Johnny does what he probably ought to do. He puts his hands into his trouser pockets and walks towards the end of the street. Overhead, Shakespeare swings on his sign. Johnny is somewhere else, then somewhere else again.

III
Seven Months Later

26

WHAT A FUCKING nightmare. That's what people would say. I see myself groaning in a pub, a half-drunk ale in my hand. I'm tossing my pupils to the tops of my eyes. I'm going, what a fucking nightmare. Seriously. I'm like.

Draw breath and realise that we're in this together. Doomed to swallow more talk of tits and in and out and blood. The truth is leant against the bar and it's staring at you and me. We continue to talk, to hold each other's eyes. But we feel its gaze and are excited. We wonder which of us the truth would like to smooch.

By the way, I'm in the shit.

It's very funny. Hee hee. See. This morning I got a very special visitor. Not my Narrative Health Aid, Susan. No, not her. I looked up from my work to see our illustrious governor, overweight in the doorway, his grey head drifting like smoke from the collar of his red shirt. I smiled and decided his name is Gordon. Gordon said nothing. He gestured that I should continue writing, so I did. It has dawned on me that it was no accident that I found myself studying human history on the Evernet system. Or at least no accident that I have been allowed to complete my studies. It appears I fascinate the governor. I am special. I am a dead body. Governor Gordon watched me like the devout watch miracles. The governor knows who I am. He knows that I know who I am.

There is nothing anyone can do to prevent this story. I know that it will not earn me my release. Sod it or fuck it and certainly whatever. But the governor knows he'd be in the shit if his superiors learnt of my being exposed to Evernet. It's a screw-up. We'll be like. Fucking come on. I'm like.

I am shipwreck rusty. I can barely hold the figures on the page. I can barely read the maps. Translate them. Bring myself to life. I'll finish this tonight. My brain was never built to be so full. It was built for fresh air. Its pipes were intended as slides but now, sadly, friction has occurred. My mind is dry with turned earth, history and information. I'll finish this tonight.

I'm thinking about death today. My own, I think. I see myself wilting on to a large stone, far away from the bright pine that surrounds me now. I bring a hand to my forehead and think for a second, trying to capture a few memories. Is it because there are too few? Or too many perhaps? Either way I don't remember a thing. Not one second of my life falls before me, split with a knife. No images or sounds. No cause to smile or be satisfied. And as my eyelids droop a figure leans above me. And although the sunlight on his shoulder makes a shadow of this man, I somehow know that he is me. Or you perhaps, yes, perhaps the figure is you. Offering me your hand and dragging me to my feet.

As Gordon the Governor watched me this morning I

knew that he was horrified. I am a wobbly tooth. I am a car crash. I am a tortuous sex game. I am a freak of nature. The governor mopped his brow as I tapped like a demon, turning occasionally to smile in his direction. Gordon shuddered, turning away. He knows that I have found out who I am. You know, don't you? You wonder what I'm capable of.

My name? Not allowed.

I'm ready and so are you. Fuck Gordon. Fuck Susan. The finale is for you and me. The truth wants a three-way smooch. Ride like a piggy. We'll be like. We're leaping through time again. Stretching for the end. Seven months later. I could shout my name but the winds of time would steal it. So not yet. No matter. Seven months later. The end.

27

One Million Cokes

MARCO FRANCHESI IS a skinny Italian from Ancona. He is a ridiculous dead-tree of a man. His bony body is tightly wrapped in black fabric; a polo shirt has been tucked into denim drainpipes. He's old Europe. He sits with his legs painfully crossed, surrounded by ashtray, cigarettes and his black-rimmed glasses. He's leaking his thin, squeaky accent into the air around his face.

'Oh Jesus, Justin, is this not all a little English? Like you don't know how to make love to a woman properly?'

Justin yawns enormously. He's been coughing on Franchesi's smoke for almost an hour. Getting annoyed at the persistently rising intonation of the Italian's questions.

'It's completely to do with personal gratification,' Justin says. 'It's completely to do with happiness.'

The bar at the Malmaison Hotel is disappointingly dark. The furniture is jet black, the carpet too. The windows are tinted to the extent that they are barely see-through. Justin had hoped for more light, less atmosphere.

'Cigarette?' asks Franchesi, passing an unlit fag between

each of the fingers on his left hand. Justin declines and Franchesi seems strangely insulted. 'I'm not Catholic, you know, Justin? You can relax.'

'I know,' replies Justin, defensively. 'It's just that I don't think I smoke any more. I thought I did, but thinking about it now, it's clear I don't. I must have given up.'

The Italian nods and refers briefly to some notes he's been making since the interview began. He puts a line through one line of text, and ticks another.

'You went to work at the football stadium immediately after leaving school, is this correct?'

'Yes, that's correct.'

Franchesi adjusts the dictaphone on the table in front of him; it's not clear why. After curling the end of his burning fag around the rim of the ashtray for a moment, he sucks on it, exhales and speaks.

'What do you know about Briony Freeman?'

'Only what I read in the papers.'

'Is that happiness, Justin? Do you think Briony found this "happiness" I notice you like to talk about?'

At this, Justin smiles, the kind of smile you make when someone's whispering brilliant news into your ear. Journalists have been asking him about happiness all day. He wishes he hadn't been so exuberant on his website.

'I am the leader of nobody, Mr Franchesi.'

Justin runs a dry palm over his shaved head; these interviews are getting boring. He's been sitting in this hotel bar since ten o'clock this morning. It's four now and through the dark window panes he can make out the shapes of commuters walking down from the station with slow, exhausted steps. He's lost count of how many journalists he's spoken to today, ten maybe. Marco Franchesi, the skinny Italian from the *Spectator*, ought to be the last.

'Are you in contact with Rebecca Fields?' asks Franchesi.

'Rebecca is a friend of mine, you know that. Why ask that when you've seen the website?'

Justin pushes against the floor with his feet. His chair slides backwards away from the table. Franchesi grunts with disapproval, but Justin doesn't give a shit. He stares out of the window at the silhouettes walking home. Again Franchesi relocates the dictaphone on the table, moving forward towards Justin as he does so. The Italian is certainly a bastard, even a twat, perhaps. His eyes seem conical, a brown pupil at each tip.

'Do you know your site received over two million hits last month, Justin?' he asks, attempting to lure Justin's attention from the window. 'Are you prepared to tell me who Colin Rogers is?'

Unbeknownst to Franchesi, Justin farts gently into his leather seat. How did it come to this? he wonders. Trumping around journalists who think I'm the devil incarnate. I've made mistakes, Justin decides, I've clearly made mistakes. He turns away from the window and looks calmly at the journalist. 'Colin is a guy I met. You've seen the site. Why ask?'

'It was Colin's idea, wasn't it? To get girls pregnant? He's to blame for Briony Freeman, isn't he?'

'We don't even know Briony Freeman. She's nothing to do with me. I barely know Colin.'

Briony Freeman was a girl from Leeds. She and her boyfriend enjoyed the idea of deliberate conception and multiple abortion. Only they got bored of the depressing atmosphere at the clinics. Got bored of listening to the judgemental sighs of the staff. So one night they got pissed on cider and Briony spread herself naked on the kitchen table as her boyfriend rifled through the cutlery drawer. They were fuck-ups. They were bad surgeons. Septicaemia. Bad blood. Briony rotted away miserably from Monday to Friday.

'I don't know,' says Justin, two fingers over his right eye. 'I don't know.'

He's drunk so much Coke in the last few hours it's likely his blood has become carbonated. It feels fizzy, brown and sugary in his veins. He's getting angry. Bored by the boring Italian. He feels he might have to explode and shower him in blood and Coca-Cola.

'I have to write three thousand words on you and your activities, Justin. About this craze you've started. You're gonna have to talk about abortion. If you want fairness, I'll need more.'

Franchesi scrunches up an empty packet of cigarettes and produces a fresh deck from his leather satchel. He's lit one in seconds, so fast it must be magic. Justin composes himself, preparing to tell Franchesi exactly what he told the other journalists.

'Rebecca and I began the experiment because we wanted to find better ways of having sex. Colin's is the idea that has proven most popular. I don't want to go to prison. I don't want to break the law. We were fed up, OK? We were fed up.'

Franchesi is unimpressed. There's so much smoke coming from his face that Justin suspects he may be on fire. He can just make out his slender black figure through the white fog. He can just make out the regrettable movements of his lips.

258

'The law *is* being broken, Justin.'

'Not by me. I just want a sex life, fuck's sake . . . this constant repetition . . .'

Depending on which way you choose to look at it, the timing of Rebecca and Justin's sexual experiment is either perfect or deeply unfortunate. If you're going to partake in the premeditated termination of foetuses for one's own sexual pleasure, then it can be unfortunate if your activities coincide with a widespread re-evaluation of the issue of abortion. Alternatively, the recent controversy surrounding abortion has brought Justin's adventures to a wider audience. He's received free publicity for his crusade. Only it doesn't feel like he's saving the world any more. The experiment is fucking up in his face. But, then again, it is exciting to find oneself at the centre of national outrage.

Combined with the horror story of Briony Freeman, the revelation that a high-ranking government minister secretly negotiated and fast-tracked as many as six terminations for his various mistresses sent the issue of abortion splattering over the front pages. Of course, once the scent of a particular issue has been established and the journalistic hounds have had a sniff, then sick revelation can be found everywhere. It wasn't long before newsex.biz was the talk of the tabloids. The idea of recreational abortion shocked and disturbed the population. The people raged and grew red in the face at the idea. They seethed. Spluttered. They clenched their fists and willed that the blood of the damned be spilled.

And it was, kind of. The minister resigned and was replaced by another minister, and Justin was identified as the pitch-black-minded devil behind newsex.biz and the idea of recreational abortion. Since the story broke, Justin has agreed to as many interviews as he can bear. With every article that appears criticising him and his circle of deviants, his circle of deviants seems to breed. It grows. So it is that Franchesi has been sent to Manchester to meet the beast. So it is that he's referring to his list of questions, wondering which one to ask next.

'Tell me about "unseen lives",' asks Franchesi, after some thought.

'Life's a piece of shit, Mr Franchesi. We wanted to create life without the shit,' replies Justin, for the tenth time today.

'Is Colin a dangerous man?'

'I hardly know him . . . But no, no I don't think he is.'

Franchesi stubs out a fag unsuccessfully; it continues to smoulder in the tray. As if attempting to compensate for this blunder he leans forward through the smoke and pushes the dictaphone right to the edge of the table to where Justin sits. The Italian's eyes flash briefly, then appear to darken two or three shades, like an evening sky collapsing quickly into night.

'Is Rebecca still capable of giving birth, Justin?' His voice is rotten and vindictive.

'Yes,' Justin replies instantly, splaying his fingers across the tabletop, admiring their innocence. But the Italian won't stop.

'What's your connection to Frank Jacobs, to the White Love organisation? Can you explain that, Justin?'

For a moment it seems as if air doesn't exist in this awful bar, as if it's been completely replaced by enormous hedges of bright green stinging nettles. Justin yawns and sips from his millionth Coke.

'No, I can't explain that. That's something different.'

28

Trinkets Our Element

IF YOU'VE GOT enough energy to walk with your head held high and with long confident strides, then the experience of exiting Piccadilly train station and walking down towards the Gardens can be extremely pleasant. Particularly when the weather is good and the sunlight is reflecting off the large glass hotels. The Rosetti, the Malmaison, the Holiday Inn. There's nothing quite like the experience of public transport to instil a sense of urgency and purpose into a person's behaviour. Businessmen gallop with briefcases held close to their chests. Students saunter, overgrown with eclectic luggage and beaming with a sinister sense of freedom. For those moments, on those rare warm days, the world you experience between Piccadilly train station and Piccadilly Gardens threatens to be your oyster.

It is six-thirty in the evening. The sun begins its descent and the automatic doors of the train station glide open, prompted by the arrival of Steve. Although he's only carrying a small rucksack, his walk is laboured. It's like he's giving a piggyback to a lanky corpse. He creeps out of the station and begins stuttering past the restaurants and the newsagents, down towards Piccadilly Gardens. This world is not his oyster.

Steve's role in establishing the White Love company was minimal, largely financial. In recent months, Frank has grown closer to Justin. He tends to seek his advice on most issues concerning the business, rather than Steve's. The fact is, Steve struggles to be outside. He struggles to keep the company of others.

He takes a few steps from the station. The prospect of seeing people causes his anus to loosen; he needs a shit. In fact, he's needed a shit for days, but the prospect of taking one causes his throat to throb with confusion. The ape in him has vanished. I'm a manmade man, he maintains. His eyes glance up from the stooping curve his body has assembled in time to see a surge of people power walking straight for him. He winces, shielding his body with his rucksack. He sidesteps cautiously towards a shop doorway to avoid the breaking wave of business-orientated life. As the people pass by, he holds his bag over his face and seems to bend his limbs inwards in an attempt to hide their precise function and appearance.

'Are you coming in, sir? Would you like something to eat?'

A small Asian guy cuckoo-clocks out from a curry house, his face painted in jet black facial hair. Steve shakes his head and continues to sidestep alongside the row of shops, his chin hard against his collarbone as if his neck has been broken in the interests of hiding his considerable shame. In his peripheral vision the Malmaison appears, sunlight dimming quickly on its expansive glass structure. Nearly there.

On Frank's instruction, Steve has spent the last week with his parents, in the hope that some kind of rehabilitation can be achieved. But the situation remains critical. His state of mind deteriorated rapidly following Carly's release from hospital. He began to buy clothes and fashion accessories on a daily basis at an alarming rate. He started early in the morning when the shops opened, only returning to Carly and the flat late in the evening after the last of the boutiques had brought down their shutters and closed. It wasn't uncommon for shop assistants to find him still on the premises long after the shop had shut. He'd be discovered fondling garments in some concealed alcove, running his fingers over the fabric, trying to work out exactly how fashionable the item was.

Financially, Steve's discovery of retail hasn't been much of a burden, coinciding as it has with Carly's affair with the Sex Machine and her sudden apathy towards clothes and shopping. Carly spends every day in the flat with the machine. She liaises only with Frank when he calls round to assess her state, feed her and ask her questions about the machine. She nibbles at the food that is brought for her. She showers occasionally at moments of clarity; those rare moments of stillness that follow large periods of time spent in the company of the machine. Although Frank is retailing the machine under the name White Love 1000, Carly insists on calling it 'Darling'. Her neighbours comment to each other about the late-night screaming; the near-deafening cries of Darling! Darling! Darling!

Steve darts across the road only when he's convinced there isn't a car in sight. His run is the run of a spindly-legged fairly-tale villain, his hands and his torso wrapped around his rucksack like it's a snatched child. Passing cars are one of Steve's biggest fears; you can never be sure of the expressions on the shadowed faces within. Never be certain they aren't mocking your appearance, doubting your fashion. Once across the road, Steve scuttles the remaining few metres to the entrance of the Malmaison where he is due to meet with Justin. He enters, head bowed, eyes staring deep into the centre of the earth's core.

'Steve, over here!' a voice calls to him from a table over by the window. Steve recognises it as Justin's. And thanks God.

Justin had been reluctant to meet with Steve. He dislikes him. He finds it very difficult to believe the stories told to him by Frank regarding Steve's past. In Justin's eyes, Steve has always been a jabbering wreck, but this image jarred with the stories of the handsome and athletic academic told by Frank. At this moment, in Justin's eyes, Steve is a giant pantomime rat, sniffing his way over to the table in a Stetson and a vile flowery shirt. What the fuck is he wearing? thinks Justin as Steve arrives nervously at the edge of the table, his lips quivering as if muttering minuscule words. Justin stands for the introductions.

'Mr Franchesi, this is Steve, an acquaintance. Steve, this is Marco, a journalist.'

Steve lowers his arse carefully on to the seat beside Justin, refusing to look at anything but the floor. With eyes still nailed to the carpet, his mouth opens and addresses the Italian in an uneven, trembly voice, reminiscent of the croaking of reptiles.

'Hello, Mr Marco . . . and are you a fashion journalist? Do you write about clothes?'

'Eh no, I do current affairs, culture, politics etc. But I must say, my friend, that is quite an outfit you're wearing today.'

With a sudden jolt, Steve straightens his spine hard against the back of his chair. He throws his neck back so his head is facing almost directly upwards. He looks a little bit like he's lost, deep in some unfortunate thought.

'Well, you see, Mr Marco,' Steve begins, 'what I'm wearing is incredibly fashionable today. On my head is a Stetson, like a cowboy. My shirt is crimped floral satin from Vivienne Westwood, if you look, it's crimped floral satin, you see? If you could see my trainers, you would notice the beautiful gold embroidery and the shiny crystals in the tongues . . . You must see my trainers!'

Steve and Justin lurch suddenly in unison. Steve stands up and brings his left foot crashing down on to the table in front of Marco Franchesi. Justin dives forward and grabs the soft packet of cigarettes and begins lighting one with a matchbook.

'Of course I smoke, I remember now,' says Justin, his heart attempting to stop at the sight of Steve's trainers on the table in front of him. His cheeks apple-like with embarrassment.

'They are certainly a lovely pair of trainers, my friend,' Franchesi mutters with a snigger, addressing Steve but with his eyes fixed on Justin.

'There are small shiny crystals in the tongues,' yells Steve. 'There is golden embroidery. Look, Mr Marco!'

Justin dispatches the first lungful of smoke into the air and stares firmly into Steve's eyes, offering a look that suggests he would rather he took his foot off the table. Franchesi sniggers again; an Italian sort of snigger. Hee hee hee as opposed to ha ha ha.

'Look now . . . I suppose all I need to know, Justin, is what are your ethics?'

Justin, his eyes still on Steve and his brain simmering slightly at the Italian's snigger, decides to scratch his head before speaking, it takes a moment.

'I believe people should follow their instincts, should do what they want,' begins Justin, turning at last to the spindly Italian. 'People should disregard the modern beauties and the muscly foreheads, the websites, the star signs. I believe people should be a little dangerous.'

'You mean that people should partake in recreational pregnancy, multiple abortions?'

'No, I just mean that people should be a little dangerous. That's my ethic, Mr Franchesi.'

The Italian is disappointed. He had hoped to learn more from Justin. He puts his cigarettes into his satchel and swings the strap over his bony shoulder. He looks at Steve, who's licking his fingers and trying to remove tiny scuff marks from his trainers. 'I think it's time I left you boys to it.'

Yeh, so do I. So he does; the Italian leaves. He gathers up his dictaphone, and departs, clutching his satchel. He probably says things as he leaves, things like goodbye and good luck.

Justin neglects to smile. He swigs the remainder of his Coke and wishes, as we sometimes do, that his life was completely different. He's fairly satisfied with today's set of interviews; he's given them nothing, as usual. He's made no real sense; the last thing he wants to have is a proper opinion. He watches the Italian as he disappears into the hotel lobby. Moments later, he sees him again through the dark window, crossing he street, phone to his face.

At Steve's request, Justin books a room in the hotel so they can be away from the public glare. Steve's perspiring like mad and it's causing his hair gel to liquefy, skim down his forehead and sting his eyes. Steve's brief interaction with the journalist is as social as he's been in a while.

The room in the Malmaison is what you'd expect: plush, dark, richly upholstered. The kind of room some people call 'sexy'. Steve lies down on the bed and begins smoothing out the creases in his trousers and shirt.

'I've come to the decision that I'm going to be more like you, Justin,' says Steve, hopelessly fighting the creases in his satin shirt. Creases are my death, he thinks, hee hee hee. His brain is shrinking by the second, it sloshes about in tap water. 'Yes,' he says as Justin arrives at the edge of the bed, 'I shall make Carly pregnant, hee hee hee.'

Justin sighs and looks at his watch, then grabbing his supposed colleague firmly by the neck, he pulls the Stetson down off Steve's scalp so it's covering up his entire face. A muffled voice squirms out from under the hat: 'Sorry, Justin, I'll stay under here for a while, it still smells new . . . delicious.'

By the window is a table and chair. Leaving Steve under the hat Justin takes the seat and finds Frank's number in his phone. On the bed Steve continues to blindly locate creases in his clothing and iron them out with his ringed fingers. Justin's call connects.

'Frank . . . I need you to come to the Malmaison and pick up Steve . . . yeh, I know, but it hasn't worked . . . he's worse than ever . . .'

From underneath the hat Steve can be heard muttering the word 'Frank' to himself, although it sounds more like 'rank'. Rank, rank, rank.

'Just come and get him, room sixteen. You'll understand when you see his clothes, he's still fucked. Chances are I'll have already left.'

As soon as Justin hangs up his phone it begins to ring. It's his mother; she's been calling at least once a day since his name was splashed all over the tabloids. He cancels the call and sets his phone to silent.

'You can remove the hat now, Steve.'

'Thanks.'

Steve takes the hat from off his face in time to smile at Justin as he sits down beside him on the bed. Justin takes a moment, breathing deeply and staring into Steve's glazed eyes, then at his dreadful floral shirt. Can he really have once possessed a brain?

'What do you remember of your economics degree, Steve?' Justin asks, noticing that Steve has at least two rings on each of his fingers and thumbs. Steve spikes his hair and adjusts his collar nervously.

'Well . . . the thing is, Justin . . . I can barely remember anything at all.'

Justin watches as a layer of moisture develops on the surface of Steve's eyes. The delicate skin that surrounds them begins to quiver frantically, his eyebrows crease into Ms and his cheeks clench.

'I don't remember anything hardly, Justin,' Steve says, his voice delicate. 'I mean, your name – I remember that, and Frank, Carly, the Sex Machine. Clothes shops. Colours. Cuts . . . but it's like every day is a new life, for me. Entirely different from the previous one, and the next . . .' The first tear falls from Steve's left eye. He battles to get his words out. 'It's like clothes are the only real thing . . . trinkets our element . . . and . . . and fashion the only real time.'

Justin picks up the hat from the bed and once again places it over Steve's face. He returns to the table and his mobile phone. Sobbing can be heard from under the Stetson, muffled, like a man weeping privately in an adjacent room. Justin locates a number in his phone and waits for it to connect, straightening his back and staring out the window towards Ancoats and its numerous renovated cotton mills.

'Colin?' he says.

There is a lengthy silence as Justin listens carefully to the voice on the end of the line, tapping his finger against the thick window pane to drown the sounds of Steve's crying. It's almost a minute before Justin speaks, by which time he is pacing the room angrily and occasionally slapping the window with the flattened palm of his hand. Steve continues to moan, both his hands pull the Stetson hard over his face in an enormous and desperate attempt to mute his distress.

More seconds pass until Justin slaps the window so hard he's convinced it's going to shatter and shower innocent people in broken glass. Steve screams and the window holds firm. Turning towards the door Justin holds his phone out in front of his face like a microphone. He's shouting, his face stretched and red.

'Is Rebecca pregnant or not, Colin? What the fuck have you done to her?'

29

A Good and Useful Life

COLIN KICKS REBECCA several times across her body. He bends down, lifting her by the neck, pointing her disastrous face at his own. Blood runs from her chestnut hairline. Blood runs from her mouth.

'It's love, is it?' he says, crooked fingers digging into her. Rebecca. His last chance. Broken on the bathroom floor.

He allows her head to fall and join her body on the red tiles. He moves to the sink and watches his reflection in the mirror. He sniffs. Is this it? He wonders whether he should wipe his scarlet hand across his reflected image. But he doesn't; what would be the point? In his inside pocket his phone begins to sing, the word 'Justin' flashing in the centre of the screen.

'Hello,' says Colin, somehow politely, one eye fixed on its reflection. Justin says his name and Colin walks calmly from the room.

'She hasn't been aborting them,' he says, on the landing

now, banging on the banister in an attempt to stay calm. 'She's been lying to us. She killed my first, but since then, nothing. She's been carrying your kid for six months. She's been lying to me and lying to you. Making us believe that she killed them at the clinic.'

Colin begins to turn in circles, kicking the same place on the wall with each rotation. 'So it's over,' he says. 'I've dealt with it and dealt with her. She should have known.' The wallpaper splits and plaster trickles to the floor. 'It has to be so boring now. Do you see, Justin? I've dealt with the kid. But all along it's been lies. Do you understand? It has to be so boring from now on. Not a party, only a funeral!'

Colin pulls his foot from the wall, dropping his phone as he does so. Back in the bathroom. More kicks. Rebecca's bloated stomach. Tears in both their eyes. Snakes alive in Colin's veins, kicking her again and again, the treacherous dog, dressed in blood, kicks between her legs. Broken hearted.

'Do you see what you've done?' he shouts, fists at his eyes. He lets out a piercing high-pitched scream. 'Do you see what you've done?'

Rebecca watches as Colin leaves the bathroom once again. Her senses are shadows of their former selves. Colin exits in a sequence of jumping images and scratched sounds. Rebecca is hurt. She has been vandalised by Colin's heavy feet and fast legs. Her body feels like scattered stones. It's incomprehensible to her. The pain is a powerful throb, like a heart beating inside her skull. Her blood surrounds her. It's as if all agony is, is a pulse, a countdown, a mindset where all memory is rendered absurd. She can make out little of her surroundings. There is bleach where she lies. There is rat poison, too. Rebecca closes her eyes.

She has seen this situation before. In her mind. She has

seen herself beaten in Colin's home. She always knew it might occur. For months she has concealed Justin's child from both him and Colin. She has continued to visit them both in ever more loose-fitting attire. Both boys have been surprised at their ability to conceive with Rebecca. Always at the first attempt. Both have declared their joy at creating a wordless, lightless being, unscathed by the shining boredoms of the outside world. Both have thanked her like rewarded infants as she left for the clinic to terminate the foetus and complete their fetish. But there was only ever one abortion.

Seven months ago Rebecca knocked on Colin's door. It was as his arm wrapped round her and pushed her up the stairs that her mind began to change. She had lost interest in Dostoevsky. She had quit her job and abandoned her degree. She was enjoying the sensation of her life being dismantled, like a completed jigsaw puzzle being broken up into larger sections, then being frantically reduced to its hundreds and hundreds of different pieces. For Justin's sake she went to Colin. She hoped that it was love all along.

Sex proved a protracted arrangement of mysterious jolts; Colin's body whacking and aching around her. He came with eyes melted shut and Rebecca had to resist the temptation to laugh. She was certainly far from tears, even given the stench of Colin's stale blue room. Experimenting with Justin had long since blunted her sexual fears.

A week later she pissed on a pregnancy test. She pissed on it in the very room in which currently she bleeds. She watched as Colin wept as it turned a chemical blue. Positive. Colin stroked her flat belly with a clenched fist. 'A life that will never see light. Innocent,' he whispered, causing Rebecca to shake her head and just watch as his tears fell.

Afterwards, at the clinic, it was the sound of wails that woke Rebecca. It was minutes before she recognised them as her own. The anaesthetic wore thin and a nurse smiled above her. Women lay in silence on each adjacent bed. Some stared at magazines; crisp, old and hardly held by their hands. One woman held a lipstick and seemed to contemplate applying a coat. But what was the point? Rebecca watched as the scarlet stick was wound down and discarded. It was then that she decided: never again. Nature was talking. Not dead after all. Rebecca pictured her womb, disgruntled and suddenly emptied, its contents sucked out and flushed to God knows where. Never again.

Things were already moving beyond the control of her and Justin. Antiporn protested at the clinic's gates. Rebecca had to barge through placards and loud screams. Women with faces full of shadows grabbed her clothing. Women with colourless hair and old coats. Appalled at the concept of abortions carried out just for fun. Some placards even mentioned newsex.biz. Rebecca's deceit began that day.

A month later she and Justin conceived. Justin had been identified as the boy behind the website. There were reporters outside the house. As the test turned blue, Justin talked of unseen life, of happiness, of answers, finally. After all the prostitutes, domination, dogging, Gandhi-shagging, celebrities, the various probes and gangbangs. Happiness, finally. He looked out of the window, prompting an explosion of bright camera flashes from the pavement below. Rebecca left, to abort it, she said. But instead she walked home and wept.

On the bathroom floor, Rebecca tries to turn on to her side. The rat poison is paddling now, encircled by her blood. She thinks of Justin. Was it love all along? He's hounded constantly nowadays, by the media and by Frank. She sees him too rarely. She needs to see him. She needs him now because she is bleeding to death. Their child presumably dead inside her.

It was this afternoon that Colin discovered her secret. Rebecca had tried to remain clothed as he made his usual manic advances. The strange hoots and groans that always precede their sex. For Justin, all this for Justin? I'm an idiot, Rebecca thought. I'm a fucking idiot. She was surprised when Colin demanded that she took off all her clothes. 'Get rid of them,' he shouted, tugging at her blouse. To Rebecca it seemed antique to shrug her garments off. But it seems a fondness for nudity survives in this era of new sex. Colin began tearing at her clothing, pulling at it until the seams began to break. He couldn't be stopped. It wasn't long before he ripped off her blouse to reveal her round stomach. Their eyes met. Both hearts sank.

'It's Justin's,' Rebecca said immediately, gathering up her limbs and making naked for the door. 'I love him,' she added, turning back to Colin as she left. 'I really love him.'

That's when Colin turned blue. When the rats retreated. When the air suddenly dried. The screwed-up structures began to unfold; detritus came to life. Pizza boxes flexing into something like their original form. Beer cans unscrunching with loud scraping sounds. Colin's shoulders hunched as if wings were sprouting from his back in an agonising but ecstatic metamorphosis. His lips curled and his mouth made a distant sound, as if his voice was coming from a gnarled recess at the bottom of his diaphragm, echoing up his throat, over his tongue and barely tapping at the sound barrier.

'But I was becoming happy,' he said.

'It's getting out of hand.' Rebecca's voice was an attempt at calm. It had an American inflection, as if by imitating a mainstream culture the situation could be diffused.

'We've failed,' said Colin, softly. 'And it's time to get extremely boring.'

At this point, he ran to Rebecca and punched her several times hard in the face. He knocked out a tooth, the blood on his knuckles confused itself with the blood that poured instantly from her soft face. She couldn't struggle, she just fumbled amid the shock of painless punches. She hit the floor; the jigsaw was being dismantled, every piece separated and scattered.

In the course of the beating she was dragged here, to the bathroom, underneath the sink where she now lies. It is only now, having been beaten to the creosoted touchline of consciousness, that Rebecca realises that lately she's been living in a trance. Her ear rests on the wet red of the bathroom floor. Below, Colin can be heard. How can he be stopped?

Down in the kitchen, Colin's hands are full of bullshit. Full of many different panini: chorizo, mozzarella, pesto and Parma ham. He throws them into the microwave and sets the time. He'd bought them for the cruel-brained slut factory bleeding to death upstairs. Bought them because, until now, he cared for her. He wanted her to eat what she liked when she came to stay. He was willing to cede ground to her world of lifestyle and fucking crap.

Ping! The panini are done. He takes them out and replaces them with a series of coffees he'd bought for her. The bitch, he thinks, remembering the stomach, setting the time. The lie. How could she?

It killed Colin to buy these items. The coffees and the food. To shop around in the mud and the free and easy aisles for the dog shit that devours him. He holds a jar of sundried tomatoes up to the light. He watches them bob about in their oil, seasoned and packaged. Oh, the bastard betrayal and the word love.

He returns to the bathroom holding the food and the drink. The piping hot, Italian-inspired bollocks: cappuccinos, lattes, brain-rot, sundried tomatoes. Rebecca hasn't moved, maybe squirmed a little, breathing like a breathing machine, dying because he's fucked it up at last.

'It's a funeral,' he shouts. 'Because the world will never change.' His lips are nibbling at each other, squabbling. He places the food and drink beside the bath, arranging them neatly like a buffet. Turning to look in the mirror he's convinced that he's invisible, that his reflection is just staring out at an empty room.

'It's a funeral,' he says again, staring down at Rebecca before turning and leaving once again.

Rebecca hears the key turn in the bathroom lock. Moments later she hears the front door slam below. It's a blessing. He's gone. She turns and looks towards the bottles under the sink. Since she smelt the scent of pesto and saw Colin arranging the food beside the bath, her mind has been on the rat poison. She reaches for it.

Her breathing reminds her of a kettle in the middle phase of its boiling process. But it's her blood that boils. Thick angry liquid drips from her face in red-hot drops. I should never have returned here, she reminds herself. I'm an idiot. She attempts to climb on to her hands and knees but is forced to give up. Body and mind are in moods with each other, back to back with folded arms, making her desire to poison the panini hard to realise.

Having recalled a series of popular films in which people perform complex physical tasks while teetering within inches of their lives, Rebecca falls and squirms in the direction of the bath. With one hand she holds her bloated abdomen, with the other she pushes the rat poison across the floor. She recalls Colin's face as he'd arranged the food. His white light eyes. His entire face grinning like teeth in a vice.

The lid of the rat poison is a nightmare, not designed in the interests of girls with crooked, broken fingers and bloody, slippery hands. Eventually the lid's off and, breathing like a building site, she's able to lift the tops off the panini and sprinkle the turquoise pellets among the lukewarm ingredients. Rebecca looks at the tomatoes and the coffees and she wonders what the fuck? And where is Justin? She gasps. Where is Dostoevsky and where is my lovely life?

Using a towel to erase the skids of cranberry blood left by her journey, Rebecca works her way back to the sink, returning the rat poison to its home by the bleach.

Quite naturally, she's dying. Her baby, too. She pats her stomach with her hand, like beating wet sand with a toy spade. Her knickers are horrifyingly red and her legs are streaked with blood, like dire, dated, patterned leggings. She settles under the sink using the bloody towel as a pillow. She believes that Justin will save her. It's been love all along. He'll track me down, she thinks. Somehow he will.

Her body looks like Mars. The mountain of her stomach is coated in a layer of dried brown blood. Beyond it lies a lake of deep red, where the Martians holiday, perhaps, where they sunbathe. But what of such description? Time is dripping like a tap into an empty sink. Din. Din. Din. Where has Colin gone?

I know where Colin's gone. You can always rely on me. I'm.

Colin strides out into Withington. The weather looks more like a weather forecast; simple representation of clouds, suns, showers of rain. The culture of cool days has spread. Withington is a selection of warm colours; outlets selling a busy day, a chilled convo, a snatch of tradition, preoccupation, a bite on the run. Colin struggles to believe anyone has jobs any more. But if you stare through the colours and the freshly baked confectionery, you will notice faint signs of human industry, its yellow scaffolded grin.

Colin is going shopping because he needs more supplies for the funeral. On the wall of the One Stop convenience store an Antiporn protest is being advertised on a large poster. The poster has been made in haste with a marker pen and a photocopier. It reads: ANTIPORN. EMERGENCY PROTEST. 3 p.m. MALMAISON HOTEL. Below the poster is a sleeping tramp. A trickle of piss leaves his groin, bound for the gutter. But Colin doesn't notice any of this. He strides into the shop and begins collecting magazines from the shelves. He gathers up all the celebrity magazines he can manage, which is nowhere near all of them, and takes them up to the counter.

'Hello, mate,' says the lad at the counter. He's Chinese and seems unnecessarily intelligent.

'Hello,' says Colin, miserably, as if he's been told his entire family has been set on fire and he's demanding confirmation. Really? Are you sure no cousins survived?

'OK, sir, would you like a bag?' says the Chinese lad, tearing one from beneath the counter.

'It's probably about leading a good and useful life, isn't it?' says Colin, squinting, talking to his pelvis.

'I don't know, sir, but perhaps, yes.'

'And, of course, I'm going to be a murderer.'

The Chinese lad smiles absently. Casual confessions of murder aren't abnormal in Withington. And, in any case, behind Colin a queue of people is beginning to snake.

'OK, could you type in your pin, mate?'

Colin types in his pin number, his eyes computer screens. He allows the carrier bag to be threaded on to his wrist like a weighty bracelet.

'Ha . . . a good and useful life . . . ha.'

He takes one step out of the shop, then another to his left. His head feels like it's got a lagoon inside it, like his brain's a small island in the middle of a beautiful lagoon. He pictures Rebecca, waving from his lumpy brain, a red sarong around her waist. I've buggered it. He leans back against the wall, then scrapes his way to the pavement where the tramp sleeps. By beating up Rebecca I've buggered it. Bollocks.

Could I wake him, the tramp? wonders Colin. Could I wake him up and get him to help me? The tramp stirs, emitting odour as he does so: piss, shit, smoke, semen, soil. Life itself. Colin sits on his magazines, legs bent, hugging his knees to his chin with both arms.

It was wonderful the first time Rebecca came round seven months ago. She was angry for a while, but she was there, at least she came. He had shared his rice and peas with her, watched her as she ironed her clothes, straightened her hair and, yes, finally, watched as she undressed before they . . .

how can I describe it? Did it? Had it? Made it? Fucked? Screwed? Loved? None fits quite right, not for Colin. 'Schemed' is perhaps the best word. He schemed a foetus into her, then destroyed it before it could be born and become incredibly disappointed. Yes, for even the womb is a source of disillusionment, believes Colin. All that warmth and bobbing about quickly becomes banal. 'We must kill it quickly,' he'd said, 'before it realises.'

But none of this matters now because of Rebecca and her various deceits. Colin coughs into his fist, noticing, as he does so, the blood marks on his boots. Beside him the tramp's eyes open, like barn doors, to reveal eyes the colour of haystacks.

'All right, mate?' asks the tramp, reaching for his crotch to confirm he's pissed himself.

Colin nods, looking into the tramp's ageless face with envy. Yes, envy. Better to have pissed yourself and have a face like a brimming ashtray than have a house with a sink and a dying pregnant girl beneath it. Colin knows this by now. He's realised. But life's a waterslide and we're born with sunscreen on our backs, there's no stopping us, we just slide to the end. He has to get back. He's gathering his magazines and getting up from the ground when the tramp seems to cough half his face off, then speak.

'What do you do, mate?'

What do I do? wonders Colin. What kind of a question is that? What do I do? He doesn't reply. He begins to scurry away. What I do is I . . . I . . . well . . . I get them pregnant because . . . well . . . and then abort because . . . mate . . . I guess. What a weird question. Yes. I do things. I blame happiness. I blame happiness.

For the first time in a long time Colin thinks of his job

at the university last year. What do I do? All the names he'd processed, the new students; their hobbies, desired living arrangements, study choices, all those fucking hobbies, all those fucking names. So much leisure. Colin begins to march along the pavement like a soldier parading on some nostalgic-looking street in China. He's sending his legs firing out in front of him with military precision, clutching the celebrity magazines like he could massacre the whole street with them at any moment. He's shouting orders like a general.

'Table tennis! Polo! Orienteering! Gilbert and Sullivan! Snowboarding! Art! Travel!'

Shouting at the top of his voice, Colin is drawing attention to himself. It's a bit of a laugh actually. A few lads in tracksuits are chuckling and even the elderly snigger, given the harmless nature of his words. People are cracking up as he walks down Wilmslow Road bellowing at the top of his voice.

'Football! Theatre! Socialist politics! Drinking! Rock climbing! Ballet! Knitting! Rugby! Swimming! Monasteries! UFOs! Computer games! Sex! HAHA! Tudor architecture!'

'Sounds like a busy day, son!' shouts an old man, humorously, as Colin arrives home to check on the pregnant girl he's been kicking to death. She's fine, though, still gurgling away as he unlocks the bathroom door and sets down the magazines.

'Rebecca?'

Rebecca's eyelids lift to reveal a roadmap of intricate red lines sketched over the whites of her eyes. He notices she's taken one of his towels from the rail and covered it in blood. Bit annoying.

'It's about leading a good and useful life, isn't it,

Rebecca?' he says, prodding her cheeks with his fingers, forcing her awake.

'Am . . . bu . . . lance . . . you're . . . a . . . a . . . good boy,' gurgles Rebecca, eyes like gobstoppers.

'Yeah,' continues Colin. 'It's all about being busy during the day. I get it now.'

'Ple . . . ase . . . C . . . olin.'

'But bitches like you messed it up. You were more than just beautiful . . . and you know it.'

Colin perches himself on the side of the bath and begins to unpack the celebrity magazines.

'And so this has to be a funeral. But I've bought you your food and your magazines.' Colin's voice is a cheerful scream. He's bounding about now, preparing his party. When he's happy that all is as it should be, he emits a satisfied sigh. Then he turns to face Rebecca, a panini in each of his hands.

'Eat, Rebecca . . . it's time to eat.'

30

Murderer

'THERE MUST BE a back door!'

'They're covering every exit, sir. The police are on their way.'

Justin's trapped inside the Malmaison; it's entirely surrounded by Antiporn protesters. Justin assumes they were tipped off by one of the journalists, Franchesi perhaps, but more likely the woollen-skinned bitch from the *Mail*. He swings his car keys round his fingers, scratching at his shaved head. Rebecca. The voices of the crowd thunder-clap all around the foyer:

'MURDERER! MURDERER! MURDERER! MURDERER!'

And as the crowd shakes their fists, they howl. Through the hotel's dark glass the faces of the protesters can't be made out, only the dropping of their jaws and the craning of their necks. The flashes of the cameramen and the camerawomen. Justin stares at the young porter standing beside him. What does he make of all this? The porter avoids his gaze.

At the front door, the shadow of the crowd becomes disturbed; it begins to separate like a parting sea, like a tank's being driven through the throng. The police, assumes Justin, hands dancing by his sides in the manner of an athlete preparing to sprint. But no, it's not the police. An enormous figure jostles its way through the most devoted protesters at the front and bangs on the glass of the front door with a gammon hand.

'Let him in,' shouts Justin, shoulders hunching and relaxing, fists clenching and unclenching at speed. The security staff unlock the door and squeeze the colossus through, then slam the door in the frenzied faces of the mob, their fingers blistering at the glass, forks of lightning streaking from each extremity. While the door is open the voices amplify, screeching with a commitment and fanaticism of footballing proportions.

'MURDERER! MURDERER! MURDERER! MURDERER!'

On entering, the gigantic man brushes down his suit and smiles that familiar smile; each cheek rising like calf corpses being winched.

'Oh my boy, my dear, dear boy.'

'Hello, Frank.'

'What could they possibly have against a child like you?'

Justin ushers Frank under a spiral staircase. The fat bastard's jittering about with excitement. He can't wipe the smile off his face; it'd be too big a job.

'Frank, I need your help. Rebecca's in trouble. Colin's got her down in Withington and I think he's fucking flipped. He's a lunatic.'

'You've sent your beloved into the arms of a lunatic? Oh, Justin.'

'I think he might hurt her,' says Justin, harshly, desperate to make Frank see the serious side of this. Frank's hands meet in the middle of his chest, resting on his huge gut. Fingers fiddling with each other. His smile flickering like a looped image, cycling unrealistically.

'I'm afraid I shan't get involved, Justin,' he says, slowly and almost seriously. 'I must maintain a distance from your other activities, for the sake of the White Love brand and our business venture. We really shouldn't meet in person any more.'

'She might die, Frank.' Justin grabs Frank's arm and instantly regrets having done so; it feel like a bladder. But there's no convincing Frank. He doesn't like saving people because he's a twat.

'I'm sorry, Justin, but I shan't get involved. I'm making you a great deal of money. You'll have half a million on the first month's sales alone. It really is my time at last.'

Justin's halfway through figuring out why half a million quid means nothing to him when the front door bursts with neon yellow. He takes the long way round Frank and walks towards the police.

'I'll take care of Steve, my boy. Good luck,' shouts Frank over his huge shoulder.

Justin doesn't listen. He approaches an officer with his arms outstretched. The officer frowns.

'It's gonna take at least an hour to get this crowd dispersed, son.'

31

Darling Death

IT'S HAPPENING. REBECCA bleeds and Colin kicks, Steve is mad and Justin's trapped. And Carly, dear Carly, is where she has been for several months now: locked in the Green Quarter apartment with the Sex Machine.

After hours with the machine, Carly hums while breathing. She's too weak to separate her lips. She draws air in through the sides of her mouth then releases it slowly though her nostrils with a high-pitched and wistful hum.

She slowly removes each of the pleasure-pads from her body. Smoke rises from her nipples as she frees them from the machine's electric grip. The skin between her legs is scorched black. Her hair is falling out. From certain angles she looks noticeably bald, her enlarged forehead falls like melted wax to her patchy eyebrows. Then her eyes, hollowed hard; lids the texture of biscuits.

'Oh, darling,' she murmurs, entwining her legs among the wires and straps of the Sex Machine – darling: White Love 1000.

She hasn't left the house in six weeks. She barely eats.

Her limbs are flesh golf clubs, hardly capable of allowing her to stagger out of the bedroom. Frank has masterminded the cover-up operation. He can't afford bad press in the months prior to the UK launch of the White Love 1000. And Carly is certainly bad press. Her parents were told she had a sudden attack of moral heartache and that she's currently involved in aid work in Sudan. But she isn't, not at all. She lying on her bed waiting for her body to cool down. So she can start again.

A layer of dust has settled on the room. A layer of grey on the always-silent hi-fi and the abandoned screen of the television. Where did all this come from? wonders Carly, utterly confused by everything but the machine. Steve is rarely here. He's always out, she knows not where. She is always in. There's no other way to describe this place. It is Carly's lair.

She scurries to the floor, leaving the machine to recover on the bed. 'Distraction,' she whispers. 'I need distraction.'

After using the machine Carly has to find ways of killing time. Ideally she'd never turn it off, but in rare logical moments she knows her skin would blacken further and it's likely she'd pass out. So she must try to give herself periods of recovery.

She crawls to her dressing table and begins fondling the objects that she finds there. She can't remember many of their names. She knows that the small bottle containing thick pink liquid had something to do with her fingers. But she can't think what. The colours of her make-up seem awkward to her now. She reads their names and wonders what it was she had once seen in the various shades. 314 Hot Lilac. 28 Sheer Blossom. 49 Violet Magnetique. 30 Foxy Lady.

She throws the make-up down and pulls open a drawer. Inside she finds a stack of greasy paper. She knows what this is. She's sure she's seen it before. She smells it and feels her memory returning, it smells of stale sweat. But, no, she can't think. Can't remember. Each sheet is incredibly creased, somehow memorably. There are different colours, immense amounts of detail on each side. She compares the different designs, lines them up and stares. But it's useless. She can't work out how they could possibly be used.

'Twenty pounds,' she reads from one, the words awkward on her tongue. 'Twenty pounds,' she says again, allowing the piece of paper to fall.

It was the boredom, of course, the absence of anything else to do. That's what caused this. And then it was that delicious desire for more that we shivering idiots possess. After all, birth then death is a fairly old-fashioned sequence of events. It's only proper to punctuate it with years of heightened pleasure. So Carly allowed the Sex Machine to electrocute her for increasingly long periods of time. Hours on end.

But it wasn't love of sex that brought Carly to this situation, nor was it love of orgasm, really. It was that colourless sludge. Existence: that feigned yawn. The surprising tedium that draws thin cotton curtains around your brain and makes life seem like an inconsequential disaster. You know? Being alive. Socialising, knowing people. Things like that.

Carly was so sensationally bored. Baffled by the world of bombs, speeches and ambition. Gutless in the face of a planet dilly-dallying with effort and energy.

Beside the bed now, Carly discovers a band of silver metal around one of her toes. She pulls it off and holds it to the light. It seems so useless, she thinks, what could this possibly be for? She climbs on to the bed and drapes herself lovingly over the machine. So much greater than cock and balls, thinks Carly. No more grunts and clumsy thumbs. She looks down at her blackened chest and at the areas of her body that no longer recognise touch. Darling doesn't mind. Darling doesn't care what you look like and nor does death. Her mind empties. She begins to attach the machine. She hates men. Cockless arseholes. Carly only likes incessant fatal orgasm. Put simply, she was bored and liked sex machines. Now she's burnt black by their effects.

32

Sundried Eyes

THE DELICIOUS SOFT dough of the panini absorbs the blood from around Rebecca's mouth. But her jaw won't work; it refuses to accommodate the food that Colin prods her with.

'Eat, Rebecca, eat your lovely food.'

Colin's eyes are frozen wide, stuck in an expression of foul surprise. He repeatedly pushes the panini at her lips, staining the food with a thick mix of blood and lipstick. Rebecca's throat pulsates in a cycle of small gags, the sharp scent of pesto scraping the walls of her nostrils.

Giving up on Rebecca momentarily, Colin takes a large tear at the panini with his teeth, colouring them a glassy red. With his jaw munching up the food, he kneels and brings his face close to Rebecca's. She can't see because her eyes won't open. Her lulled senses just recognise the sound of chomping and the deep bassy curdling of Colin's Adam's apple. She wishes he'd start reading the magazines again, give her a moment of peace.

But instead she feels the cold drip of liquid on her face, landing on her cheeks like light pin pricks. She's reminded of time, how it sort of drips, how it's running out. Colin's holding sundried tomatoes above her head and allowing their oil to fall on to her face, watching it slide though the creases of her skin and into her cuts.

Irritated by her lack of consciousness, he pulls at the lids of Rebecca's eyes and looks into the shocked, stationary pupils underneath. But he can't hold her gaze. Her pupils fall upwards as if she's straining to stare at the roof of her skull.

'Ears working, are they, Rebecca? You bitch.'

Colin lets her eyelids fall, then with steady hands he places a dainty tomato on to each of her eyes. Rebecca doesn't notice, maybe she feels a coolness around the eyes, soothing perhaps. But she doesn't move. She is a dead ogre with red, wet, pippy peepers. Colin sits back on the edge of the bath. He picks up a magazine and tries with difficulty to get the blood from his hands with the glossed paper of the front cover.

'This is a nice little ending, just as it should be. Sundried tomato and a good magazine.'

His voice is full of flat jarring notes. Fizzy and deep. Rebecca coughs a minuscule cough. Colin flicks through the magazine until he settles on a page. He reads it aloud, pink dribble seeping from the corner of his mouth.

'For most people, breast enhancement marks the beginning of a sexier, more confident life. But not for Lianne Buckell, who travelled to Los Angeles to have her A cup transformed to a double D. All had gone smoothly until the flight home, where her boyfriend Gerrard picks up the story. "They were looking brilliant, really American, higher and firmer than most British boob jobs. I just couldn't wait to get my hands on them. But then I woke up suddenly from a kip on the plane to what sounded like an explosion. At first I thought it was terrorism, which is bad enough, but then I saw the blood and the blubber, and I realised that Lianne's tits had exploded over us both."'

Colin stops, suddenly bored, then roughly turns over three or four pages and once again begins to read.

"'I caught my husband in bed with my mother-in-law".' He spits a cherry red gloop on to the bathroom floor. Another page is turned.

"'My boyfriend only wants anal" . . . "Why is he obsessed with tits?" . . . "Him and his rugby buddies took it in turns" . . . "My ten-year-old raped my best friend".' Colin's reading manically. Rebecca is incapable of reacting. 'Wake up, Rebecca! I'm reading at your funeral . . . "My Internet fuck buddy" . . . "Why my dad and I made love".'

Colin stuffs another slab of poisoned panini into his mouth: chorizo. Mozzarella is spilling from his mouth; crumbs suicide from his gob as he barks.

"'Hollywood's golden couple are on the rocks" . . . "Where to find the style queen's look" . . . "The perfect blow job" . . . "What to do when you can't be satisfied" . . . "Make him jealous" . . . "How to tell when you've been betrayed".' Colin glares at Rebecca, then screams: 'What to do when you can't be satisfied!'

On and on. Colin's voice enters Rebecca's ears, it rattles around among the delicate bones and the tubes and blows faintly towards her brain. She pictures the interior of Justin's car, the vanilla newness of it all, the splash-effect upholstery and his pale, steady hands.

33

The Jam Jar

JUSTIN SPEEDS DOWN Princess Parkway with the radio blaring, smash hits seething from his car speakers. I CAN DRIVE A CAR AND I CAN FALL IN LOVE. Does he really listen to that crap? Oh, yes, of course he does. Because from this moment on, life must have a spellbindingly appropriate soundtrack. It's civilisation. It has brought us Lycra skin and polymer eyes. Look pleased.

Justin left the Malmaison under police escort. Some protesters had loitered about waiting for him. A woman waved a jam-jarred foetus into his face and several others pointed, not sure what to say while so close to the beast.

Justin looked at each of the protesters closely. He felt he ought to make the effort to seem interested, to acknowledge their hatred and horror. The jam-jar lady had a long white scar which travelled from her forehead down to where her pink lips curled, then onwards towards a congregation of blemishes on her chin. Justin found it captivating. Like a little history running down her face – one of civilisation's smaller stories. A moment of anger or just a silly accident.

But frankly, the woman seemed a little lost for words. A little embarrassed to be waving a foetus in the face of a young man. When everything is finished, when the sex machines are winning and the foetuses are all in jam jars, then, well, I don't know – the only thing that ever remains is the shame.

But anyway. Justin is in his car, motor raging like a child imitating a car engine. I mean, the motor zooms like a distorted siren. He's going fast, his eyes fixed on the road, his body hunched forward attempting to make the car move more quickly. He jumps a set of red lights and turns left on to Mauldeth Road East. He takes a deep breath; he's a minute from Colin's house. Rebecca. I CAN DRIVE A CAR AND I CAN FALL IN LOVE.

34

Super Slut

BY THE TIME Frank gets to room 16 at the Malmaison, Steve has already left. So Frank orders an enormous braised steak from room service and sits down to await its arrival.

Luckily, I know what all these creatures get up to. I know exactly what happened to Steve. He left the Malmaison via the back door, where he couldn't believe his eyes; he retched at the sight of the protesting crowd, his eyes still red with tears.

'Don't look at me!' he screamed as he threw himself into the front of the crowd, feeling the warmth of the other people heating his face, their placards scraping at his clothes.

'Fashion! Fashion! Fashion!' he squealed as the crowd's gaze hit him like a high-speed train. He thrashed his body wildly and the crowd parted in front of him. Young children screaming 'MURDERER' were steered away from the strangely attired, whirling young man.

It was only when he was finally through the crowd that he realised he'd lost his Stetson. He looked over his shoulder at the swarm of protesters; there was no going back. He dropped to his knees and wretched again on to the pavement, this time coughing up small pieces of moistureless gunk.

'Excuse me there, but are you all right?'

A protester bent down beside him and began patting him curiously on the head. A man with a banner which read 'I STILL BELIEVE IN THE FAMILY'.

'Please don't look at me,' said Steve, refusing to turn his gaze from the pavement and the contents of his stomach. But the man was persistent, as moralists often are.

'But you're OK, are you?'

Steve looked at the man's face, something he hadn't done in weeks. Actually looked at someone. He was about fifty. His eyes were flanked with wrinkled skin, the texture of a scrotum. As he squinted, the mottled layers gathered up, each wrinkled layer on top of the next like a neat pile of dying skin. His eyes were coated with a thin white membrane, like milk spilt on glass. The turquoise of his irises was barely visible.

'I've lost my hat,' said Steve, recalling his delightful Stetson and the happiness it had brought.

'Well, I've lost my sight, young man. Be thankful you can still see.'

A rare euphoria bubbled up beneath Steve's cheeks, and, in what seemed like the most alien motion, he felt them rise. He was suddenly shocked by the sensation of actually smiling. The man offered his hand, Steve took it and felt weightless and superb as he was pulled from the pavement. Looking down, he noticed that the man's dreadful trainers had become spattered with his vomit. He laughed, not maliciously, but as a result of a brief sensation of hilarious despair. The man, too, smiled. The kind of smile you might construct in a world without mirrors or reflection. Toothy and lopsided.

'There we are, son, it'll be all right.'

But the blind man was already alone. Steve was jogging towards a cashpoint, smile intact, ready for the finale.

But, oh, my friend, that was half an hour ago. Thirty minutes in the past. This is now. Ha. Now.

Having drawn out as much money as he possibly can, Steve goes shopping. Going from shop to shop purchasing whatever takes his fancy. He's walking down Market Street with six or seven bags of clothes in each hand. He's taken his flowery shirt off. He's topless. He passes Primark; its entrance gurgles customers. He walks under the glass over-pass that houses the Arndale Food Court. Children stare down, burgers in their mouths, fries for fingers, laughing at the half-naked Steve. He flexes his large chest. His arms tensed by the weight of the shopping.

At the corner of Cross Street he's stopped by a hen party: about fifteen women with yellow hair, orange skin and matching white T-shirts. Each T-shirt has been person-alised with a slogan across the chest in black lettering: 'Blow Job Kate', 'Cock Muncher', 'Becky Big Box', 'Penny Piss Flaps', 'Super Slut'. All the women are laughing. All of them are drunk and having a brilliant time.

'Super Slut' is the first to spot Steve's naked torso. She charges at him and clamps her lips around his nipples, sucking them amid a masterpiece of shrieks and yells. Within seconds, all the girls have gathered round and are stroking at Steve's toned chest and groping at his denim cock.

'Take a photo! Take a photo!' yells Super Slut, bending

down in front of Steve, simulating doggy. Anal. Penny Piss Flaps follows Super Slut's command and produces a camera. She edges back to fit Steve and the girls into shot. Through the lens of the camera, Steve can be seen. Centred. Flexing with all his might, the muscles in his face pulling a rock-hard grin. Around him, the girls strike a variety of poses. Two of them lift up their T-shirts to reveal their tits, then push them together to make an awkward tit-bra. Others simply cup their breasts. Cock Muncher crouches by Steve's groin with her mouth wide open. Fingers in her mouth. Munching at pretend cock.

The camera flashes and all the girls instantly lose interest. Only Super Slut pauses and shares a lingering kiss with Steve. She's struck by the tension in his lips and cheeks. It's like kissing human bones, wrapped in frozen ligament.

'Well . . . thanks for that, mate . . . bye bye . . . haha . . .'

Steve reassembles his bags, his smile still stretched like a tendon across his face. He looks down at his perfect pink nipples, perched and shiny upon tensed pecs. He feels like his entire body is growing by the second, with every moment of tension and smiling he feels larger and larger. Will I even fit through the door at home? he wonders. Carly? Will I even be able to get to her?

The two-legged creatures in the streets are of little concern to Steve now. He allows them to stare at his naked chest, permits them to laugh. He meets them with eyes of the finest silk; tensed skin of the most modern plastic. Because we jittery little time-titterers should never have laid Tarmac or dug foundation. We should never have scraped the sky like dense bastards. And now, perhaps, our grand way of life is being replaced by something else. By nothing perhaps.

Nothing but a bawdy, pitter-pat, pulsy nonsense and a pinchy and pathetic selection of breathing strategies.

But where is the grand annihilation? The loud bang? Why on earth does weather still occur? Surely the clouds have become tired of all this armpit sniffing, combing, styling, killing rubbish. Surely the sun and the moon no longer give a shit.

Steve puts the shopping bags on the pavement. He disentangles the different handles from his fingers, admiring the brands on the bags; the sorts of bags you keep and reuse: Gucci, Prada, Vivienne Westwood. Ha, the trendy primates! He searches through the various bags until he finds what he's looking for: a red silk tie, decorated with pin-thin stripes of black. With his head turned towards the yellow sky, he ties the tie around his head and fluffs his blond hair out of the top. This isn't fashion. This is a sartorial salute to the end of the world and his life. Steve breathes through his clenched teeth. Will I even be able to get to her?

Further down the road, up some stairs and through a couple of doors is Carly. Carly has crawled into the kitchen of Steve's flat to find some food. The cool air of the fridge soothes her frazzled body. The refrigerated breeze brings to mind the outside world. She hasn't thought about outside in ages. Not since she was last there, which was months ago. She suddenly remembers her shopping trips to town. All the money. The trips to Versus and the cold beers in the bars of Deansgate. She's confident she doesn't miss it; outside, I mean. It was shit, she thinks to herself, it was boring.

The area of charcoal skin is expanding. It stretches now between her bellybutton and her knees, and over and between each breast. It crossed her mind a long time ago how much damage she was doing to herself. The shattered coffee table left her with scars that will never fully fade. But what was the point in beauty when it meant missing out on her darling? And, of course, life is simply the pursuit of pleasure, she believes. And she's right; we bend ourselves in leisurely ways.

As she sips water from a glass she only had the strength to half fill, Carly considers weeping. Wondering, for a second, whether Darling is worth the scorched skin and the hair loss. Worth enduring the pain she feels in its absence. She hasn't seen Steve in weeks. Does she owe him an apology? She supposes that she does. Simply for becoming a shadow of her former self.

The thermostat on the fridge cuts out suddenly; a silence floods Carly's ear, annexing her little brain. She coughs to break it and begins scurrying in the direction of the bedroom; tears in her eyes and a babyish cackle rabbiting from her mouth: 'Darling, Darling, Darling.'

Steve heaves his shopping bags the last few steps to the front door. Ice in his eyes. Carly's shrieks in his ears.

'Darling, Darling, Darling.'

He opens the door and swings both arms forward, throwing bag after bag on to the floor in front of him. Carly stops dead, crouched still on the floor. Her mottled grey scalp visible through the lonely strands of her hair.

'Darling, Darling, Darling,' she bleats, edging backwards extremely slowly on all fours, purring air into the room. Steve stands with his legs wide apart and his hands on his hips. The bandanna around his head. Sweat trickling down his back.

'What have you done, Carly?' he says, looking down at her. She appears primed to pounce, like a large, fast cat: a leopard. A starving leopard.

What a cock, Carly's thinking, her dry lips crisping into a grin. A bandanna? He comes to me after so long, topless and with a bandanna? Slowly and with considerable difficulty she rises to her feet. Her body uncreasing into a heavily curved but essentially upright position. Completely naked, the horror of her injuries is clear. Her cotton-thin limbs. Wasted waist. Her pelvis protrudes like antlers from her charred midriff, pointing towards her blackened tits and her haunted face. Tears rest in the crusted rivets of her eyes, forehead steaming like thick lava. A blessed anger and not a drop of shame.

'I was bored, Steve,' she says, in a slow voice of near masculine depth. She's struggling to keep her balance, large blue-cheese veins pulsating in her feet. The lovers observe each other in total stillness. A gloopy tear the consistency of semen drops from Carly's eye. She sniffs and growls, her lips pursed and her back arched in agony. Steve attempts to plot the history of her decay; he examines her loins and tries to excavate their perfection. Carly glances down to where her conspicuous ribs suck into her barren stomach.

'Well, what have *you* done, Steve?' she says, throwing a circular smile in the direction of his bandanna. Steve reflexes his pectoral muscles and fills his lungs with gallons of air. What could he say? Have I collapsed? he thinks, or have I simply gone mad? Or am I a victim of change and dreadful circumstance? He sighs. Can I turn this fucker around and affect the world?

'I've gone out of fashion,' he says, walking towards her as he does so, preparing to hold his burnt lover and bring her close to his chest. 'I've gone out of fashion, my love!' he says again, this time with tears in his eyes and snot choking from his nostrils. As his large hands reach for

Carly's cheeks she drops to the floor; he lunges at the tiny space her face had once occupied.

'Darling, Darling, Darling!'

Carly crawls towards the bedroom with her face close to the carpet, as if sniffing for insects.

'Carly, please.'

Steve follows her in. Carly's on the bed when he arrives, grappling with the Sex Machine, attaching the pads with a revolting energy and reaching for the switch. Steve dives for her body, grabbing her tissue-paper skin. His hands grip her arms but the machine is already on. He feels volts of electricity searing up his arms and into his shoulder blades. Already she's shrieking: an incessant squeak located halfway between life and death. Oh, what to do here? We waddling tragedies; what to do amidst this titillating sham? This absurd life: so day-to-day. What to do here but watch and wank? Yes. Ha. The age of watch and wank. Steve withdraws his hands and pulls the plug from its socket, causing Carly to take a deep breath with a ghostly dry howl.

'I'm out of fashion,' says Steve.

'Turn it back on,' shouts Carly, her fingernails breaking off as she claws at Steve.

'I love you. You're taking me from me . . . me, man!'

Steve kicks off his trainers with their shiny, crystal-studded tongues. He tears off his denim legs and leaps for his love.

'I'm a man,' he shouts.

'Turn on the machine,' she screams.

'Man!'

'Machine!'

Steve grabs the machine, ripping the pads from Carly's body in one victorious tug, causing her to scream. He falls on to her, almost recoiling in disgust at the membraney insubstantiality of her skin. Carly makes a lunge for the floor but her strength is long gone. She feels herself being grabbed by the remains of her hips and pulled into that familiar position. Sex, she recalls, that dead dog of a pastime. That distant age of in and out, back and forth. Pah! That spitty, grovelling land of love. She almost gags as she notices her buttocks being parted and feels Steve's manicured fingers looking for an orifice.

'Darling, help me, Darling,' she cries, but the Sex Machine lies limp and confused in the corner of the room. Steve stares down at Carly's body. He holds his cock in his right hand. Oh, the blighter; the silly instrument. Could I guide it past the sharp mounds of burnt dead skin that spoil her loins? He thinks. Is this what is left? He prods at her with his penis. A prodding penis. A blushing one. Wobbling about in the air around a girl. I can't do it. Steve feels a revolting gurgle in his throat. The distant age of in and out, of back and forth.

Carly's neck is bent crooked, her eyes straining at Darling; the betrayed machine scattered in the corner, forced to watch her with a man. The activities taking place towards the southern boundary of her body seem entirely alien. Like a foreign custom that she fails to understand. Steve has a hot hand on each arse cheek. This seems so strange, so unreasonable really. Where was the development, the exciting change? It's an exhausted lifestyle. The feeling of human skin on human skin has all of a sudden lost its aura. Its attraction. To Carly, it seems like the most unnatural sensation.

Steve continues to watch his cock. Awaiting its decision. Carly listens to his whimpering; a bedraggled smirk drifts over her face. She pictures her womb, something she's never done before, the sorry organism slumped among the other stuff. Bladder, bowels, lungs and kidneys. What a strange little hostel to be carrying around. It suddenly seems so out of date. The kind of bizarre appendage that evolution ought to have forgotten about. A stupid container of no use to her. Because time is simply not our element. We inhabit something more akin to forgetting. A sort of gloopy forget-fulness, where sex is a niggling memory and reproduction its perverse effect.

Steve holds Carly in place. A cock full of blood. A big body. A mood bulb brain.

'Man meat, eh? I could do you. I'm a sex god,' he shouts. 'In bed, I'm really brilliant.'

'Mach . . . ine,' says Carly though gritted teeth.

'I could take you to heaven, baby. I'm a guy. I could take you to heaven.'

Steve grabs Carly's hair, tugging at a clump till it tears from her scalp and she yelps in horror. He grabs her tiny waist. She's so light he can almost suspend her in mid-air. He traces the dotted bones of her spinal column down from her neck. We are growing thin. Us lot, we're pretty dirty. Life is unsatisfactory. My poor little penis, thinks Steve. It never knew. He brings his head to rest on Carly's charred back. A tail bone pressed into the socket of an eye. We could have made love into the small hours. We could have fallen side by side and exhaled through smiles. Steve weeps. Another world finishes to the sound of its inhabitants hissing.

Steve feels a heaving weight of semi-digested matter battling up the pipes in his neck, too dry and large to surface. He gags, struggling to breathe. Carly takes her chance and falls from the bed and scuttles over to the machine. Steve's at his knees on the bed, Carly's struck by some strangely unnatural red blotches on his arse. How does nature find the will to decorate us in deformities? Who would have the patience? She holds one of the Sex Machine's pads to her black breast, an explosion of what looks like sympathy occurs, deep in the technologies of her eyes. And then she sings.

'Oh my darling, oh my darling, oh my darling, Clementine.'

A smile bubbles to the surface of Steve's face. It's a nice surprise. He pushes it to its extremes by stretching his grinning mouth and raising his cheeks as high as they will go. Carly continues to sing.

'You are lost and gone for ever, dreadful sorry, Clementine . . .'

Steve turns his head to see Carly softly serenading the Sex Machine, her head tilted, stroking it gently with her knuckly hands. Her vocal is broken but pure and from the heart.

'You are lost and gone for ever . . .'

Steve's features drift to rest, pulling the kind of face a hermit might pull; a face unfamiliar with the world of expressions. He gets down from the bed, his penis shrivelled to a fist, bloody and mangled from the fight.

Carly doesn't even glance at him as he walks past her out of the door to the living area. She continues to sing gentle lullabies to her machine. But the machine – does it wink at Steve as he leaves? No, no of course it doesn't. How could it?

Limping into the living room, how wonderful. Steve stares at his flat. How funny. An amusing shelter. The empty space of the flat reminds him of Frank, the large bastard who so often filled it with his excessive proportions. He thinks of Justin, too. His easy manner, how the three of them will soon be so rich. How they've pimped the Sex Machine for millions.

He goes to the sink and runs the cold tap on full tilt. Running water always seemed the most blissful example of civilisation. The intricate system of underground pipes and pistons, it makes him want to laugh out loud when he compares the project to his own current state. The weeks he's spent buying. The blind man. The efforts he's gone to to avoid the gaze of others.

His nude body seems a cosy arrangement of traditions, jokes and sporting references. His shapely thighs, firm feet, rounded pectorals. What a joke. And the people in the streets; the hen parties and the protesters. It's best that their mysterious motives and thoughts remain just that – a mystery. Parliaments and markets; proud fake ideas. Pop concerts, peace rallies, carnivals, birthdays, fetes. Public transport and the bombs that are detonated on it. It's all so curious. So incredibly curious. The actions of a minority, in whose bodies energy inexplicably remains.

Steve can still make out the sound of Carly's singing voice seeping through the walls. So strange of her to sing, especially such an old song. He can't help but imagine those fascinatingly crusty sections of her brain. The parts he'd never known where she must have stored all this gentle sentimentality. The nineteenth century, the twentieth, the past; so cute.

He turns off the tap and moves over to the pile of shopping bags by the door. He kicks half-heartedly at one of the bags. Isn't football wonderful? he thinks. The way they rip down the wings, cross, score, celebrate and rue with such sincerity. Yes, it's truly wonderful. But reality's ice must always thaw, so Steve moves towards the cutlery drawer. From which he removes a knife.

Looking back, Steve assumes that deep down all he ever wanted was money. If you hold your breath and dive under rocky pretence and swim over the brittle coral of honour, well, all you ever find is the barnacled shell of cash, and in it the pearl of guilt; shame. The large compromise that loving Carly represented was little more than an odorous truth. As I said so long ago, Steve doesn't know anyone who can resist someone who is as fit as fuck. Was it that? I don't recall.

He takes the knife and sits with it among the shopping. Carly's singing has stopped. He imagines life as the Sex Machine and there is a brief flare of joy right at the back of his head. The lucky fucker. Nothing but a selection of straps and electrical pads to contend with. And just one purpose. It's surely the rainbow of responsibilities contained in life that makes it such a game. Think, dress, eat, be nice, love, earn. What a creature of idealism the human is. Make me a Sex Machine, thinks Steve. Forget society and make me a Sex Machine. Then I'll show you the meaning of fun.

Steve places the tip of the knife just under where his perfect jaw curves and heads up towards the childishly smooth skin around his ear. He pierces easily. He's amazed at the self-control he retains. He's able to cut a misplaced red smile across his neck while maintaining full conscious-ness. He feels the blade strike the corresponding bone on the other side of his face. Success. The blood flows and warms his chest.

'I'm out of fashion,' he murmurs, as the blood dribbles down his sides and is absorbed by the shopping bags around him. The up-to-the-minute designs soak up the rich brown muck.

As he bobs hopelessly on the surface of life, spurting blood pulling him down, he hears the sound of Carly screaming; a shriek of Darling, Darling. He reaches out and delves into the bags around him. He feels the fresh fabric. The distressed denims. The silks. The satins. The old skins; spilling on to them his blood.

'I'm out of fashion,' he whispers, bobbing on the surface of life. He sinks perhaps, dies, of course. Is pulled down, or up; whatever.

35

Computer Game Hell

SMILE. THERE ARE things to live for. We'll list them together later. For now, there's one last end. Back to the bathroom. Everything important happens in bathrooms.

It was the unexpected desire to vomit up each of his vital organs that made Colin a little nervous. Now he's on his hands and knees, back looping and arching, tongue dangling above Rebecca's corpse, hacking and hacking. His Adam's apple is lurching up and down his neck. He suspects he's sweating his brain out through the pores of his forehead, that's why his thoughts are losing clarity and he's so nervous. He'd barely come to terms with the fact he'd murdered a mother and her unborn child, when he himself began to die. It seemed an unlikely coincidence.

But Rebecca isn't dead. She's listening to Colin's strange sounds in some quiet corner of her consciousness. It feels as if the pain and the blood loss have reduced her to a small individual who inhabits the innocuous nooks and crannies of her body. Gone for her are the days of living in her head. She's convinced her consciousness and thoughts exist only in her kneecap, or her armpit perhaps. It's hard to tell. It's a fitting form for humanity to take, she thinks. We should never have been so big. We should never have used our heads. As her heartbeat becomes faint, she can still hear the strange groans and drillings of Colin's body. The sound of the rat poison taking control.

She's been pretending to be dead for so long she's anxious she might have indeed died. Certainly, she presumes her child is dead. She must. But her eyes won't cry, weighted as they are with exquisitely fresh and sundried tomato. When you think about it – which she does – life's a funny business. It is, isn't it? Particularly when you think about it while dying on a bathroom floor. Pretending to be dead and listening carefully to the slow death of a young man you've poisoned. Yes, life is brilliant and simple.

With an awful groan reminiscent of a birthing cow, Colin's head falls into Rebecca's stomach and the sounds and smells of him shitting himself drift through his legs towards the two young people. With his head still buried in Rebecca's stomach, Colin breathes a deep breath, then he throws up over the girl and over the floor. Little bits of Italian-style bread. Mauled chorizo. Styled and treated meats. Blood-red mozzarella. It's then that Colin notices the rat poison. The small turquoise pellets among the regurgitated food. Moments later he notices Rebecca's heartbeat.

. . . dudum . . . dudum . . . dudum . . . just a slight pulse – she's still alive. Before Colin can react he's dragged off into another disgusting cycle of shitting and vomiting. It's colourful: red from his arse and turquoise from his lips.

Downstairs, through the door and down the street, Justin turns the steering wheel of his Peugeot. Justin, finally. He pulls up outside Colin's house and gets out of his car. He skips neatly around the bonnet and strides heroically to the front door, which he kicks down. He lets out a small blurt of laughter as the door swings open ahead of him. It was only on the latch. His leg bones jolted as the door opened with unexpected ease. He sniggers again, feeling embarrassed; a slight shame.

'Colin!' he shouts, stepping into the hall and looking up the steep stairs which begin almost as soon as you enter the house. 'Colin!' he shouts again, forcing anger into his voice. He feels strangely guilty about breaking down the door and trespassing. He steps to his right and glances into the living room; a foul brown three-piece on a thin brown carpet. On the far side of the room on the mantelpiece, Justin recognises the bright blue of a used and positive pregnancy test. He chuckles at the sight of it, covering his mouth with a sideways palm. Who keeps piss-stained paper on their mantelpiece? 'Colin!' he screams, turning again to the staircase, his voice containing a slight smirk.

Sensing that the element of surprise is already lost on account of the giggling and the shouting, Justin runs up the stairs. He reaches the top, where again his confidence fails and a smile appears on his lips, keen to graduate to a laugh.

He's never been to Colin's house. It's disgusting. He thinks back to the Malmaison, to the jam-jarred foetus and the woman's scar: one of civilisation's smaller stories. What am I? he thinks. A twat, presumably. Another smaller story.

The experiment wasn't meant to include episodes like this. Where are the cheering Africans? The liberated call-centre staff? The keys to the city? I've made no one happy, Justin confirms, wiping yet another smile off his face.

It's nerves, naturally. He's only nervous. I'm not a hero, he thinks, I'm to blame. He recalls meeting Rebecca in the Nude Factory. There must have been a simpler way. We could have holidayed together. She could have chained me to the bed. We might have laughed. Been happy.

He composes himself and reaches for the fake porcelain doorknob on the bathroom door. He turns it and the latch gives with a click. He steps cautiously into the bathroom. More embarrassment: Colin's shit himself and it absolutely stinks. But then, Jesus, the blood. Justin watches as Colin squirms on top of Rebecca; his throat gurgling like a plughole.

Justin catches his reflection in the mirror above the sink. Staring into his own eyes, he identifies something he believes to be himself. A glint. A memory pool. But this self exists only in his eyes. He doesn't recognise his body at all; neither the head that surrounds his eyes nor the torso on which his head is perched. He feels he couldn't possibly manoeuvre his shoulders or his arms; he feels completely paralysed. He's distracted by a long and sudden burp from Colin. Justin's gaze lowers: all this bloodshed, all of it just for sex.

Colin crawls to Justin's feet. His head lifts up with a disturbing jolt, as if only flaps of skin are keeping it on his shoulders. He tries to speak but succeeds only in spewing a green gloop at Justin's feet.

Justin is motionless. He's waiting patiently for anger and shock to make him move. Where is my rage? he thinks. He aids the process by staring at the blood, the unnatural curves of Rebecca's body. The coffees sit unsipped on the side of the bath. He wants to laugh out loud.

'Well, it's gone too far,' says Justin, immediately shocked by the uselessness of his words, as if they hadn't come from his brain but had been lodged between his teeth and had suddenly come loose and fallen from his mouth.

'Help,' barks Colin, his gob a gaping blue, the entrance to a cold computer game hell. Justin notices Rebecca's eyelids flicker, forcing a sundried tomato to fall on to the floor. But he can't look at her. This is cowardice, he thinks, his life fucked up all over his face and shaven crown. He sits on the bath and picks up a magazine.

'I could do with some advice, you know, guys? I could do with writing off for some wisdom, you know? Guys?' says Justin, flicking through magazines as the guys die beneath him. He executes an enormous yawn, so big it almost sends him tumbling back into the bathtub. After completing the yawn with a rather camp cooing sound, he nonchalantly takes Colin by the hair and carefully brings his face smashing into a radiator. There, he thinks, a bit of anger, at last. There is a dull flesh-on-metal thud. A tingling sound reverberates around the acoustics of the radiator. Then pushing Colin's body to one side, Justin kneels over Rebecca and kindly removes the remaining tomato from her eye.

'Rebecca, wake up.'

'Justin?'

'Yeah, it's me.'

Justin stares at Rebecca's stomach. My child? he thinks. I'm some sort of dad. There are tears in his eyes but they were put there by his yawn. He takes Rebecca by the shoulders and turns her on to her side. She splutters approval.

Nature, thinks Justin, it gets you in the end. We thrash about like plastic fantastics, talking of romance and success. But nature gets you in the end. It arrives late at the house party with its two able wingmen, death and birth. Before you can strike a pose they have taken over. Death is on the decks, spinning records like a pro. Birth is on the dance floor, showing up our sorry moves. Nature is in the corner, chatting up your love, winning them completely. Justin can't think what to do. Nature has won. Against all odds. He looks at Rebecca. He wants to nurse her wounds with a warm sponge. Is this my fate?

He can't stop yawning. He has to turn away from Rebecca to unleash one of the windiest yawns he's ever done in the direction of Colin, whose nose is scattered all over his face like bird seed. Tired of pretending to be dead, Rebecca returns to the same spluttering sort of life she'd been leading an hour or so ago. She fires up her traction engine lungs in an attempt to prevent Justin from nodding off.

'Justin . . . Come on.'

Justin shakes his head vigorously from side to side then stretches his eyes open. He expels a large lungful of air and with it the same cooing sound we heard a few moments ago.

'I'm sorry, Rebecca. It's me, isn't it?'

'Yes,' says Rebecca, her words brittle. 'You're the idiot.'

Justin nods. Rebecca puts a hand on his knee. He can't feel any squeezing although her hand is clearly straining. He looks again at her uneven stomach. She never aborted my child, he recalls. It was all complete bullshit.

'It's funny, isn't it?' says Justin.

'What is?'

'The way things work out.'

'It's hilarious,' says Rebecca. 'Were you going to call an ambulance or . . . or would you like me to do it?'

Rebecca's voice sounds barely human. That is to say, too human. She's in danger of dying of anger. What is Justin doing? With every wave of rage she's sure that the blood accelerates from her cuts and that her bruises darken.

'Save me,' she croaks.

'I am saving you.'

'This is real life!'

Rebecca splutters and recoils deep into her consciousness, once again taking up residence in her kneecap or her elbow joint. Somewhere small. She barely notices as Justin lifts her head into his lap and begins to tuck the loose strands of her hair behind her ears.

Justin's thoughts are wordless as he massages her scalp. He drifts through his past. Its principle characters turn on him then freeze. Noises leap from mouths but desist just short of making sense. Episodes merge. His mother sits at the table in the restaurant, strippers faking it beyond her shoulder, celebrities falling to bits. He sighs. All of it just for sex.

It's minutes later when Rebecca feels her head being gently lowered to the floor and hears Justin dialling nine three times into his mobile phone. Her eyes open in time to see him place his hand over the receiver and stare at her with a beaten gaze.

'I don't want a girlfriend, Rebecca,' he says, his lips exaggerating the shapes of the words. He grins. 'And I do realise this is real life. Yes . . . this is real life.'

Epilogue

YOU NEED TO know my name. That's what they've told me. And, like all prisoners, I have a grudging grasp of obedience. It seems that however much time passes, our species still gets wet at the prospect of revelation and truth. So yes, they've told me to write about myself. Me. Really me. I smirked at the idea. But Governor Gordon has had it with my story. Susan, too. It's a screw-up. Truly. It's a screw-up. And existence, it seems, boils down to little more than a selection of pronouns: my story wasn't *for you* or *about them*. It was about *me*. How disappointing.

I am called Theo. A stupid name, I'm sure you'll agree. To me it sounds like a process. A verb. To Theo. A word to describe a quick and hysterical slip into total despair. When I was younger, they used to take me out of here on day trips. I used to go to schools to see how I behaved around children my own age. I didn't do well. They suffered, the little girls and boys. Don't, Theo. Don't.

Other than that I've been here all my life. Writing silly made-up stories for Susan and for Gordon. Finally,

I discovered the truth thanks to the Evernet database. I served it to them sour, in chapters. Now the two of them are trapped and angry. They've requested I tell you about myself. Relax. I have very little to say.

The date. I know how society feels about dates – you're obsessed. I almost certainly can't share your enthusiasm for years or specific days. I've spent so much of my life in a kind of dateless sea. I've been aware of some form of duration but never really found myself in the wash of time itself. Only in recent years have I begun to understand the full significance of dates. Jesus, 1945: that's a big 'un, I've gathered that. 1789: woo hoo. 2001: it must have been extremely exciting.

It's not the same for me. Time, I mean. I recall having been alive in the past; certain lights and the odd feeling. But realistically, I remember bugger all. Just the odd sensation that I touchingly allow to masquerade as memory. Agewise, I reckon I'm twenty-odd. Yeh. I'm a jolly young twenty-something looking forward to the future.

I need to tell you more about my research on Evernet. To those who watch my text this will seem superfluous, no doubt. But to me it matters; the research counts. You see, my most recent story isn't the same as the other grotesques I've submitted previously. Though no doubt Susan and Gordon see it as consistent with my earlier writing. I maintain that it is a history; a real life, of sorts.

Around six months ago (forgive me, I'm hopeless at estimating passing time) I began researching my personal background on the Evernet system. What I was looking for was some evidence of me having been born. I had learned very late about the concept of reproduction and human evolution – it came as quite a shock. Throughout

my life I've been continually bewildered by my own existence. I've always felt originless, as if my body had burst
suddenly out of nothing. The notion of civilisation was kept
from me. For many years I assumed existence to be little
more than a selection of toings and froings, carried out in
brightly lit rooms.

Slowly, through an untrustworthy mixture of rumour
and fact, the full extent of mankind's project became known
to me. In theory, none of us 'real lifers' were expected to
know the principles of reproduction, for our own safety.
But these things have a way of becoming known, even in a
place like this. In fact, this is an important point: the present
Authority really is a bumbling misery of posturing. Little
more. It's wonderfully inefficient. Many people see the
Authority as extremely repressive – but I must confess, I've
never found it so. I remember meeting a drunken warden
on a late night trip to the lavatory. I must have been pretty
young. He described, in slurred English, a distressing sexual
disease he'd contracted from his mistress; the poor man
was beside himself. It was through such encounters that I
began to understand more about gender and reproduction.
I now know that on the outside world infidelity is an impris-
onable offence. Alcoholism, too. I've learnt a little about
power and repression as well, thanks to my research. I know
they're both practical jokes; both always the same.

There was no record of my birth on Evernet. I was able
to learn that I didn't possess any form of citizenship. I
wasn't melancholy, I had no idea what it was. But I had an
increasingly heated belief in my own innocence. I realise
now that this is a very old-fashioned conviction. But it was
strong, nonetheless. My slow life had culminated in a
quaint desire to know where I'd come from. The guilt that

I'd lived with so comfortably for so long had suddenly become alien.

Eventually (a silly word to describe hours spent trawling Evernet) I located my prison file. It wasn't especially difficult to find; the computer wasn't intended for patients and, as I say, this so-called 'repressive' Authority has always struck me as rather casual. I shan't forget that moment, suddenly seeing my name on the screen. Theo: the embarrassed squirm at seeing it in print.

I learnt that my mother's name was Rebecca and that my father's name was Justin. I instantly liked the names, probably just because of my own self-loathing. They struck me as clean, healthy names.

I had hoped for a sudden pang in what Susan calls my 'soul' when I discovered my parents' names. But what I felt was a sudden cramping in my bowels. Besides the names of my parents, I learnt a little more about my beginnings. I was born in the city of Manchester and was placed, almost immediately, in an institution. My mother, Rebecca, appears to have died in childbirth. It was this last piece of information that dropped a pinch of what I know to be sadness into my brain. Of course, I didn't miss her or even have an enormous desire to have known her, but it felt a little awkward that she'd died giving birth to me. I admit to feeling guilty and a little embarrassed that, in death, she had spawned such uselessness.

My file contained written accounts of my behaviour on the various trial excursions I'd been taken on as a child. I didn't recognise the events they described; I have no memory of the excursions to the outside world. The reports made terribly severe accusations of my state of mind. They cast me as a troublemaker, spoke of nascent sexual urges that could only cause trouble. This struck me as laughable. Sure, I caused some stirs in my youth after a snort or two of dog dirt, but that powder made fools of us all. I didn't even know what a sexual urge was. But they're idiots, this Authority. I know that now. The system stinks.

I learnt that I'd been placed on 'Creative Therapy' when I was seven years old and that I've been writing stories for fifteen years in total. The comments on my stories were unrelentingly damning. Even at an early age I'd apparently produced 'unstable' stories, crammed with enough immorality and baseless violence to make my release unsanctionable. The comments you made hurt me, Susan. I'd always hoped you might have understood. I enjoyed the writing, did it with honesty and conviction. I hope that you experience some regret.

The most significant part of my file was right at the bottom, in a section titled 'Risk Assessment'. There I found just four words: 'Original Deviancy. (High Risk)'. It was these words, the allusive significance of them, that really stoked the fire in my belly. I remember walking back to my cell with the four of them rattling round my skull. I couldn't sleep. I just lay awake trying to fit things together: Original Deviancy, my mother Rebecca, the scraps of knowledge I possessed about sex and the Authority.

Those were muddled times. I confess that it was then that I grew weak: I surrendered to the dark shuffle. Oh, it hurts to admit it, especially to you, Susan. But yes, it was the only solution to my sleeping problems. I would masturbate over and over again till I was exhausted and couldn't think but just sleep, finally.

With every session on Evernet, I felt different; more complicated and prone to daydreams. I devoured the world

I found on Evernet. I read the magazines, viewed the TV programmes, the websites, the recipe books, the films, I became a right little shit. Serious. I was well fucked-up. No doubt.

Truth is. I'm all right.

But I knew what a woman was, finally. I knew what you were, Susan, at last. Because I found nudes on Evernet. I couldn't believe my luck. The nude sites were usually medical in origin; the only places you could legally display the female body in all its glory. I bit into those bodies with my brain. I tore off their limbs with my teeth and put fists down their throats. Those sterile specimens were quite enough for me. Enough to send my imagination trembling into the shadows. When I happened upon a turn-of-the-century pornography site, I couldn't believe my luck. It was, I think, the last of its kind. The last remnant of the civilisation of porn. I was over-joyed. With a computer's assistance, I became sexual, or rather, horny.

I found the concept of 'Original Deviancy' easy to trace. It referred to a sort of commotion that surrounded my birth, as well as to the widespread use of a sex machine, about which I was able to discover more. The White Love 1000. My first response was one of amusement; the notion of a sex machine was completely at odds with my basic grasp of reproduction and sex. I couldn't begin to imagine the purpose behind such a contraption. In my isolation, I felt far superior to a machine. My late-night flights of fancy took me to some grave situations. I'm sorry to say I've contorted you on more than one occasion, Susan. I have placed you in situations that would make you shriek. I have shut my eyes and conducted my experiments upon your flesh.

As my research continued, I was able to piece together a fairly clear picture of the context into which I was born. I learnt about 'unseen lives', 'recreational abortion', the old Internet site 'newsex.biz'. These were revelations to me. I got a strong impression of civilisation as a stuttering little creature. A kind of disorientated dwarf, chasing itself without exhaustion. A little runt, collecting things then misplacing them altogether. This was a surprise. Whatever I had imagined took place in the outside world was clearly wide of the mark. I had always seen society as a tremendously ordered and transparent affair – I was shocked to the core by its grim secrets, its neediness.

So I became a historian. I began tirelessly researching the world I had almost known. I would have liked to have gone farther back and learnt more about the twentieth-century wars, but with the rise of this petty Authority so much was repressed: history, the Internet, almost all the blessed porno. I am, how did they put it? Absolutely gutted.

The current Authority governs under the name 'Future Love'. Its roots lie in the Antiporn movement and in the public horror provoked by 'unseen lives' and 'sex deaths'. I realise now that they keep the information on Evernet as a warning, as an example of the vile affairs that Future Love replaced. Why else would so much information on turn-of-the-century society exist? It's virtually all you can find on the Evernet system: documents relating to that civilisation and its people. They left so much information behind, stacks of it. The fashions, the media, the maps, the curricula, restaurant menus, sporting statistics, government documents, the endless blogs. I pored over everything. I'm fascinated by that period. Desperate to consume its colours and its freakish nosedives.

And my dear parents, such icons of that lost world, sometimes I feel so incredibly proud of them. Of myself, too; a real pride. You see, I feature as a kind of martyr in some of the founding texts of Future Love. I am the poor child that narrowly survived the reckless and sick attempts on his life. But sadly, they tell lies about my later life. They say that I work for the Authority and that I live with a wife and children in a place called Wolverhampton. But I suppose I'm cheerful anyway, simply to be associated with that strange old world.

I think about my father most of all. Justin was arrested shortly after my mother's death and put on trial. There was enormous press coverage. I've seen so many pictures of him being bundled into cars or booed by large crowds of Antiporn protesters. He's a real hero. And innocent, too. He'd done nothing wrong and he got let off. He'd never have got off nowadays, they'd have thrown him in here for just a whiff of sexual misdemeanour. But the government was keen to make it clear he'd done little wrong. I admire his innocence. Although, at times, I wish they'd found him guilty and that he'd become a real cornerstone of all this Future Love idiocy. But it wasn't to be. That honour was given to Colin.

My bowels are cramping again, I think it's this chair, this dreadful hard pine. I'm sure they'll be turning my light off soon. They do it without warning but I've developed a strange ability to predict when it will happen. I'll be typing away when, suddenly, I'll get a weird, vulnerable feeling. I'll stop and look up. Then be buried in pitch black.

In any case, I've said too much. These kind of bumbling descriptions won't win your approval, will they, Susan? But perhaps you understand me now? Ha, that's a joke. But maybe you get it, that I'm making a stand? That sounds funny – making a stand. Like some old-fashioned rebel. But my story is the truth, near enough at least. That should be in my favour. Let me out of here, I'm ready, let me out!

Wait – I feel vulnerable, here it comes, then –

This morning, I returned from the lavatory to find Susan leaning on my desk, flicking through some notes I've been making. She isn't pleased with me. Her forehead was lightly coated in a small frown, her eyes were desperately trying to appear piercing. So I smiled, and apologised for the naughty things I've been saying about her lately. And yes, as you can imagine, it was a little awkward. She stood in a variety of absurd postures, attempting, in vain, to hide the precise geography of her body from me. But, Susan, honestly, it needn't have been so tense. You could have relaxed, laughed perhaps. We could have reclined on my thin bed together. We could have smooched and giggled about these stupid lives we're leading.

Susan tells me that Gordon certainly won't release me. No shit, I remarked. Then I told her that my face wasn't listening. Old world slang. Whatever else I might be, nowadays I'm so cool.

I'm the son of gods. I should never have been allowed to find out. If you let me out now, I'll just start blurting my mouth off wherever I can, and, if your hilarious logic is to be followed, then I'd probably start raping women. No, I confess, I have no hope of release.

Susan wants me to write about my innermost feelings. The mistake she makes is glaring. I don't have any innermost feelings. For twenty years I wandered contentedly between the rooms of this bright hell, unaware as to the precise nature of my suffering. Yes, at times, I grew strangely weary, but I shrugged it off, not knowing how to comprehend what I now recognise as melancholy.

My mind is rooted firmly in my origins, my eyes averted from the future and fixed on my past. A past I know only through the medium of a computer screen. But there seems to me to be an honour in completion, in finishing the story that I suspect will be my last. I was fond of my characters, of Carly and Steve, Johnny, Colin and the others, my parents. I'm nervous to ask, but did you like it? The story, I mean. No, actually, stop, don't answer that.

I'll finish. Some truth at last. Jesus, I'm biting my lip so hard it's bleeding.

According to the testimony of the paramedics, Justin was loitering outside when the ambulance arrived at the house in Withington. Apparently he seemed nervous, jumpy, pacing the pavement as if he might flee at any moment. But he went with the paramedics to the bathroom. Crucially, for the spiny whiners who cheese out judgements on people's characters, Justin offered no help to the medics. He was asked to identify the young man who was barking blood from his arse and the dying fish of a girl, who was flinching around in her own guts. But Justin just shook his head. He claimed not to know either of them. And, instead of helping with the body lifting, he just turned and walked away.

Dear, dear Father, don't think I begrudge you this decision. But I do wonder where you went. I like to think you went to a pub, to a quiet and old-fashioned affair off the beaten path. I picture you sitting at the bar on a high stool, leaning on to polished mahogany, chatting idly to the elderly punters. And then, of course, you drink too much. So much so, Justin, that you violently resist the landlord's attempts to get you out at closing time. I picture you spilling on to the streets with tears in your eyes, just because you're drunk and not because you care.

But at his trial, Justin had no idea why he'd not identi-fied either victim or where he'd gone to after he left the house. He stood in the dock with a face that was devoid of emotion. I like to imagine the skin of his face growing quickly and enveloping his eyes, creeping over the angles of his nose and sealing his mouth. I like to imagine him with no features whatsoever, completely illegible, just a thick slab of skin stretched across his face.

Colin survived the attempt made on his life by Rebecca. It seems she overestimated the strength of the rat poison. It harmed him, of course, but because he had vomited up so much of it at an early stage, doctors were able to bring him round. If my mother was the martyr and my father the fool, then Colin was the Devil in the eyes of the public. Once he was fit enough to face charges the legal and media establishments really went to work on him. Austere black and white prints of his face were featured on the front page of all the major newspapers. For a man whose only real crime was two counts of attempted murder (I count myself, though the courts didn't), he faced an extreme amount of national hate.

After the disappointment of Justin as a hate figure, with Colin they really felt they'd found what they'd been looking for. An icon around whom they could organise, repent and end their wicked ways.

These were the origins of Future Love, the laughing bundle of sexual repression that waltzes law through parliament as I write. Antiporn provided its fanatics, but Colin's story brought support from across the nation. People who read of his playful desire to kill the unborn were appalled. Liberals winced then smirked, amazed that the erotic apparatus they'd invited people to lose themselves in was finally being rejected. But I suppose I'll never know the whole truth. I offer you only my skinny little theories, so be gentle with them. Maybe things just fall into place or get out of hand. The twitching casualty of history rolls on to its back, creating a progress of sorts.

From what I've seen, it's laughable that anyone ever tries to make sense of anything in the outside world. There's always some smirking alternative making fun of your theories. A minxy demon holding a mirror to your self and your thoughts, showing them to mean nothing at all.

So as Antiporn and Future Love held hands and attempted to swoop over all the two-legged totterers of England, the number of recreational abortions soared. It's true. As millions opposed it, millions couldn't resist trying it. There's too many of you, that's your problem. That and your appalling self-delusions. You can't agree on anything.

I've read so many accounts of dumpy young couples from Dorset spicing up their stewed love with acts of destruction, by aborting the sloppy mess of life they'd humped into being. The age of the tit-bra had ended. Sex had escaped from the magazine racks and made for the abortion clinics. Pregnancy and abortion became fashion. Became fun. Money was made. Bodies ruined. I suppose it had to be stopped.

Colin, I guess, still resides in the wing adjacent to my own. I think of him from time to time. I wonder if he's on creative therapy, too. I have been unable to trace his file on Evernet. His, more so than any other, had to remain secret, I suppose. But I'd love to read his stories. I'm rather jealous of the quality of filth he must surely possess. Or perhaps he's sick of his poisoned instincts and scrapes together tales of innocence from the dry rotted basement of his brain. Yes, I can imagine that. Tales of picnics and parlour games. I'll never know.

I was unable to find any record of Justin's activity; his trail fades shortly after he was found innocent. Rumour takes him to Moscow where I've heard it's very cold. I hope this is true. I like to picture my father surrounded by snow and wrapped in long jackets of thick tweed. He'd be OK in a land of ice.

The funny story is Johnny's. Ah, Johnny, you thought I'd forgotten about him, didn't you? Johnny Simkins, whose handwritten diary of sexual turmoil is easily located on Evernet, becomes the redeemed hero of this tittle-tattle Authority. He resurfaces at a General Election. He's elected in Rochdale East and becomes part of Future Love's inaugural government: Minister for Sport. He was eager to publicise his troubled origins, made a real show of the perversity of his youth: the prostitutes and the phone sex. This approach was seen as fresh politics, or so it seems. The Future Love party loved him for his gaping soul. Can you believe that? Perhaps not. Too farfetched? Oh, but do believe, it's healthy and, of course, it's true. Good old truth. Johnny was a friend of Rebecca's. He seemed to have loved her very much. Rebecca was never a stripper, though. I don't know where she met Justin either. Forgive me for all the lies.

Oh, finish this, you fool. The lower lids of my eyes are quivering. They do this when I feel a sense of loss. My bed

333

is luring me. I'm getting that feeling, that hunger for the dark shuffle. But you don't need to know that. I know what you need to know. 'From the heart, Theo, from the heart.' I'll save that for the morning. I'll save the story of Sex Death, too. That's a tale for tomorrow. I need to get under those sheets, clear my throat of this nagging desire. Turn the lights out, you perverts, turn out the lights.

People wanted to defend Western sex against the frigids from the East. Am I right? Susan? As if you'd know, your brain is flatbread. But anyway, allow me to theorise. The baby-killing recalled in people their worst fear, that, deep down, we are a disobedient flock in whose minds sex whizzes so freely we must certainly be destined for a dimly lit and erotic annihilation. In contrast, the White Love 1000 was a timely reminder to Western society of its achievements.

Back then, people enjoyed lifestyle. Enjoyed lattes, bruschetta, holidays and cash. They enjoyed preparing personalities and then releasing these gassy concoctions publicly and seeing how they reacted with those of others. So it was that the windows of pubs, cafés and restaurants were forever steamed up with love, hate, hobbies and quirks. Whether babies were being killed for fun or not, many people were reluctant to give up on all the identity, catch-phrases and anecdotes that freedom's rule had given them. And the White Love 1000 seemed the perfect answer to all the abortions. For some, at least, it seemed controlled, clean and somehow moral. Sex was already taking a beating from sections of Islam. All the extremism. The bombing, beardy bullshit. As worrying as recreational abortion was, many still hoped to save complex sex and lifestyle for themselves.

So journalists began representing the White Love 1000 as an icon of our great culture. A talisman around which to reorganise and move on. A way of showing just how liberated and daring the way of the West was. Sex as a perfectly blissful piece of machinery and economy. In an effort to goad the fanatics and break Britain's swelling waves of conservatism, the machine was offered as a piece of cultural artillery. It was closely attached to female freedom, to male tolerance, to a kind of time-cranking perfection of life.

I wish I could be more clear. I wish I could draw neater lines from A to B, from year to year. Although perhaps my point is a simple one and concerns the general disarray that people inhabit. Perhaps this is the conclusion to my studies: that there is too much to and fro in the world of events and trends, too much criss-crossing and contradiction. So it is that dead foetuses share the front page with adverts for fuck machines. My point is simple and concerns the end of the world: you won't see it coming. It will be extremely untidy. It will be unclear. Because of humans and their collective indecision.

Frank Jacobs, who did exist but to my knowledge never met my parents, his meeting Justin is another lie, was delighted. As expected, the sales of the White Love 1000 were great indeed. All his projected profits had to be torn up when it became clear that men were buying the machine, as well as women. Yes, men were quick to fasten its pleasure pads to their anuses, nipples and, eventually and mistakenly, to the tips of their inquisitive dicks. It helped that the product was so brilliantly domestic. We're talking about a time of war after all, when people were scared. The White Love 1000 seemed to commentators to be the ideal form of freedom and fun for those times. The solution to a boring blitz mentality that was widespread. A way of maintaining the tradition of dizzying fun while people trembled and awaited the loud bang.

But, of course, I wouldn't be here now if this hilarious emancipation had taken place. If we'd won the war of conflicting funs. That, Susan, is why this story is important to me. Why I fret and moan when you tell me to write from the heart and that you know all this. Just marry me, Susan, untie your hair and strip off. Get me out of here and marry me. Ha. Oh, just let me continue, there's an honour in it and blah blah blah . . .

It's true that a girl named Carly Keen was the first registered Sex Death. They found her because of the smell: a nostril-stripping stench of burnt skin, sour blood and rotting insides. The neighbours were bound to complain. It's also true that they found Carly's lover suicided in the living room, naked and surrounded by shopping bags. But I've been unable to find out why or what his story was.

The medical establishment had seen the fatalities coming. Frank had too; he escaped to Bangkok with the first flex of profit. But the government was slow off the mark. It was in disarray. And who listens to doctors when there's fun to be had?

There are numerous accounts of the smell on Evernet. The smell of Sex Death as it came to be known. But it wasn't really sex at all. It was the scent of people electrocuting themselves in the name of repetitive fun, white love, a constant enjoyment, utopia. They say that before the penny dropped, entire areas reeked.

On days such as this, when I can't bear the brightness of this place any longer, I often think about the sex machine.

I fancy a crack on one. I reckon it'd be a fitting end for me, a way of compensating for the scarcely detectable life I've led. I think about raping Susan, too. But they wouldn't execute me for it and I doubt I could live with the shame. I'm a nice sort, deep down, I know this to be true. And I seem destined to survive, to just write. A virgin. Oh, it makes me snort. I shouldn't be embarrassed but I am. My cheeks go red. My fingers shake. Are there any more loose ends?

The Sex Death crisis snapped the existing government and paved the way for the Future Love regime. A crimson-coloured class lost its nerve, realised the problems freedom had caused at the more innocuous levels of society. When the news of the thousands of Sex Deaths came through it was clear that something was finished: an era, or perhaps something less significant. A style of life. It was clear that human instincts had been damaged. There was a comical amnesty to try and collect and destroy the existing sex machines, but customers tended to keep their purchases. Reports of Sex Deaths continued to filter through until quite recently.

Humans adore understanding. They've been at it for centuries. Thinking this way and that. Structure, no structure, God, freedom, language. They'd continued to think beyond the advent of exchange and the opening of the market, when perhaps they ought to have just given up. But, in the end, they were just damaged. Desires burned too fiercely. Some common courtesies remained intact, but the breed seems finished. Confused and chilled out. Ready for a colourless and awkward crackdown.

So these were my origins and this is beginning to sound like the end. Thank you. As for the outside world nowadays,

I couldn't tell you. I'm sure it's some fruity cocktail of embossed appearance and secret shit. But don't take my word for anything. One thing that strikes me about creatures on the outside is the amount they leave behind. It's too much. If you could only see the size of your archive. The unclaimed baggage of loose lives. The slimy trail that sludges behind you. You give too much away and it doesn't make the historian's task any easier. You're neither coming nor going. You'll never make sense.

I'm getting angry and my mouth's dry. In a moment of daring Susan recently suggested I write about my own sexual frustrations. The woman clearly has no critical faculties, just a snail's-shell head and a grey brain. But I suppose she has a point. I've never really touched another person, just read your pious accounts of the sensation. There's no end to your mutual regard, is there? Your caresses. Embraces. The running of fingers down silk cheeks. The wiping of tears. Your comforting, ah, it makes my eyes gurgle. But it's jealousy, jealousy, I'm sure. My torso was never removed from its packaging. My thighs seem transparent in the absence of a woman's touch; neither my mother's nor that of any old whore. My cock's an appalling source of shame; a fleshy civilisation, gift-wrapped, then lost.

Can I be the hero? Of course not.

I have thoughts so dark your spying peepers can't register them, relying as your eyes do on the presence of slim light. Chinks of hope. Tragic, biological poetry. Do I wish I'd been aborted? Would it have been better to have trickled on to the bathroom floor as a beatless collection of little guts and early versions of limbs? Well, it's the obvious question, surely. Sniff sniff sniff. How did I become such a weakling?

338

Do I wish I wasn't here? Well, compared to this . . . no, I can't answer. But these awful bright walls. Paint – who invented it? I hope someone forgave them.

Rebecca, Frank, Carly, Steve, Johnny. Let me say their names one last time. Justin. I won't write again, I'm tired of it. I'll refuse to write and do something stupid instead. When you read this I'll probably be dead, or, better still, I'll be out of here. I'll make my brain explode and I'll blow out the cell wall and run off to meet you, buy you a drink and woo you with a well-turned phrase. But who's you? Don't ask me.

There's a terrible whiff of the end to all this, I can see it coming at me from down the page. I want to love, I wish I could be a part of things. No, forget I ever said that; it was a lie. But make the most of yourself! Oh, definitely forget I said that. Just imagine me laughing out loud, that's how I imagine you.

If I could see a panoramic landscape, then the sun would be setting on it. Certainly, if I could love, then my lover would be dead, rigid in my arms. If I could fight, then the battle would now be won, or lost in the extreme. And, if I believed in human endeavour, then I promise someone would be doing something exceptional and hopeful by now.

But instead.

Acknowledgments

Thanks to my family and my friends. Especially, Tony Weymouth, Nicholas Royle, Joe Cross, Kristian Scott, Lív Lamhauge, Laura Marsden, Edward Evans, Gareth Buckell and Jude McWilliams. Also, to John Saddler and Beth Coates.

www.vintage-books.co.uk